DEMIGODS AMONG US
[The Shemihazah Files.]

Written by
Elliott Eddie

Copyright © 2014 by P&E Publishing
All rights reserved. No part of this book may be reproduced, scanned,
or distributed in any printed or electronic form without permission.
First Edition: September, 2014
Printed in the United States of America
ISBN: 978-0-9904963-9-7

To My Wife Pamela: The one person on God's green Earth I can truly say has my back. I trust you, I appreciate you and most of all I love you.

Elliott Eddie

This is a work of fiction.

Names, characters, events and incidents are either products of the author's imagination or used fictitiously.

Any resemblance to actual persons, living or dead, or actual events is purely coincidental.

Chapter 1

Tonight is the clearest night anyone has seen in years.

Tonight is the kind of night where the stars seem to shine even brighter than normal; millions of tiny dots in the sky- millions of tiny eyes watching…waiting to see what their next move will be. All of Heaven and Earth seem to be gazing intently…eyes wide, mouth gaped: the collective breath of the unseen universe holding back it's exhale to see what the outcome of this night will bring.

The air that patrols the streets this evening is brisk, not too chilled as to be outright cold, but brisk; the type of cool air that stings the inside of your nose and lungs with every deep breath. The type of cool air that makes your eyes tear up if you stubbornly leave them open for one moment too long. Yet it is a beautiful night; a night that all of those endearing Christmas stories are made of…a night that also bodes perfect for a winter time tale of horror. The strange thing- it is the middle of July in Central Virginia.

And the streets are deserted.

There is no traffic on the streets, no people milling about. There are no lights flashing, no horns honking, no music playing…just the soft hushed sounds of the wind as it rushes pass. If anyone were walking down Leigh Street in Richmond Virginia's warehouse district at this very moment, they will have noticed something a bit out of place amid all of the things that are out of place. A discerning eye might notice three figures running between buildings, trying to keep to the shadows of the night. The three figures run on, trying to avoid the tall street lights which stand guard and casts their ever watchful eyes down the streets and across the sides of the buildings. These tall steel guardians of the streets are focusing their intense gaze deep into the corners of the alleyways behind every building. Even as these sentient street guardians train their gaze down the length of the street, three figures dart quickly across the street; as if sheer determination is enough to mask them from being caught in the angry gaze of the steel guardians.

Our three visitors are desperate to find a place to hide from the peering lights. They are desperately seeking solitude from the heaven's relentless gaze so they can regroup; lick their wounds and plan their next move. Three weary individuals pressing on, running in and out of the shadows, behind buildings, over trash cans and back into the shadows wherever they can find them. These three warriors know the importance of their mission. Everything rests on their shoulders. It has come down to the three of them; if they fail their mission tonight, the entire world is in danger of being destroyed.

"Wait guys, I think I see the building."

The three figures run into the alley and dive behind an empty dumpster next to an old bakery. The three people huddle together as if it is possible for them to physically become one- one giant mass ready to move in sync at a moment's notice. The mass becomes quiet; the only sound between them is their synchronized breathing in the chilled air of the night. This group has learned the ability to completely control their breathing so it is hardly noticeable; a feat that has come in handy several times over the last few weeks. There were a few times they had almost been caught by their stalker; an enemy who's very presence on this Earth broke dozens of natural laws.

Vic slowly raises her head above the dumpster they are crouched behind. The rusty and filthy dumpster is empty and smelled of decayed sewage. Vic intently surveys the street, looking for movement or any other sign that signals that they are not alone. It has been a long journey and Vic is tired; tired of being chased, tired of being hunted, tired of constantly moving with no rest or sign of relief. Vic has traveled many miles with only the company of the two men beside her. One of the men is her younger brother named Brandon whom she has taken care of since her parent's recent and untimely death at the hands of a killer. The other man with Vic is Cliff. Although Vic has only known Cliff for a little over a month, she has grown to despise him. Vic despises Cliff because he is not like her. Vic believes Cliff is a liability. The only reason Cliff is here with them now is because he inadvertently saved Vic's life. As Vic looks Cliff in the eyes while they crouch behind the dumpster, anger begins to rise up in her towards him. However, this is not the time for Vic to indulge in her personal thoughts. Right now the three of them are in trouble and it is once again up to Vic to find a place for them to go so they can figure out their next plan of action. Vic knows that at some point they will have to stop running and face their enemy, and that is a day Vic is not looking forward to.

Chapter 2

Vic was born Victoria Harper, but she has always been known as Vic. Vic was the first born of three children to the late Col. Benjamin Harper and Dr. Rose Harper. Vic's parents were great people who showered her with love from the day she was born. Most of Vic's friends thought that she used the name Vic because her father wanted her to be born a male child. However, this is not true. Actually, Vic's father was happy that his first born child was a baby girl. It was Vic who wished she was born a male child. Vic believed that if she had been born a boy, she would have been even closer to her father as she became older. Vic was a bit jealous of her brothers because she believed that no matter what she did, their father loved Brandon and Charley more than her. Many times while growing up her father and brothers went places without her and seemed to have so much fun and so many stories that they shared over family dinners. Vic and her father had stories they shared as well, but their stories seemed somewhat less important. Vic's stories with her dad usually centered on shopping, going out to dinner or seeing a movie together- very date like. Her brother's stories seemed to revolve around playing sports together or going fishing or any number of activity related experiences. Vic went into the military straight from high school to follow in her father's footsteps.

Vic retired from the military after 20 years of service and accepted a job with NASA. Within two years of being hired, Vic was promoted to Chief of Security; a job detail with access and clearances to information she could not even share with her father. Although Vic's father understood he was not privy to the information surrounding her job and life at NASA, their relationship seemed to degrade from the moment she accepted the position. Vic's father highly disapproved of some of the secret projects that were transferred to their underground facilities that of course, didn't exist.

One night while at work, Vic ran into a situation that proved to be beyond her clearance level, and beyond her ability to comprehend. At the beginning of her lunch break, Vic was walking towards the elevator on her way to what she thought was the basement of NASA. Usually Vic was one of the most perceptive and observant people on the face of the Earth. However, this particular night she was distracted- looking over an email on her phone. The email was from her dad saying he would be home early this evening and wanted to take her out to dinner. As Vic smiled and began to email him back on her cell phone as she entered the elevator, forgetting to press the lobby button so she could go outside to her car.

The elevator's doors closed but Vic's attention was on the email, not realizing that the elevator was traveling down further into the facility instead of up towards the lobby. Vic did not notice anything wrong until the elevator came to a halt. Vic finally looked up; ready to walk out of the elevator and go on to her car, but the door did not open. Instead, the elevator began to move sideways. Finally putting her phone down, Vic looked at the elevator lights to see what floor she was on and that is when she realized something was horribly wrong. Vic was now in what she believed was a restricted portion of the underground base. Vic knew this was a restricted level and that she should not be here at once; she knew this because to her knowledge, there was no floors 'R: 1-12'.

As the elevator went sideways, Vic's heart began to drop. How did she end up here? If this was a restricted level, then how did she even access it? Wouldn't a person need a special code or card to get the elevator to access this part of the facility? Vic's heart started pounding quicker. Underground rooms that someone with her clearance did not know about should not be easy to access, even by mistake. She did not remember pushing a button when she got into the elevator, but even if she did something was still wrong. Vic has worked for NASA for five years now and had been in this particular elevator over a thousand times and she did not remember ever seeing a button for R: 12. Vic immediately looked at the buttons on the elevator wall and that is when she noticed it; a secret panel below the floor number. She had never noticed that before. Vic saw that the secret panel was not secure and moved in closer to inspect. Opening the panel, Vic saw twelve buttons with different words on each button. One of the buttons with the letters "SEMI" on it was covered in blood, along with the 'Lobby' button which was covered in blood as well.

The elevator began slowing down and would soon come to a stop. As the elevator slowed, Vic began hearing noises- sounds of gunfire and screaming. Vic grabbed her service weapon from its holster and crouches low, ready for whatever is to happen. The gunfire stops and now Vic can hear whistling. It sounded like a tune Vic had heard before, *but what is it?* As the volume grows, the tune begins to sound even more familiar...and very disturbing. It makes Vic think of all of the nightmares she had as a child- and all of the horror books she has read over the years. It was so familiar...she had it; it was from the movie Kill Bill by Quentin Tarantino. Vic had seen that movie several times with her father and brothers and she knew why it disturbed her. Vic associated that tune with killing and with blood...lots and lots of blood.

That's when she heard the screams again. Blood curdling screams.

The elevator came to a stop and the door open. Vic peered down a long dark hallway. The darkness in the hallway almost seemed as if it were...*moving*. At first it looked like it was moving down the hallway and away from her, until the beep signaling the opening of the doors betrayed her presence. Now the darkness stopped moving down the hallway and started moving back towards her in the elevator! Vic pressed the button for the lobby and waited for the doors to close back, but the doors did not want to close- and the darkness in the hallway at the other end was creeping a bit faster towards her. It wasn't Vic's eyes, the darkness was really moving! It was a living, breathing darkness and it was alive. Vic's presence on the floor had been detected and she had been deemed an enemy. Now the darkness was coming after her. Then the screaming began again, but this time it was a different type of scream. It sounded like someone was saying something. Vic had her gun pointed towards the darkness in the hall, frantically pressed the lobby button...

"Come on, come on...let's go"

Vic could now make out the words being yelled at her from out of the darkness,

"Hold that elevator. Don't leave me here. Don't leave me here."

Vic pressed even harder for the elevator to close. Fear like she had never known was now coursing through her body. That's when Vic saw a figure appeared out of the darkness. The figure was screaming and running towards the elevator at top speed.

"Don't leave me, don't you dare leave me. If he gets this bag, the world is over."

As Vic frantically presses the lobby button over and over, time itself was moving in slow motion. Vic's first instinct is to shoot; shoot the man running towards her, shoot the darkness itself. Vic steadies her hand and waits. She has no idea why or even *how* she is able to stay so composed, but she does.

As the running man gets closer, Vic can see pure terror in his eyes. Vic estimates the man stands about six feet one inch tall from and weighs about two hundred fifty pounds. The man has curly red hair and he is running full speed towards the elevator, carrying what looks to be a green tote bag over his shoulder and a small object in his hand.

"Come on elevator, close."

"Don't leave me! Don't leave me down here with him!"

Just as the running man makes it to the elevator, the doors begin to shut. The man's momentum carries him into the elevator and slams him against the back wall. As the elevator closes, Vic can make out another figure *inside* the darkness. It looks like a human figure veiled inside the darkness with fire red eyes. The whistling begins again and the living darkness now seems to speed up; as if it intends to make it on the elevator as well. The door closes just as a figure steps out of the darkness. Vic can hear a voice...a voice scarier than any monster she has ever heard in all the movies she has seen with her father. Vic doesn't know it yet, but this voice will haunt her dreams over the next few weeks and send her on a desperate trip through six States. The doors close and the elevator begins to move sideways as the voice on the other side calls out to Cliff and his new acquaintance...

"I'll see you soon Cliffy. And tell your new friend Victoria I'm coming for a visit real soon now, ya hear!"

Chapter 3

"Okay, ready...now!"

Vic, Brandon and Cliff dart from behind the rusted out dumpster and run full speed towards the warehouse at the end of the street. It is an old building that looks like it should be condemned- and it may have been, but that is not a concern for tonight. Tonight there are greater concerns, more pressing concerns. Tonight *he* is coming for them. The three of them have been running for six weeks; ever since they left the facility in New Mexico. There has been no rest for the weary ever since '*he*' has been chasing them. Truth be told, their 'hunter' would have had his prey by now had it not been for their sheer dumb luck; a well timed snow fall in Chicago, a crying baby in Ohio, a nosey old lady in Baltimore. Everything seemed to be working out in their favor...that is until today. There is no way of knowing how *he* found them again. *Did someone tip him off? Had they left evidence behind at one of the sites?* Not likely. There is always the "*supernatural information gathering*" possibility. After all, he is supernatural.

"Shhh... I hear something"

Vic and her companions stop in their tracks and hug the wall on the side of the building, next to the warehouse they are trying to reach. As luck would have it, the moment the three of them fall into place, a cloud completely covers the brightly shinning moon, providing them a bit of shadow for cover.

"Wait, I heard something"

As comically as a slap-stick television show would do it, Cliff bumps into the back of Brandon, who in turn bumps into Vic, sending her momentarily into the light. Brandon quickly grabs Vic and yanks her back into the shadows.

The wind howls as if it is trying to inform someone that it has spotted them.

"You think he's still following us, Brandon?"

"Come on Cliff, you know he's following us"

Vic turns to them both and repeats her firm, stern order...

"I said quiet"

Silence.

Vic and her companions stand perfectly still as if stillness will offer them the gift of invisibility. They listen intently, but hear nothing except the soft wail of the wind and the gentle hum of the street lights in the cold deserted night.

"Okay guys, listen. I think the safe house is inside that warehouse right over there, on the second floor. All we have to do is make it to that building and we should be safe. We should be safe at least for a while."

"You don't know that Vic."

"Shut up Cliff, I know we will be safer in there than we are right now on these streets. All right, on the count of three we are going to run straight to that back door. No stopping. Just run."

"One..."

"Wait!"

"What is it Cliff?"

"There are no more shadows. We have to run in the light."

"Yes. Cliff."

"I don't think this is a good idea. If we run in the light, someone will see us. You know 'he' has spies everywhere."

Vic grabs Cliff by the shoulders and looks straight into his eyes...

"Cliff, we have to go. We can't stay out here or we'll get caught for sure. Now put on your big boy drawers and get ready. You got that key ready Brandon?"

"I got it ready."

"Okay, One...two...three..."

The three of them simultaneously leap out of the shadow provided by the moon's cover and dash across the alley like bats out of hell. They run at top speed; almost become living shadows themselves. The group reaches the back door of the warehouse in mere moments, although it seems like it takes forever in the bright light of the still, cold night.

Once the group reaches the back door as planned, they notice the huge bright light hanging just above the door. The light fixture is perhaps fifteen feet in the air, too high to unscrew by hand. Brandon takes the key and puts it in the lock, but the key won't fit.

"Open the door Brandon"

"Shut up Cliff, what do you think I'm trying to do?"

"I don't know what you are trying to do, I know what you are not doing and that's opening the door."

Vic pushes Cliff out of the way and stands next to Brandon.

"What's wrong B?"

"This must be the wrong key, it's not working."

11

While Vic tries to help Brandon figure out the key and lock issue, Cliff is nervously surveying the streets- looking for their unwelcomed follower.

"We are sticking out like a sore thumb. We're going to be seen. Open the door."

"I'm trying..."

"Get us inside Brandon"

"Shut up Cliff, I'm doing the best I can; the key is not working..."

"You're going to get us killed...."

Vic goes into action. Vic spots a nice size rock on the ground near the door and grabs it. Vic takes off her jacket in a flash and puts the rock inside her jacket. Vic breaks the window, reaches inside and unlocks the door. All three of them rush inside the warehouse and close the door behind them. Ducking down in the darkness they wait...and listen. They listen for footsteps, they listen for breathing, they listen for movement...they listen for any sounds that gives proof that they have been spotted.

Nothing.

Nothing but the howling of the wind and the hum of the street lights standing guard in the dark of the night are heard outside the door. After a few moments Vic stands up and walks past both of her companions. She stops short before she exits the room.

"I'm going upstairs to check for supplies. Keep an eye out down here for a little while and then come on up when you think it is safe."

Vic turns and looks Brandon in the eyes. When Brandon returns her gaze, she nods towards Cliff and leaves the room.

After ten more minutes of listening in the darkness, Cliff lets out a nervous laugh. Cliff realizes that his laughter is audible and offers an excuse for the sudden noise...

"I'm sorry Brandon. I'm just scared, that's all. Lord help me, I am so scared."

Cliff is an imposing figure. It is quite a sight to see a man of Cliff's stature sobbing like a three-year old child. Brandon walks over to Cliff and stands next to his sobbing body. Brandon is a thin man with a classic baby face; except for the scrappy beard and dark sunken eyes that he's been sporting these days. Cliff and Brandon have been on the run together for a while now and it is starting to show on Brandon's face. Brandon always fancied himself a lady's man and he did look the part. Although Brandon never thought of himself as "metro-sexual", he did secretly fancy the term. Brandon was always well put together; manicured fingers, regular facials and massages. Brandon paid special attention to his clothes, particularly his shoes. If everyone truly has a vice, shoes would be Brandon's vice of choice. Some people believe you can tell a lot about a man from the way he presented himself, particularly by the type of shoes he wore. Brandon believed it wasn't about having the most expensive shoes he could find, it was about style...and Brandon certainly had a lot of that.

Being the youngest of three children brought up in the Harper household, Brandon was always spoiled with the finer things. By the time Brandon came along, all of the family's financial struggles were a distant memory. Brandon's father was now a well respected military leader and often advised the President of the United States on matters of foreign policy. Brandon's mother had been the head of a successful medical practice for many years and now her only wish was to shower love and attention on her baby boy. Brandon was privileged, while most of his acquaintances and friends were not. However, Brandon never let his privilege skew his perspective on life. Brandon was a hard worker; he took responsibility for his actions and always tried to do the right thing- even when the right thing was not the easiest thing to do.

Brandon loved his big sister and he would do anything for her. He respected her because she had always been straight forward with him. Even when they disagreed hard enough that they could come to physical blows, she never let them walk away angry. Vic would stay in his face and press him until they settled their disagreement. They didn't always see eye to eye, but Brandon always knew that even at the height of Vic's anger, she would never turn her back on him. Brandon loved his big sister for that and he would do anything for her…even lay down his life to save hers, no question. When their parents were recently *murdered*, Brandon thought he would lose it. He literally thought he heard something "snap" inside his head. Brandon was in darkness; but, somehow Vic found him in that darkness and pulled him back into the light. Of course, once Brandon got into the light, all hell had broken loose. Vic was screaming about being followed by some *"thing"* that was not completely human- some type of human and alien hybrid or something. Vic was talking like a crazy woman; saying their parents did not die, that they were killed and that this *"thing"* was now after them and they had to leave. Brandon was not sure what was going on, and he is still not sure. All he knows is that Vic is convinced that their constant running is the right thing. Vic believes the entire world is in trouble and that this guy sitting here in front of Brandon, sobbing like a little girl who lost her pretty little bow, is now their responsibility to keep alive. Brandon does not understand any of it, but if Vic says it is so then it is so. Brandon will follow Vic to the ends of the Earth and back twice if she said it was important. So for now, Cliff is Brandon's friend and he will protect Cliff with his life as well, because Brandon loves his sister that much.

Brandon takes a seat on the floor next to Cliff and stares at him in the silence. Even though Brandon is not known to be the patient type, he can understand the emotions that have gripped his companion. Brandon would say the word *friend* is a strong word to describe the relationship between Cliff and himself, but in moments like these all they have is each other. After a few minutes, Brandon reaches out and puts his hand on Cliff's shoulder in a gesture to offer comfort.

"I know Cliff. This is hard on us all." But we have to keep it together. We have a job to do."

Cliff looks into Brandon's eyes, hoping to find the same comfort in his eye's that his words suggest. Instead, Cliff is met with a cold hard gaze; devoid of caring, devoid of faith. There is no comfort in Bandon's eyes and this makes Cliff sob even harder. Brandon knows why Cliff is sobbing. Cliff no longer believes they will live- he no longer believes that they will be able to accomplish the job that has been placed in their laps. Brandon would probably be sobbing right now too, if he had any tears left. However, Brandon has no tears left to shed. Brandon's only mission now is to protect his sister with his dying breath, which he believes he will be taking sooner than later.

"Come on Cliff. Let's go upstairs and check on Vic."

Chapter 4

Once upstairs, Brandon and Cliff walk into an open room which now serves as a graveyard of unwanted objects. Old furniture such as sofas, beds and dressers are scattered about the room. There are also light fixtures, wooden objects and memorabilia of days long past spread about. Boxes of all sizes are dispersed around the room as well, making it almost impossible to navigate through the room without bumping into something. There is one wall on the opposite side of the room where the boxes are stacked up halfway to the ceiling. Cobwebs hang from the ceiling like giant pieces of rope. The dust that has settled on the boxes, furniture and all about the room look to be an inch thick. *Surely no one has been in this place in years.* Perhaps Vic was right on this one, perhaps this is the perfect safe house for them. Maybe they will be able to hold up here for a while and collect their thoughts. *How great would that be?* It has been a long time since Brandon allowed himself to hope. It felt good to hope again, even if it is premature hope and even if it only lasts for a short time.

To the far side of the room, is a faded banner that hangs limply above an old table. The banner reads, "Stop the Violence". Brandon spots Vic sitting at the table. Vic has already claimed her spot amid the dirt and chaos of the room, sitting quietly at the table which is covered with a cache of guns, knives and hand held weapons of all sorts. Brandon moves in closer and upon further inspection of the weaponry, he notices that it is all old and not in the greatest of shape. The blades of the knives seem dull, the batons seem brittle and he wondered if the guns would hold up under the strain of being used in battle. Right in the middle is Vic, cleaning out the barrel of a nine millimeter glock pistol. Vic slowly raises her head as Brandon and Cliff enter the back the room. Brandon does not hesitate to take a seat next to his sister. Brandon picks up a shotgun and inspects it. Taking the lead from his sister, Brandon begins to clean the gun.

Cliff approaches the table and stands in front of brother and sister with a look of fear and dread on his face. Cliff asks the question that seems the most obvious to ask; not because he is curious about the answer, but because it is a habit for him. When Cliff gets nervous, he talks.

"Where did you get all these weapons Vic?"

"They were left here for us by a friend of mine. Someone I can trust."

Vic and Brandon carefully inspect each gun and clean them thoughtfully, as if this were the most important job in the world.

Cliff begins inspecting the various weapons on the table. Cliff hones in on one hand held weapon in particular and picks it up. The weapon looks like a hand held scythe. The scythe is light in weight, aerodynamic and the weapon seems to fit perfectly in Cliff's hand. Cliff begins to pace back and forth, drifting off into a memory of his own. Vic and Brandon continue to clean their guns, all the while keeping a sharp eye on Cliff who seems to be going through some sort of mental break. As Cliff paces back and forth from one side of the table to the other, Vic and Brandon pause briefly and exchange worried glances. Brandon knows exactly what his sister is thinking; she is wondering if they can trust Cliff to do what needs to be done when the time comes.

Amid all the weapons on the table is one green tote bag. It is the same tote bag Cliff had wrapped around his shoulder the night he and Vic met; the night in the elevator that changed their lives. Cliff paused briefly and fixated on the green tote bag, wondering if all of the important items and information that are supposed to stop their formidable and resourceful enemy are really in there. In all of the weeks they have been on the run, Cliff has never actually searched the bag. He assumed everything would be in there because that is what he was told. Cliff remembered putting the syringe in the bag the night Cliff met Vic in the NASA lab over a mile below the surface. Cliff was just supposed to be helping out a friend; he was not supposed to be there. *How did they know it* would be him to walk into that building- him, the perfect scapegoat?

Maybe, just maybe he was *set-up*.

Cliff stopped pacing and stood over the tote bag, longing to reach out and pick it up. Cliff wanted to go through the tote bag to see its contents. At the same time it was taking all the mental and emotional strength Cliff had to fight the urge to run out of the room screaming at the top of his lungs in fear. Just as Cliff's imagination began to morph into full blown fear, Vic jammed a clip into the glock she had been cleaning with enough force to startle Cliff out of his mesmerized state.

Looking at Cliff, Vic breaks the silence.

"Are we ready?"

"Ready? How the hell can we be ready for what we are about to face?"

Immediately Brandon jumps in the conversation.

"That's enough Cliff."

"No it's not enough. What are we doing here? Do you honestly think that we can win?"

"That's enough Cliff! What are we supposed to do? You know that we are the last line of defense. If we don't stop him you know what's going to happen."

"Well then fine Brandon, let it happen. At least we'll live to fight another day."

That's when Vic takes back control of the conversation she started.

"Enough Cliff, that's enough. I'm not trying to hear you anymore.

If you want to leave, then leave."

Silence.

"We are here to do a job and we are going to do it. Too many good people have died and too many lies have been told. But we're here now, in this moment we are here. No one else is here to do this but us. So take those bad images out your mind and let's do what we need to do."

Cliff takes his rebuke and begins to pace back and forth. Clearly agitated, Cliff uses the dull side of the scythe and runs it across his check. A little blood is drawn but Cliff doesn't notice, nor does he feel the blade digging into his skin.

The crash of a window is heard downstairs. Next, the sound of the downstairs door exploding reverberates through the hollow halls and rooms of the old warehouse.

This is it. The revolution has begun and it is not being televised.

Brandon jumps out of his chair and turns off the single light bulb that is burning above the table and the room goes dark. Vic, Brandon and Cliff sit in darkness for what seems to be an eternity; listening…waiting for any signs of movement that suggests someone knows they are in the building. They wait; barley breathing as if the thought alone will betray them in these vital minutes. After a few moments, their eyes adjust a bit to the darkness that surrounds them. Vic taps Brandon on the shoulder. Vic points to him, then to her ears and then opens both hands as if asking the question, *"Do you hear anything?"* Brandon responds by shaking his head no.

Out of the silence, a faint whistle is heard. The turn sounds eerily familiar. The sound brings an uneasiness and fear with it that chills their very bones. Vic knows this tune very well and it disturbs her greatly. Brandon knows the tune, but for some reason, he just can't place where he knows it from.

"What is that?"

Vic turns towards her brother who is looking at her with a puzzled look on his face and whispers so softly and lovingly that Brandon is momentarily confused.

"It's the tune from Kill Bill."

Cliff slides in closer to them both as the whistling continues. The sound becomes louder and louder as it comes closer and closer. Now the sound is coming from the other end of the big room that the three are in. Then the whistling stops mid tune. That's when they hear his voice.

"Cliffy, Cliffy, Cliffy...you know I can smell ya."

The sound of a butane lighter clicks open and a single flame is revealed; the flame can be seen across the cluttered room as a cigarette is lit.

"...and you brought some friends."

Brandon can stand it no longer...

"Man, forget this hiding shit."

Brandon turns the overhead light back on revealing their positions in the room. Vic stands armed with two nine millimeter glocks pointed at the intruder. Brandon wheels the double barreled shotgun he is holding in the direction of the room's newest visitor. Cliff backs up slowly as a small stream of fluid collects at the bottom of his pant leg. Cliff slowly moves away from the intruder looking for a way out. Cliff sees nothing; no exit door, no elevator shaft, nothing except for the wall sized window in the back of the room behind a bunch of boxes stacked one upon another halfway up the wall. Cliff grabs the green tote bag that is on the table along with his scythe and moves behind Vic.

Vic glances at Cliff as he moves towards her, not because of his movement but because of the sound he makes when he moves. It sounded to her like Cliff stepped in a puddle of water. As she quickly glances down, she can see Cliff's pant leg is wet and realizes that Cliff is so scared he has literally pissed his pants. Ordinarily she would feel disgust for him- even anger, but right now she can understand. It is not merely the appearance of the newest guest in the room; by all means, he is not intimidating in looks. The room's newest visitor barely stands five feet five inches tall. He is a small man with a small stature. The visitor is dressed in ordinary clothing; black on black cowboy boots, faded black jeans, a burgundy leather jacket with a black button-down shirt underneath and an old tan cowboy hat that suggests too many years in the direct sun. He is wearing various rings and necklaces with ornaments and designs that would make a gothic teen jealous. He carries a black cane with a rams head ornament at the top and a skulls head ornament at the bottom. His appearance is not intimidating at all; except for the eyes, his bloodshot red eyes peering *into* you. Those eyes seem so empty, so lifeless, and so dark. Mostly, it's his *presence*. Being in the same room with this man is like being suffocated by the air itself. And the name; there is something terrifying about his name…something inhuman…something ancient…..

Back in the lab at NASA, they called him Shemihazah. Some people nicknamed him 'Shemi'. While there was only one person in the lab when he came 'alive', everyone who was associated with the project knew deep within that they had gone too far. Due to his unique *genetic make-up,* some even said that Shemihazah is *Nimrod Reborn-* a human created son of the chief watcher from among the original *'fallen ones'*.

Shemihazah stood there staring at them, smiling and smoking his cigarette.

"Something tells me you all are not happy to see me. Now why would that be?"

Brandon tightens his grip on the shotgun…

"It's not going down the way you think it is chump"

Shemihazah takes a drag of his cigarette,

"You know, that's what they all think chief. Now come on people. You know those little toys you have right there are not going to harm me. I am immortal."

Vic is not intimidated,

"Not while you're walking on this Earth. On this Earth you are Earth, which means you are in some way- mortal."

"Not quite. I am something more than Earth. Much more…

Shemihazah takes a long drag from his cigarette. The red light from the tip of the cigarette blazes bright, causing his eyes to look like blood red liquid swirling in the dark. Shemihazah releases the smoke into the air in front of him. A mixture of the darkness in that portion of the room coupled with the smoke, made Shemi's body seem to 'shimmer'. It looked like Shemihazah was phasing in and out of reality. Brandon let out a deep sigh.

"To tell the truth, to call me Earth is an insult to me, especially coming from someone like you Victoria Harper.

Vic seemed stunned that he knew her entire name. *Who the hell…what the hell is this thing?*

Shemi looked into Vic's eyes and a weird grin slowly lit up his face, exposing a grim set of teeth. Shemi took another drag of his cigarette…

"You seem amazed that I know you Vic. I know a lot of things. Now hand over what's mine. You have until the end of my next cigarette drag."

Vic speaks without ever taking her eyes or her guns off of Shemihazah.

"Cliff, you know what you got to do right? Right?"

"Yes."

Shemihazah raises the cigarette up to his mouth to take a drag.

"Brandon, you ready?"

"I was born ready for this shit right here sis."

"Well then, let's make daddy proud."

Shemihazah finishes his drag and flicks his cigarette. Cliff barely begins to move before all hell breaks loose. Guns begins to fire and Shemihazah lets out a blood curdling scream like nothing Cliff has ever hear before. Cliff moves as fast as he can towards the only window in the room. Cliff's plan is to throw himself at the boxes and go flying through the window. Admittedly, in Cliff's mind this is a heroic move right out of the pages of the best of Hollywood movie scripts. It is a Blockbuster move, he should be the leading man in his own action film, forget Duane "The Rock" Johnson.

Cliff is hoping that by flinging himself into the boxes, the boxes themselves will take the brunt of the impact from the shattering glass as he heads straight out of the second story window and down to the ground. Cliff doesn't have a clever line like Sylvester Stallone, Arnold Schwarzenegger or Will Smith. Actually, the only thing Cliff can think of to say as he plans his very own Blockbuster move is…

"Oh God, please let there be something soft in these boxes."

Chapter 5

Cliff was not always a scared man.

This fear that Cliff has developed is rather new. As a matter of fact, the bulk of his fear just began to surface a little under two months ago.

Cliff was a laid back type of guy. He grew up in New York City, in an area called Bensonhurst. Bensonhurst is a large, multi-ethnic amorphous area consisting of several neighborhoods, in the southwestern part of the borough of Brooklyn.

As a youngster, Cliff was always in church. He can still remember the long days and longer nights at church where his father was a youth minister and his mother was the organ player. Cliff never did like church much because he thought it was too *click'ish*. As an only child, Cliff grew up rather spoiled and never did quite learn how to play well with others. Some of the biggest misunderstandings of Cliff's young church life were because he could not get along with the other children. Most of the "preacher's kids" in the church were snobs and they always had to have top billing in everything. Cliff was in a constant struggle; a struggle for attention, a struggle for power or some other struggle that made it hard for him to socialize with the children and adults at the church. Cliff could not wait to grow up. He wanted to get to that age where he could go to church when he wanted…which would eventually translate into not going at all.

Cliff was an above average student in school. His teacher always clamored on about how smart he was and what a bright future Cliff could have if he would just apply himself more. Cliff would have done more, but he just hadn't found anything in particular that interested him for any substantial period of time. Once he matriculated to college, Cliff chose the path of least resistance by going to a Liberal Arts College in Clinton, New York named Hamilton. Cliff studied Theatre at Hamilton and became very good. He didn't particularly like being on stage, but he did flourish behind the scenes. Cliff took on various jobs like; Properties Master, Light Designer, Stage Manager and any other position that did not require him to be out in front of people. Actually, Cliff found that he was great at everything he tried. He spent more hours than anyone he knew studying his craft and researching new ideas. His social skills developed greatly in college; in part because Cliff found he could be himself and people could respect that. People respected Cliff just because of who he was and how he operated. Cliff was the type of person that would help anyone he could. He would never be party to talking behind someone's back or sabotaging anyone else's efforts or dreams. Cliff was amazed at how many people just appreciated the fact that with him, what you saw was what you got.

After college, Cliff took on a number of different jobs. He never really stayed in one place for more than a year. This movement was not a plan per se, it just happened that way. All of Cliff's life, he had been looking for something that interested him. Cliff was in constant search of himself and it wasn't until about ten years ago that he found himself, by mistake.

About ten years ago, while working for a non-profit organization, Cliff finally found a subject that interested him. Of all of the subjects in the world, Cliff was surprised to find that this interest lie in the sciences. Cliff fell in love with the science of Genetics. He did not go back to school to learn it, but rather learned on his own by researching the subject and devouring every single book, article and video he could find on the matter. It wasn't until he had been researching the subject for three years or so that he ran into a term that captured his imagination. The term was; Trans-humanism- via genetic engineering.

The science was relatively new when Cliff first started researching it, so it was very hard to find books on the subject. The idea of trans-humanism was to greatly enhance human intellectual, physical, and psychological capacities to the point where they would become something *more than human.* Cliff had always been a comic book fan while growing up and was fascinated with the idea of superheroes and mutants. Because of this fascination, when Cliff read about the goals of the trans-humanists (which he equated with turning people into real life superheroes and mutants), he was amazed. Could it really be done? Could human beings create a real life "Spider-man" or "Incredible Hulk"? Could we create cyborgs- half man, half machines that were sort of human but better- like the Six Million Dollar Man? The very idea fascinated Cliff and he went all in to study this science.

While studying about the possibilities of creating real life superheroes, Cliff met a scientist that would eventually become one of his best friends. The man's name was Dr. Hugo Larceny. Hugo was a geneticist- a biologist that studied genetics. Genetics is the study of genes, heredity and variations of organisms. Cliff fell right into this line of science because it touched on some of the other joys of his childhood. Cliff had always been fascinated with science fiction characters; the ones you find in old Greek Mythologies, in movies such as Clash of the Titans (the original, not the crappy remake) and the entire world of characters he came to love from his college days of non-stop marathons of Dungeons & Dragons. Cliff can still remember the day his friend Hugo told him about a secret experiment one of his colleagues had done, before regular people ever heard of the term *gene splicing*. A secret experiment was done in an underground lab where his friend Hugo and a few other scientists created a cross breed or "hybrid" life form. These scientists took a regular farm cow and introduced into it the genes of a human being.

Cliff's jaw almost hit the floor when Hugo told him about the experiment. At first he was repulsed, *how could people be so irresponsible? Would it be a human-cow or a cow-human? What did it look like? Who would drink the milk? Yuck.* Cliff thought of becoming a vegetarian; he could not imagine eating a piece of steak that was part human. Would that make him a cannibal?

Suddenly, a different thought began to develop in Cliff's mind...a human cow? The idea was not new to him, but why? That is when

Cliff realized that he had read about human cows all of his life; he had fought against them in his Dungeons & Dragons adventures, he had seen them in his movies and comic books. A human cow mixture was a Minotaur. Hugo and his scientist friends had created a Minotaur!

That is when life began to change for Cliff. He spent his days and nights researching two subjects; trans-humanism and genetic engineering. Cliff read every book he could get his hands on, he went to every lecture he could find and he stalked and harassed every scientist he thought would be dabbling into this new version of "the Black Arts". Cliff soon became one of the most knowledgeable men on the subject although he had not taken a science class since he left high school.

After about six years of steady research on the subject, Cliff began giving lectures on the subjects. The science was still in its early stages as far as the world knew but in secret, it was thriving from private funds and secret underground laboratories. Cliff became a wealth of knowledge; *real scientists* were seeking him out to get his opinions on the subject- the possibilities, the positive and negative effect, the moral dilemma. For a person who had not been formally educated in the sciences, Cliff had become a leader in the field- in the theory of the science, not the application.

It was about a month and a half ago that Cliff received a telephone call that changed his life again and set him on the path to where he is at this very moment. The call came in one morning at 5:23am. Cliff remembers the time exactly because it seemed like time itself had stood still from the time he picked up his phone until the moment he put the phone back down. The phone rang and it was a woman's voice on the other end that began the weirdest conversation he had ever had...

"Hello. My name is Myra Tenney. Am I speaking with Clifford Vale?"

"Yes, this is Cliff"

"We have never officially met Mr. Vale, but I am an admirer of your research. I saw you speak recently at The University of Nevada on the subject of Trans-humanism. I believe the title of your speech was, "Building a Better human Being- Should we do it?" It was a fascinating speech and very intriguing I must say."

"Well thank you. Did we meet afterwards?"

"No. I wanted to meet you though. Perhaps you noticed me in the audience?"

"Well I can't say that I did. There were a lot of people there and that speech was about a year ago."

"Fair enough. I was the one in the front row with no panties on. Does that help jar your memory?"

Actually, it did. Cliff remembered being on stage and seeing a beautiful red head woman in the front row wearing a sheer dress with a plunging neckline. Cliff also remembered that the woman kept crossing and uncrossing her legs, all the while giving him a glimpse of her bare womanhood peeking at him from underneath that skirt. Cliff would never forget that particular lecture because that had never happened before. Cliff remembered thinking, "Man, *I must be a rock star!*" Cliff remembered looking around the stage throughout his lecture to see if there were multiple pairs of panties lying somewhere nearby. When Cliff finished speaking he tried his hardest to make it over to the woman who had been teasing him, but he kept being interrupted by some person or another wanting to talk about something *"sciency"*. Cliff distinctly remembered thinking, "*Well this sucks*".

"I vaguely remember something that might fit that description"

"Come now Clifford, I think you remember it quite well."

"How may I help you Mrs. Tenney?"

"It's Miss. And please, call me Myra."

"Okay, how may I help you Myra?"

"Well, I happen to head a team of, shall we say, scientist- for a very well known organization. We recently came in contact with another interesting individual that may fit under your idea of a trans-human and I wanted to know if you would be willing to come and chat with us concerning this individual."

"Who is this person?"

"Now now Clifford, I am sure you understand that this is not the type of conversation I should be having over the phone...just given the fields of study you are in and the possible implications should this person indeed be what you describe. Perhaps we can chat a bit over a cup of coffee?"

"That sounds like it could be nice. When would you like to chat?"

"No time like the present, right?"

At that very moment, the line went dead and there was a knock at the door.

"Who in the world..."

Cliff went to his door to look through the peephole and found two men standing outside his door. The men were dressed in black suits, black tie, black shades (at five thirty in the morning?) with crew cuts.

This definitely made Cliff nervous.

"Who is it?"

"I believe you have a coffee date with Myra."

"Who are you?"

One of the men held up his wallet with his identification card in it. According to the card, this was Bill Simms…from NASA.

Chapter 6

This night is not fit for man or beast.

Outside of the warehouse in the cold of the night, a mangy dog wandered into the same alley that Vic, Brandon and Cliff had been running through less than an hour ago. The dog was undernourished and dirty. As the dog slowly moved from trashcan to trashcan along the partially lit alley, the wind began to blow harder. Wincing from the cold and discouraged from the lack of food in this alley, the dog quickly found a spot between the old warehouses and stopped for a minute. The angry gaze of the street lights trained their eyes into the alley at the very spot where the dog stands. Becoming a bit uneasy, the dog moves out of its hiding spot and slowly walks back to the center of the alley. The dog's ears suddenly raises to attention; as if they are listening to a conversation off in the distance. The dog begins to growl as it grows more uneasy. The seconds pass and the dog's demeanor changes even more- it goes from giving an angry growl to a fearful yelp. The dog backs up slowly, looking all around as if it senses danger but is not sure from where the threat is coming.

In the still of the night even the air itself seemed to be getting tense. The soft wails of the wind grow louder and louder. It seemed as if the wind itself was holding back a scream that would begin at full pitch at any moment. The soft hum of the electric street lights had now become a constant and unmistakable growl of its own; the very lights voicing its disapproval of something happening around it. The dog notices the change and begins to cautiously walk towards the warehouse at the end of the street.

Suddenly the silence of Leigh Street is replaced with the sounds of gun fire. The gun fire is accompanied by defiant voices.

Then there was laughter.

Not the warming laughter of someone being entertained by

comedic jokes and not the nervous laughter of a first date, when the two try to find a comfortable way to have their first kiss. This laughter was awful. This laughter was mixed with evil; with pain and with death. This was the laughter associated with madmen, with psychopaths…with murderers.

The dog retreats faster and growls; a deep growl signifying that it is about to fight. The dog still has no idea where the fight will come from so it is walks backwards, turning its head in every direction it can.

Suddenly the night is interrupted with the sounds of breaking glass. The dog runs like the dickens, yelping all the way like his name was…Cliff.

Chapter 7

Upstairs in the warehouse, as the guns sing their songs of death and destruction, Cliff throws his entire body into the boxes that cover the windows and crashes straight through. Cliff can hear the sounds of bullets firing, the glass window breaking and screaming…it's all happening so fast. Soon he finds himself falling…gravity has grabbed a hold of his body and the boxes that surround him and drag them all down to the cold ground below. Cliff is on the street again.

Cliff lands on top of several boxes which are filled with old clothes. Perhaps the clothing was from a theatre company that stored its unused items in this forgotten storehouse years ago. Perhaps it is overstocked clothing that has been purchased but never given to the individuals that were meant to receive them. Perhaps it is clothing from all of the storage sheds in the City of Richmond. Whatever it is and where ever it came from, Cliff is glad it is there. With his luck, Cliff would have thought the boxes would be filled to the brim with broken glass or something. Cliff believes his luck is just that bad. However, maybe he should start thinking differently because this is just the kind of 'miracle' that has happened to him over and over since he met Vic and Brandon and started their recent, *How to Narrowly Escape Death*" tour.

Cliff hits the ground hard, but landing on top of the boxes helps him survive the two story drop. The wind is knocked out of him for a few moments. As Cliff lays there on top of the boxes, struggling to catch his breath and regain his senses, he looks up into the sky and sees all of the stars of the heavens staring down at him.

"Wow, there must be millions of them…they're so beautiful."

Cliff is lost in the beauty of the stars until he hears his name being called in the still of the night…

"Cliffy…Cliffy…When I finish with them Cliffy, I'm coming after

you buddy…and boy am I going to make you SUFFER!!!"

With that, Cliff is up and running again …

…he is running like his life depends on it.

Chapter 8

It's a beautiful day in the neighborhood.

Today is a beautiful day; the perfect day for a road trip. Rick barrels down the I-95 from Richmond to Petersburg. All he can do is look at the sky and marvel at how beautiful this day is.

"It's nothing like last night."

Rick woke up at four o'clock this morning and went to the window to peek out. Rick was shocked to find the window completely frosted over- a layer of thick ice had formed on the outside of the glass. Rick remembered thinking to himself,

"That's odd. Why is there ice on the windows in the middle of July?"

What Rick thought was odder than the icy windows was the fact that he was awake at four o'clock in the morning. Rick had not seen the clock strike four am for the last three years; not since he stopped doing cocaine.

Rick was going on a road trip with his buddies today; they all had been planning this trip for months. In fact, last night Rick had thrown a party in his apartment to celebrate going on vacation. It was a small party consisting of some childhood friends and a few other people. Just tell a few people you were providing free pizza with free beer and *presto change-* you had a party.

Rick was one of the few local boys that had done well. In the last few years Rick had done a one hundred eighty degree turn around. Rick graduated from high school and was now attending VCU- Virginia Commonwealth University. Rick had even made it through the first three years of college without one arrest- something he failed to do even as a junior high school student.

Rick was in a good place in life. This was Rick's senior year. The last time Rick had come out of jail, he promised his mother before she died that he would go straight and makes something out of his life. Rick decided he would become a journalist and declared it as his major the day he was accepted to VCU. For the last three summers Rick worked various non-paid internships for television stations between New York and Alabama. Rick had never been one to back down from a challenge; his stubbornness and determination finally came in handy and helped propel him to the top of his class. Rick had already been offered an entry level position with ABC World News upon graduation. It was the opportunity of a lifetime. For Rick, things could not get any better.

However, ABC World News was still a few months away. Today, Rick is on his way to Petersburg to pick up two of his friends for the trip. There are a total of six of them going to the cabin- three couples; Rick and Sheena, Bobby and Stormy and Moon with his newest girlfriend Mimi. This was going to be an epic road trip; Rick could feel it in his bones. They all chipped in and rented a cabin in the Blue Ridge Mountains and were leaving today to spend an uninterrupted four day weekend together for fun and games. Ahhh, life doesn't get any better than this.

The first stop on the list today was Virginia State University to pick up his friend Moon and he was almost there. Rick and Moon had been friends for over fifteen years. Both of them grew up in the Church Hill area of Richmond and they had gone to school together all the way through high school. While Rick had a promising career in journalism that he had all mapped out, Moon was a cinch to be a first round draft pick in the next NFL draft. Moon had a breakout season his sophomore year which was even better than his record breaking season his freshman year. In Moon's junior year, he was a beast, breaking three national records in one season. The media had done numerous stories on Moon over the last two years and there were those who even thought Moon had the chance to be picked as a Heisman Trophy winner this year. Virginia State turned out to be the perfect choice of schools for Moon, who at first, almost chose to go to VCU just to be closer to his friend. In the end, Moon made the right decision by choosing to attend Virginia State.

Moon and his girlfriend Mimi were excited to be going with them to the cabin. Although Moon was a national college star and local celebrity, he was still a simple boy at heart who was enjoying the ride. For Moon, this little vacation was all he could talk about for the last two months…ad nausea. Moon called Rick probably ten times in the last two days alone, just to ask about the cabin and the trip. The cabin itself was the same one Rick and his family had gone to hundreds of times while he was growing up. Rick loved that cabin. It was Rick's idea for the six of them to go up and relax for a weekend. Rick wished he had not invited Bobby to the cabin. Bobby had also been their friend for over a decade but Bobby and his girlfriend Stormy were having some type of relationship problem at the moment. Rick was concerned that their problems would put a damper on the weekend. However, Moon would not hear of leaving Bobby behind because Bobby had been a good friend to them both for many years- even if he did attend Virginia Union. Moon was not so excited about having Stormy come along because he didn't think Stormy had ever gotten over him turning her down.

"God this it is a beautiful day."

Rick continued to roll down the I-95 South to pick up Moon and decided to give Bobby a call to let him know they would be at their apartment to pick him and Stormy up in less than an hour. Bobby needed a little advance notice because he was always late. Rick must have told Bobby a million times if he said it once, *"man, you will be late to your own funeral."* Bobby always tried to laugh it off, but truth be told, Bobby knew he might be late to his own funeral. Rick decided that it was a matter of life and death that he calls Bobby and tells him to be ready. Actually, Rick planned on telling Bobby that they would be at his apartment in thirty minutes- that way, perhaps Bobby would be ready in an hour.

Chapter 9

Bobby Timmons was at home on the recliner, playing basketball on his Playstation 3 before the phone rang. Bobby had been in this spot all morning, trying to win the championship for his latest season in the game. Bobby had a lot more time on his hands now. A couple of weeks ago Bobby came home an announced to Stormy that he had been fired from his job. He told her that his store was downsizing…last hired, first fired. As a result, Bobby and Stormy had not done much of anything lately. There was no money for extra-curricular activities. The only reason they were able to go on this trip to the cabin was because Moon secretly paid for Bobby's share of the rental fee. No one was supposed to know, but as soon as Mimi found out she made it her personal mission to make sure Stormy knew that her boyfriend had come up short. Of course Stormy was embarrassed; not only because Bobby didn't have the money to pay, but because this *bitch* was throwing it up in her face. Stormy did not care much for Mimi. Stormy thought that Mimi was an opportunistic gold digger, hanging onto Moon's nut sac so she could live the good life when Moon was drafted.

Actually, Stormy's anger was a little deeper than she let on. Stormy had a crush on Moon and Mimi knew it. But who didn't have a crush on Moon? The man was a football stud, soon to be multi-millionaire and he was *"fine as frog's hair"*. Everybody wanted a piece of Moon.

"And if she doesn't watch her back, I might just get me a little bit of that Moon pie this weekend."

The thought made Stormy chuckle.

"Ahhh, I'm just joking…not"

The phone rang just as Stormy was getting out of the shower. She knew it was probably Rick calling to tell them he will be there soon to pick them up. After four rings, Stormy yells out from the bathroom,

"Get the damn phone Bobby, I'm in the bathroom"

Bobby puts down the controller and picks up the phone.

"Hello?"

"Hey Bobby, its Rick."

"What's up Prick?"

"Ha ha ha, you're so funny. I'm on my way. We'll be there in about thirty minutes."

"Got it. See you in a few."

Bobby already knows the deal. If Rick is calling now to say he will be there in thirty minutes that means he is on his way to pick up Moon and it will be at least an hour before he gets there.

"I don't know why he keeps doing that."

Bobby hangs up the phone and turn back to his game. There is only about two minutes of regulation time for this game to be in the books. Just as he is about to hit the start button to finish up the game, Bobby hears a low hum coming from the back room.

"Hey Stormy, you Okay back there?"

Chapter 10

Stormy is indeed Okay. Stormy was standing in front of the mirror in her birthday suit looking at her curves. While standing there thinking of this weekend and about getting herself a piece of "*Moon pie*", she had unknowingly grabbed her vibrator out of the sink drawer and started rubbing herself with it. The soft hum of the vibrator along with her thoughts of Moon caused her to break her own record. Within two short minutes she was gushing, a puddle of her own self had run down her long, cleanly shaven legs and gathered at her feet.

"Two minutes, a personal best."

As Stormy bent over with towel in hand to dry up the floor around her feet, Bobby walked into the bathroom and caught a glimpse of one of his favorite things. As Stormy stood back up, she looked into the mirror and saw Bobby standing behind her enjoying the scenery. It had been over a week since she let Bobby touch her. Stormy was not happy with Bobby anymore. Bobby's laziness and refusal to get a job was a turn off. Bobby didn't have money and what's more, he didn't even seem concerned about it. Stormy had been the one paying the bills. It was Stormy who packed the refrigerator and put gas in both of their cars. This was not how Stormy imagined things would be when she decided to let Bobby move in with her a few months ago. It seemed to Stormy that as soon as she gave him a set of keys to her apartment, Bobby got fired from his job and started sponging off of her. Stormy felt that if she had to pay the bills herself, she might as well be living by herself. What did she need him for? She didn't even need him for sex, since she had her "pocket rocket" and her thoughts of Moon to make it real.

"You look so good Stormy."

"Do I?"

"How about a little love making session before they get here? It has been over a week."

Stormy could have stuck to her guns and said no, since she was planning on breaking up with him anyway. Stormy's plan was to get to the cabin this weekend and pick a fight with Bobby. As soon as Bobby said anything to try and save face in front of his friends, she would reveal all of his little secrets and then break up with him. It was the perfect plan; Stormy would get to have the last say, embarrass the hell out of Bobby in front of the friends he always tried so hard to impress and Bobby couldn't retaliate because nobody would let him touch her. Yes, it was a mean spirited plan and it might ruin everyone's weekend, but sometimes a person just could not avoid collateral damage. If misery did indeed love company, Stormy was about to throw a party. The idea alone made her feel warm inside; Stormy couldn't wait to get to the cabin and put her plan into action.

However, Stormy was considering letting Bobby get lucky right now. Stormy's two minutes of pleasuring herself had only served to get her into the mood. Right now she was so wet and horny that she wanted to do more than just fantasize about Moon having his way with her. Stormy thought she might give Bobby a last little taste of paradise. Stormy could close her eyes and imagine that it was Moon caressing her long slender neck...sucking her huge round nipples, entering her soft moist vagina. If she let Bobby slip in from the back, she would not have to worry about opening her eyes by mistake and ruining the fantasy by realizing it was Bobby who was inside her- fumbling around like a drunken mosquito.

Even if Bobby knew what she was thinking at this very moment, he would not care. It had been ten days since they had sex. For the last ten days, Stormy had used all types of excuses; *"no, you're drunk...no, you're high...no, you're disgusting...no, no, no."* The closest Bobby had been to a piece of coochie in the last ten days was his right hand all lathered up with Irish Spring soap. Although it did the job, it was nothing to write home about.

"Okay, we can do it Bobby, but just for a little while. You know they will be here any minute."

"Bet."

Bobby immediately grabs her and starts kissing her and reaching for her vagina. "*Damn fumbling ass.*" Stormy pushes Bobby away and leans back against the sink, opening her legs. Bobby comes back at her, reaching out and grabbing one of her round breast. Stormy pushes his hand away and smacks him across the face. Bobby takes a step back stunned, wondering what was happening. Before he can make a protest, Stormy walks up to him and puts her index finger over his lips and says, "*Shhh.*" Bobby thinks this is some kind of new foreplay, but for Stormy this is not foreplay; it is a mixture of anger along with her desire to continue the fantasy she was having about Moon. Stormy pushes past Bobby and walks out of the bathroom towards the bed. As Bobby watches her, she stands at the edge of the bed with her back facing him and bends over- revealing that special part of her that she knows Bobby loves to look at. Stormy gets up on the bed on all fours and opens wide. She then turns around and faces Bobby while kneeling on the bed. Stormy takes one hand and runs it down her body and takes her other hand and motions for Bobby to come close.

As Bobby approaches, Stormy allows herself to fall onto her back on the bed. Bobby moves in close and begins taking off his clothes. The shirt comes off, then the shorts and then the boxers. As Bobby moves to get on top of her, Stormy stops him in his tracks by putting her foot on his chest and pushes him back.
"*No, no, no, on your knees. You're going to have a meal before you get to this dessert.*"

Bobby knows exactly what she means. For a split second, Bobby looked disturbed, like a scary thought had taken over his mind. But the moment passes and Bobby kneels down in front of her. He spreads her legs wide and gets on his j-o-b.

"*Slow down junior. This ain't no pie eating contest. If you going to do the job, then do it right."*

Stormy let's herself relax and enjoy the festivities...she has played this round perfectly. Stormy has won all around; she gets to enjoy the experience and think of Moon the whole time. If she can hold out long enough, by the time her second waterfall begins to gush forth, Rick, Moon and the girls should be pulling up and she won't have to do anything else. This is the perfect plan.

"Damn, I'm good...Ahhh."

Chapter 11

"We're here."

As the mini-van pulls into the parking lot outside of Stormy's apartment, the four occupants are laughing and singing with the radio. Sheena, who is sitting in the front passenger seat, turns the radio volume down and stares at the window of Stormy's apartment. Moon leans in from the back seat to chat with Rick.

"I bet you they're not ready."

"Yes they are Moon, I know they are. I called Bobby an hour ago and told him we were on our way and would be her in thirty minutes."

"Come on Rick, you know that doesn't work with him. He probably knew you were telling him a half hour too early. I bet he's not even out of the bed yet."

"You are absolutely wrong Moon. I bet you he is waiting by the door right now."

"You want to put some money where your mouth is?"

With those words, Sheena can't help but jump into the conversation.

"Don't bet him anything Rick."

"Shut up Sheena. At least I said put his money where his mouth is...not where it's been."

Mimi hits Moon playfully on the arm.

"You are so crass Moon."

Sheena can't pass up the chance to respond to Mimi,

"No girl, what you really mean is, 'you are such an ass Moon."

The girls and the guys exit the mini-van. Moon takes the football out of his bag and throws it to Rick.

"So back to you Mr. Turnall. What about a little wager? Here's the bet. You honk the horn a couple of times. If Bobby gets down here within five minutes, you win and I will give you a crisp twenty dollar bill."

"And if you win?"

"I get to smack your girl Sheena on her second chin."

"Screw you Moon. I don't have no damn second chin."

Mimi grabs Sheena by the arm.

"Girl, don't pay no attention to Moon. You know he ain't got no sense."

"So what do you say Rick, do we have a bet?"

"It's a bet."

"What?"

"Not about your second chin baby. I mean your chin. I mean ain't nobody smacking nothing. The bet is a twenty dollar all the way around."

Sheena walks over to Rick and whispers in his ear...

"Watch yourself Rick. Don't let Moon get you punched in the neck this weekend."

Rick swallows hard as he walks over to the steering wheel and honks the horn three times. Sheena and Mimi start walking towards the steps to the apartment. Before the girls can make it twenty feet, Bobby is looking out of the upstairs apartment window.

"Alright, alright...I'm coming down now."

The girls stop in their tracks and turn to look at Rick, who is now patting himself on the shoulder. Sheena rolls her eyes and the girls start walking again. Bobby comes down the stairs of the building as the girls walk past him waving and smiling.

"Hi Bobby."

"Hey ladies, Stormy is upstairs finishing up."

Bobby walks to the mini-van, puts his bag in the back and shuts the car's rear lift gate. Moon and Rick just stare at him. Bobby comes back and stands next to Moon. Rick gives Bobby a handshake, but Moon does not move.

"What the hell is going on here Bobby?"

"What did I do?"

Rick laughs,

"Don't worry about it Bobby, Moon is just a sore loser. What did I tell you Moon... now pay up."

"This is some real bullshit. Just when I think I can count on you to be the slow ass chump that you are, you want to go and change up on a brother...you wanna get all brand new."

"Rick, what the hell is Moon talking about? You been smoking them funny cigarettes again Moon?

"Leave Bobby alone Moon and pay me my money."

Bobby shrugs off Moon's comments,

"So, you guys ready for the cabin adventure?"

"Ready? Come on man, Moon was born ready for whatever."

"Why the hell are you talking about yourself in the third person?

"Because it takes that many people just to understand the greatness that is Moon Wiggins."

Rick sighs,

"Excuse me your greatness, pay me my money please."

Moon digs in his pocket and pulls out a twenty dollar bill and hands it to Rick.

"I think you guys just conspired to con me."

"Conspired? How long did it take you to practice that word Moon?"

"Why? Are you impressed?"

"Not yet. You want to impress me? Let me hear you spell it."

"Certainly. K-i-c-k, y-o-u-r, a-s-s. Conspired."

Bobby grabs the football from Moon,

"Aw come on Moon, chill out. We are about to go to a quiet cabin in the woods with three of the finest girls in Virginia. How can you be mad about anything right now?"

Rick starts laughing.

"Shit, All that time and space and Moon still won't get none."

"Rick, are you crazy? I'm planning on knocking the back out of mine. I hope she brought some Aleeve because I'm gonna be tapping her spine all weekend."

"You want to make another bet on that?"

Moon pauses,

"Why...did Mimi tell you something?"

Bobby and Rick fall out laughing.

"Man, forget y'all. So Rick, tell us about this cabin. And for what I paid, this spot better be the truth."

Chapter 12

Inside the apartment, Sheena is helping Stormy finish packing for the trip while Mimi is in front of the mirror admiring herself…again.

"Dang Stormy, this is a bad dress."

"Thank you Sheena. I caught a good sale."

"You went shopping and you didn't call me?"

"My bad girl, you know I wanted to call you…

Mimi turns around to look at the dress.

"But she probably got it with a five finger discount."

"Oh no you didn't heifer. I got that dress at Macy's and it came with a receipt, thank you"

"Heifer? Who the hell you calling a heifer bitch?

"I'm just saying; don't get me confused with your mother."

"What? Oh hell no, somebody done told you wrong…"

Sheena steps between them,

"Come on now, don't start this. We are women. Let's leave the teenage girl stuff at home, Okay? Now, are you guys ready for this weekend?"

Mimi turns back to the mirror.

"I know I am. I'm gonna get my groove on."

Stormy used the moment to get in a personal dig...

"Humph. And how is that different from any other weekend?"

"Okay ladies. We are going to have to call a truce. We can't go out there bickering back and forth. Now if you two can't get along, just avoid each other this weekend. We are going out to a cabin in the woods to have a good time, not to be stressing each other out. Can't we all just get along?"

Stormy and Mimi look at each other and then turn their gaze on Sheena and surprisingly say the same thing at the same time,

"Bitch, shut up."

They all laugh.

"Okay Mimi, I'm down for a truce. How about you?"

"I can do that. Truce."

Sheena smiles...

"Good, now shake hand ladies."

Mimi and Stormy reluctantly shake hands. These two women have only known each other a short period of time, but the dislike is real. They don't have any history together. They don't even go to the same school. In fact, they know very little about each other, but what they do know, neither of them like.

Mimi knows that Stormy is pre-med and that her goal is to become a neurologist. Mimi only knows Stormy because of Moon and Bobby. Mimi also knows that Stormy is the only one of the girls that is actually from Virginia. Somehow, that makes Stormy think she is special or something. Stormy is always trying to look down her nose at somebody. Mimi figures Stormy is jealous because Mimi is fine and she has Moon. Mimi is aware that Stormy wanted

Moon at some point, and just wasn't woman enough to get him...or to keep him. The only piece of advice Mimi can give Stormy is not to hate the player, hate the game...and the woman who sold her that dress.

Stormy knows that Mimi is no longer a student at Virginia State. She failed out of school last semester and since then she has been hanging around hoping to catch herself a football star. Since Stormy is originally from Petersburg and most of her family and friends still live there, she does have some information about Mimi that Sheena does not know. Stormy knows that Mimi is a hoe. Not just a regular, run of the mill hoe, but a conniving gold digging hoe. Mimi only dated guys with money or with the potential to make money. Stormy knows that Mimi has been going out with Moon for about a year now; and although she hasn't heard anything about her cheating on Moon yet, Stormy still thinks Mimi is a little too fast and friendly with too many guys. Stormy knows it is none of her business but she can't help but hate Mimi...it just feels so right.

Stormy has been attracted to Moon since they met during her freshman year of college when she was still enrolled at Virginia State University. Stormy did everything she could to get close to Moon but Moon viewed her as just a friend. Stormy was so attracted to Moon that after their freshman year, when Moon spurned all of her advances, she decided to change schools. That's how she ended up at Virginia Union. Even then, Stormy just couldn't give it up. The real reason Stormy started dating Bobby last year was because Bobby and Moon were friends and this way she could be near Moon. Stormy invited Bobby to come live with her, hoping that Moon would be visiting and occasionally spend the night a few times. Stormy's plan had not worked to this point, but it was worth a shot in her book. There are no rules when it comes to getting your man.

"So Sheena, your man is the one who set this whole thing up. Have you ever been to the cabin?"

"Yes girl and let me tell you, it is beautiful. We went out there a couple of months ago and spent the week with his parents. Let me tell you about this place. It's nestled at the base of a mountain. There are beautiful views of the mountains and the water. There are flowers and trees everywhere and a ton of things to do. White water rafting, canoeing, bike riding, hiking...oh my goodness we are going to have a ball. The cabin has four bedrooms and a huge living room. It has a wrap-around porch just like in the movies. We are going..."

As Sheena is speaking, the car's horn starts honking furiously. Mimi walks over to the window to see what the commotion is. Mimi can hear Moon through the glass.

"Come on ladies, what are you doing up there? Let's go!"

Mimi turns around and put her butt in the window and smacks it."

"You can kiss this Moon."

"I got something a lot bigger for that than my lips."

The women can hear the guys downstairs laughing. Sheena walks to the window and stands next to Mimi.

"Girl, I don't know how you put up with his simple ass. Man he gets on my nerves."

"Don't even worry about him. I know just how to handle Mr. Football Star down there."

Mimi and Sheena laughed until they noticed Stormy standing in the bathroom mirror looking down at the floor and holding the towel she had earlier. Sheena walks over to check on Stormy...

"You Okay girl? What's wrong?"

"Listen. I want to tell you both something. I have a weird feeling

about this trip."

"Weird like what?"

"Last night I had a dream..."

"Oh, what...you Martin Luther King Jr. now?"

"Mimi, you promised...Okay, go on Stormy."

"Like I was saying, I had a dream last night. We were at a cabin in the woods when this man appeared. But he was more than just some man. He seemed evil."

"And?"
"Well there is not a lot more to tell. I woke up right after that, but I can't shake the feeling. It's been making me uneasy all day."

"You know that don't make no sense right?"

"What Mimi means is what does that dream have to do with anything? That was probably the result of some bad chicken or something. Don't go tripping over a dream. Let's just get our things head out to the cabin and have a great time. Agreed?

"Agreed."

Sheena grabs one of Stormy's bags and heads towards the front door as Mimi and Stormy follows suit. Once they walk out of the apartment, Stormy tells them go ahead, and heads back inside for a moment. Stormy checks the stove to make sure it is off, turns out the lights and goes downstairs.

Stormy finally makes it outside to the group just as couples begin to pair off.

"So, are we ready to go?"
Moon grabs Sheena by the head and pushes her to the side as he

walks closer to Mimi. Sheena punches Moon on the arm, and hurts her hand. Moon brushes off his arm like a piece of dirt landed on it and give Sheena a look that makes Rick laugh.

"Now back to the business at hand. I'm ready to go where I'm going, so I can get to where I'm gonna be and then get to doing what I do best."

"Really, and what, might I ask, do you do best?"

"I score touchdowns baby."

"Well. If my memory serves me correctly, the last time you held the ball...you fumbled."

With those words Mimi walks away and gets into the car. Everyone else is standing around staring at Moon and laughing.

"She's talking about our last game..."

...more laughter.

...a real football game...

"Whatever Moon, it still doesn't sound good for you."

"Shut up Bobby. Can we go please? We're wasting time."

Everyone gets into the car one by one. Rick turns on the car, puts it in reverse and off they go...vacation bound.

Chapter 13

Cary Street is busy this afternoon.

Usually if you walk down Cary Street in Richmond during the late morning on a weekday, you may bump into a few people milling about. At 10:00am on a Tuesday morning, you could have a very nice stroll; past the small quaint shops offering specialty items, vintage shops with smiling proprietors beckoning you inside, even a few coffee shops with outside seating in the cool morning air.

This Tuesday morning, Frank was not interested in the many businesses that line this favorite shopping area in the City. This morning Frank is on a mission; he has a very important meeting with a very important person. In fact, one could say this was one of the most important meetings of his entire career- perhaps even his life. Frank was scheduled to have a cup of coffee in a Sushi restaurant with a man sent to him directly from the President of the United States. This was a very serious and very delicate matter. The people to whom the President reports want to make sure this matter is taken care of quickly, discreetly and permanently.

"Sushi at 10:00am. I wonder if he'll be eating Sushi."

Frank smiles to himself; his face twisting in what look like a painful expression it was not used to making. Frank looked like he was using muscles in his face that hadn't been forced to move since his birth.

"Probably not...I don't think they eat human food."

Frank walked along the street with perfect posture. If anyone were the observant type and paying attention, they would instantly recognize that Frank was a bit out of place. Aesthetically, he looked like anyone else; a tall medium build man about six foot four with solid square facial features. Frank was wearing jeans, a simple black button down shirt and white tennis shoes. Frank completed his outfit with an old looking college cap and a pair of sunglasses. Yes, Frank looked the part, but there was still something a bit off.

To a more observant eye, one might notice that Frank's posture was impeccable. There was no particular reason that it should not have been, but with all the extra people out this morning the perfection of his gait stood out among the rest. There was also Frank's walking pace. Frank was moving at almost twice the speed as any of the other people walking about- like he was on a mission and he dared not be late. Frank's choice of outfits this morning was a bit odd when coupled with his gait and pace; it looked as if he were trying to dress down.

The fact is, Frank *was* out of pace in this scenery. Captain Frank White is the Chief of Police for the City of Richmond and he rarely went anywhere in public without wearing either a suit or his uniform. Fortunately for Frank most people are oblivious to their surroundings; choosing to see the world and ignore it at the same time, until circumstances forces them to pay closer attention. Frank was grateful for this chink in the make-up of human nature. Frank always found it funny that in this age of technological advances, we are connecting to people all over the world, yet most people are still alone. Frank's youngest son, who is on every social network on the internet and has his phone and computer and television and who knows what else connected, brags to him about how he has friends all over the world. Frank's son brags about having thousands of "friends" and million's of "likes" on his internet pages. From Frank's point of view, all his son does in sit in his room by himself, talking about how he's connecting to people everywhere. Technology, the better it gets, the stupider people seem to get. Maybe not stupid, but they are definitely more "tuned out" than "tuned in".

Frank finally arrives at Moshi Moshi, a great Sushi Restaurant at the top of Cary Street. As soon as Frank walks near, he spots the two agents standing on either side of the awning. Frank notices the earpieces, looks up to the second floor of the restaurant and spots

another agent looking down at them through the window.
The two agents standing in front of Frank move back slightly as the agent on the right nodded his head at Frank. Frank walks past the agents and proceeds into the restaurant.

Once inside, the owner meets Frank at the front door and bows.

"Welcome Captain. This way please."

Frank follows the owner to the steps in the rear behind the bar. These steps lead to a part of the restaurant that most people never get to see. The owner walks Frank up to the second floor and down a long hallway. There are two doors at the end of the hallway; the door on the left leads to the owner's office, the door on the right is a bathroom.

Frank enters the door on the left and walks into the receptionist's office, which is right outside the owner's office. Standing besides the door that leads to the owner's office is another two agents, dresses in black suits, black ties, white shirts and sporting earpieces in their ears. The agent on the left opens the door for Frank while the agent on the right welcomes their newest visitor.

"Good morning Captain White, he's waiting for you inside."

Frank walks past the agents and goes into the office. The office itself is a small cubby hole. On the walls are various local awards that the restaurant has won for excellence in food, management and cleanliness. There are also a few autographed pictures of famous people who have eaten at the restaurant, along with the owner and his family. On the opposite side of the room is the desk, and behind the desk sits the man with whom Frank has this unconventionally early lunch meeting with. Frank does not take many meetings outside of his departmental obligations, but this is one meeting he does not have a choice in taking.

"Please Frank, have a seat."

Frank sits in the chair that has been set up for him and stares at his host; a little man with a presence bigger than the room they are now sharing. Frank wondered if his feet were even touching the floor behind the desk. The agent wore a black suit just like the others, but he has no tie on. Instead, his white button down shirt is unbuttoned at the top. Frank was not told the man's name, but Frank knew he was a high ranking individual with a *Card Blanche* to do whatever needed to be done on behalf of his country. Frank knew that whoever this man is, it is in Frank's best interest to pay attention and do what he says. As Frank stares into the agent's eyes, he allows himself to quickly remember the phone call that initiated this impromptu meeting.

Chapter 14

It was three o'clock this morning when Frank received a call on the second line in his home. The second line was a reserved line, only used by a select few in cases of extreme emergencies. Frank picked up the phone expecting to hear from one of his staff on a problem in the City; perhaps a shooting of an unarmed teen by one of his officers, perhaps media coverage of some type of racial tension. It was true that Richmond had not *recently* seen the type of life and death confrontations that some Cities around the nation were experiencing- with full media and social networking coverage. Frank knew it was only a matter of time before the same incidents reared its ugly head in his city. After all, Virginia is one of the original thirteen colonies, and a lasting stronghold of the old traditions has never completely died.

When Frank received the call this morning, his officer said;

"Chief, we have someone from Washington on the other line that we need to patch through to you right away. He says it is a matter of National Security."

Frank immediately sat up in his bed and looked at the time. Frank put on his glasses, since he never wore his contacts to bed.

"This is Captain Frank White. To whom am I speaking?"

"This is Barry Swetoro. I have a problem that is heading your way and we need closure immediately. This issue must be handled with great care. Can I count on you Frank?"

"Absolutely Sir."

"Great. I knew you were a team player Frank. If we can resolve this matter discreetly, there will be a place for you here in Washington."

"That would be an honored Sir."

"Okay Frank. I have one of my close advisors on his way to Richmond right now. He will be there in a few hours. I want you to meet him this morning at 10:00am for a discussion, where he will give you all of the relevant information on this situation. Will you meet with him Frank?"

"Absolutely Sir."

"Good. Try to dress down for the occasion. We don't want to alarm any citizens. It's best if this matter is kept under the radar."

"Absolutely Sir."

"Thank you Frank. You are a good man and a patriot. I will make sure that none of this goes unnoticed."

Chapter 15

So here Frank sat with his highly recommended visitor. Frank still did not know the man's name, but it didn't matter. Frank had received a call from Washington; and whatever this man needed or asked of him, Frank would carry it out personally.

"Thank you for meeting with me Frank, may I call you Frank?

"Absolutely Sir. And how may I address you?

"You may address me as Sir. However this meeting goes, we will meet again. If the outcome is in our favor, I will see you again in Washington soon and you will get to know me pretty well as a friend and confidant. If the outcome is not favorable, when we meet again, you won't see me. Do I make myself and my intentions clear?"

"Yes Sir."

"Good. Now on to the business at hand."

The man behind the desk slowly takes off his dark shades to reveal two of the most crystal clear blue eyes that Frank has ever seen. This man's eyes were captivating, almost hypnotic. Frank has never seen eyes like these. They were alive and yet icy cold at the same time; they seemed to look past Frank's face and bore themselves into his very soul.

"NASA headquarters has been broken into; as a result, a very special project we were working on has gone missing, along with some other valuable information. Actually, more than one of our facilities have been compromised and we think it was by the same people responsible for the NASA break in. All of these break-ins happened within two weeks of each other. Edwards Air Force Base in California was compromised as well as another installation just north of New Mexico, near the town of Dulce, close to the Jicarilla Indian Reservation. Some very important items were taken from

the latter two locations that we must get back."

"Can you tell me what was taken?"

"No. That is not your concern."

"Okay. What is it that I can do to help?"

"We have reason to believe that the perpetrators are either on their way to Richmond or they may already be here. Have you had any incidents that you cannot explain in the last forty-eight hours?"

"Can you be more specific Sir?"

"Have you had any especially gruesome murders with reports of dismembered bodies or missing limbs? Have you found any bodies strung from telephone poles? Any crime scenes that seemed especially heinous?"

"No sir, no reports as of yet."

The agent stands up and peers out of the window. Although the only scenery outside of that window is the new bakery across the street, the agent seems to be staring intently at it as if the secrets of the universe lie within its business logo. The agent turns back to Frank and approaches closely. He sits on the edge of the desk right in front of Frank and leans in very close, like he is trying to intimidate Frank. Frank has never been the type to be intimidated, but this man came close.

"Frank. I want you to pay very close attention."

The agent reaches back on the desk and pulls out a manila folder. He opens the folder and hands Frank three 8'x10' photographs and an envelope.

"These are the people we suspect of pulling off the caper. Have

you ever seen them before?"

Frank looks at the photos carefully.

"No Sir."

"The first picture is of a woman named Victoria Harper. Victoria also goes by the name of Vic. She was an employee of NASA when the first incident happened about six weeks ago. Vic is ex-military and extremely good at hand to hand combat and weapons. She is intelligent and extremely resourceful. Make sure you are ready for her when you meet her, because she is a proficient killer. Understand me well Frank, she will kill you if given the slightest opportunity.

The second photograph is Brandon Harper.

"Brandon is the younger brother of Vitoria, but just as dangerous. Although Brandon is not ex-military he does come from a military background; their father being a Colonel in the Army.

"Shall I begin by calling their father to gather some information?"

"Don't bother, their father is dead. So are their mother and older brother. It seems they were in a bad car accident and none of them survived. It happened shortly after the first installations I mentioned were compromised. It was a terrible accident. The only way we could identify the bodies were from their dental records."

"Yes Sir. That does sound terrible."

"The third photo is of a self-proclaimed expert in the study of Trans-humanism and genetic engineering. His name is Clifford Vale. We are positive that Clifford is the one who is holding a bag full of very important information on one of our 'special projects'. We need to apprehend these individual...alive would be good, dead would be ok too. The most important thing is that we need that bag returned. It holds information that is very vital to the security of

the United States...perhaps even the world at large."

The agent hands Frank the folder. Frank looks at the photos one last time, and rests the envelope on his lap and returns his gaze to the man sitting on the desk in front of him.

"Needless to say, we need discretion. We don't want to alarm the general public at this time. Are you the man for the job Frank?"

"Yes Sir. If these suspects step their feet in Richmond, I will have them."

The agent smiles and pats Frank on the shoulder like a little child who has answered all the questions correctly.

"I knew we could count on you Frank."

"May I ask a question Sir?"

"You may."

"What's in the bag? How can we be certain all of the items are accounted for unless we know what is supposed to be in there?"

The agent's eyebrows furrow. Frank thinks to himself, *"Now you've done it, you've annoyed him."*

"Don't worry about the items in the bag. If you retrieve the bag...when you retrieve the bag, you give me a call and I will be there to pick it up. Do not open the bag under any circumstance and instruct your officers to do the same. We will know if you or anyone in your department has opened the bag, and let me just say, that would not be a good thing."

"Yes Sir. Is there anything else Sir?"

The agent walks back over to the chair behind the desk and sits down slowly. He picks up his sunglasses and slowly puts them on, covering up his icy blue eyes. Frank is relieved.

"No Frank that is it."

As Frank stands to walk out of the office, the agent makes one last comment that stops Frank dead in his tracks...

"Remember Frank, I will see you again. However, the outcome of this little mission will determine whether or not you see me when I see you. Understood?"

Without turning back, Frank responds.

"Yes Sir."

Chapter 16

In the past month, Cliff has found himself traveling more than he has in the past five years. Cliff was living in Arizona when he was asked by a friend to come out to Washington D.C. and sit in on a special session in a secret lab at NASA headquarters.

Cliff had never really considered himself an important person. Cliff had to admit however that in the last ten years his research had opened the eyes of many people around the world to the new experiments being embarked upon in the name of science. Cliff supposed that shedding a light on the dark side of this science perhaps was not the best avenue to take, but what else could he do? Cliff had read about people like Julian Assange and Edward Snowden. Before Cliff became a fixture in the public eye because of his desperate need to inform the people of the world to the vast changes being planned for and upon human beings, he read up on others who had gone public with knowledge that certain groups did not want shared. Cliff researched people like Edmund Dene Morel, the English shipping clerk turned journalist who reported on the atrocities in the Congo Free State and became an anti-slavery campaigner. Morel's revelations led to a strong campaign against Belgian King Leopold II's autocratic regime in his African territory, where the rubber plantations brutally exploited slave labor back in the 1890's. Clifford was familiar with Smedley Butler, a retired U.S. Marines Corps Major General, a two-time recipient of the Medal of Honor, who alleged that business leaders had plotted a fascist coup d'état against the Franklin D. Roosevelt administration in what became known as *the Business Plot*. In Butler's book *'War Is a Racket'*, he listed well-known US military operations that he alleged were not about protecting democracy as was told to the public but in furthering the business interests of U.S. banks and corporations. Butler compared these activities with Al Capone-style mob hits on behalf of American corporations and their respective business interests.

Cliff found that the list of whistle blowers was quite extensive;

covering hundreds of years and a vast amount of subjects. The thing that Cliff found curious was that almost all of these so-called *"enemies of the public"* usually met untimely deaths under extremely questionable circumstances. Cliff was beginning to believe that soon he would be named among them, with one major difference; Cliff did not know exactly what it was he had stumbled upon but he didn't think he would get the chance to find out before he expired.

Cliff was not afraid of death. As a matter of fact, in a way Cliff looked forward to the day he would no longer be a citizen of this Earth. Cliff never felt like he belonged here. The only thing that Cliff feared about death was prolonged pain. Cliff did not want to die a prolonged painful death at the hands of some sadistic murderer or some man-made disease or even as the victim of being at the wrong place at the wrong time. Cliff thought that his departure from this Earth should be with some amount of dignity, which is why he never really got involved in any protests or other acts where confrontations could lead to unwanted results. Yet Cliff now found himself in a serious situation. He had been running across the United States with two companions, breaking into and stealing from Federal Agencies. In Washington D.C. he had stolen a tote bag from the underground lab in NASA's headquarters. In California he had stolen a valuable book from an Air Force base. Cliff and his companions had even killed a few military personnel in New Mexico. It was in self-defense of course, since these individuals had their guns trained on the three of them and were ready to shoot. Cliff is still not sure how Vic got them out of that situation. Vic was a beautiful woman who was even more resourceful and dangerous than her beauty suggested. Cliff guessed that he underestimated Vic's abilities just because she was physically attractive. Cliff had learned a basic lesson once again that evening; never ever judge a book by its cover.

Now Cliff was by himself. Cliff has been on his own ever since last night's showdown in the warehouse on Leigh Street. Cliff would have stayed on the ground outside the warehouse when he came crashing down on top of those boxes from the second story window, but Vic made Cliff promise that if a situation like that ever happened, he would keep running. Vic and Brandon were the best companions a person could ask for. They were not the joking types or even the talkative types, but when it came down to it they were the sacrificing types. Vic and her brother sacrificed their lives for his; choosing to stay, face their enemy and fight until their last breath- affording Cliff some valuable time to make his escape and continue on.

Cliff was still in Richmond and he was alone. Cliff popped in and out of crowed areas, trying to stay under the radar. Surely the government had tipped off the local authorities by now and Cliff was most certainly the main subject of a State to State search. Cliff did not want to be caught; not only because of his fear of an untimely and painful death, but also because if he was caught now then all of their running would be for nothing. All of the lives that were sacrificed would be for nothing if Cliff were caught by the authorities or by Shemihazah.

Cliff remembered Brandon telling him about the death of his family. Cliff asked Vic what happened, but Vic did not want to talk about it…ever. The second time he had asked Vic about her parents Vic had grabbed her gun from its holster and slammed it squarely against his right temple...

"I swear to God Cliff, if you ask me about my family one more time I will kill you myself. You just keep up and make sure you don't lose that bag."

That was all Cliff needed to hear to confirm in his mind that something terrible happened to her family and it was because of him. Cliff didn't know how he was involved, but this seemed too personal an issue to Vic for it to be a random thing.

Chapter 17

It was in Chicago a few weeks ago that Brandon sat Cliff down and told him the story. Vic had gone asleep and it was Brandon's turn to keep watch over them. Cliff was having a bad night; his hemorrhoids had flared up something terrible and he could not sleep. When Cliff walked over to where Brandon was standing, looking out of the second floor window of the two story abandoned warehouse they were hiding in, he noticed Brandon was crying.

"What is it Brandon?"

Brandon turned and stared at Cliff with a mixture of sadness and anger.

"You know, this is all your fault Cliff."

"What's all my fault?"

"Everything. The reason we are sitting here is your fault, the reason my sister is going crazy is your fault. My parents and my brother's death is your fault. It is all your fault."

Cliff was not sure what Brandon was talking about. Cliff had not asked to be in this predicament, it was thrust upon him. Technically, Cliff didn't ask Vic to get involved. All Cliff asked of Vic was to hold the elevator that night in the basement of NASA headquarters. The next thing Cliff knew, Vic was asking him what happened. After Cliff told her, she became his guardian angel.

"Tell me what happened Brandon."

"I'll make a deal with you. I'll tell you what happened to my family if you tell me the circumstances that surrounded you and my sister meeting. Tell me why she is so intent on protecting you and seeing this thing through."

"It's a deal Brandon."

"Good. You start first."

Chapter 18

Cliff had just arrived in Washington D.C. Cliff had flown to D.C on the insistence of his friend Hugo, whom he had talk with on the phone a few hours earlier.

"Clifford, you must come to D.C my friend. I need you here with me tomorrow night."

"Why? What is so important?"

"I have a meeting with a few other people at NASA. There is a project that we have been working on for many years. If falls right in line with the things you have been talking about; Transhumanism and genetic engineering. We have found success in a way only few ever thought possible. That is all I can say on the phone. Fly in on the next plane and we'll have dinner tonight and I will explain more to you before we attend tomorrow's 'meeting'."

Cliff boarded the next plane and headed to D.C from his home in Tucson, Arizona. It was a long flight and Cliff's mind raced all the way there. Cliff was aware that many scientists had been playing with gene manipulation to create new breeds of animals. Cliff remembered when scientist first crossed a spider with a goat and used the milk to create a stronger material for body armor and other military applications; some we know about, some we don't. Cliff remembered when scientist first started growing human ears and noses inside mice, and told us that this was a wonderful application of the science. Cliff had been at the forefront of the movement against stem cell research because he knew whatever good reasons they gave us for doing it was most likely a mask for an evil agenda the powers that be would not reveal to the masses. Cliff followed cases that popped up in the regular news (which wasn't many) as well as stories of heinous creations by scientist in Europe and other parts of the world. Cliff did not believe that it mattered whether the media knew about these examples or not, because nothing would be printed either way. Cliff knew that all of the media outlets; television, newspapers, and so on, were controlled by maybe four or five people. There was a guarantee that anything the people in power did not want the masses to know would not make it into the news outlets. The news would only report on and push the stories that had been pre-approved for show. That is why Cliff was a proponent of free speech and he loved the internet. Cliff knew the internet was monitored, but sometime a person could put up some information and get a little traction before their site was shut down for whatever reason.

When Cliff's flight landed in D.C, Hugo was there to pick him up. Hugo was a great person, and secretly Cliff thought that his friend looked a bit like Albert Einstein. Hugo took Cliff to his apartment first. As soon as they arrived at Hugo's apartment, a small, one room studio in a run-down tenement, Hugo motioned for Cliff to remain silent as he took out a strange looking object. The object was black, rectangular in shape and fit in the palm of Hugo's hand. The device had two dial types of buttons on it with a series of small lights in a line across the middle. At the top of the machine, there was a circular hole with a red piece of glass or film. Hugo turned on the machine and turned it up until a few beeps could be heard. Hugo began looking through the small glass built into the machine. He turned it all around the apartment; looking into light fixtures, over the shelves that held his books and papers, under the bed…everywhere in the apartment. Once satisfied, Hugo turned the little machine off and put it back in his pocket.

"What is that?"

"It is a signal detector. I created it myself."

"What types off signals does it detect?"

"It detects mostly radio signals. It helps me determine if there are any listening devices, video recording devices or cell phones in the room."

"Are you trying to see if your room has been bugged?"

"Indeed I am my friend."

"But why?"

"You can never be too safe these days. You do remember that line in the Woody Allen movie from long ago; what do you call a person who always thinks there is someone out to get them..."

"Perceptive."

Hugo offered Cliff a cup of coffee and they sat down for a chat. At first the chat was simple; how are things, what have you been up to, how is the family. Hugo and Cliff have not talked with each other in almost two years, but their conversation never skipped a beat. Cliff was so glad to be catching up with his old friend.

After about twenty minute of chatting, Hugo's face seemed to darken.

"Cliff, there is a special meeting happening tomorrow evening. Actually, it is not so much a meeting as a procedure."

"A procedure?"

"Yes Cliff. It seems that we have been successful in creating something very new...a new life form."

Cliff sat there staring at his friend. They both knew that scientists were creating new life forms every day. They had been together eight years ago when they witnesses one of the strangest creations either of them had seen. Someone had infused human DNA into plant seeds and grew a whole greenhouse full of human/plant hybrids. The difference was that instead of using a hair follicle, they used human blood. The various flowers and plant that resulted were equipped with blinking eyes on their petals, fingers that moved constantly as the plant stood in its pot. One creation even had a face...and in the morning when the dew was fresh, this particular plant would cry red tears.

But this look on Hugo's face was strange. It was almost as if he were looking at something invisible at the same time he was looking at Cliff. *What could they have done that would cause his friend to look this worried? And whatever they did, why had they invited Cliff of all people to be some type of spectator?*

"What kind of life form has been created?"

"A man...of sorts."

Hugo went on to tell Cliff about an experiment that they did. Many people were aware of the tales of spaceships crashing and alien autopsies. Most people don't believe in such things, but there are a few that knew better than to underestimate anything. Cliff himself never believed that aliens existed...at least not what we think of as aliens.

Cliff had been raised in the church. When Cliff was old enough to make his own decisions about whether he would continue to attend church or not he choose not. Yet there were a lot of things he did and did not believe because of his upbringing in a small Pentecostal church.

For example, Cliff did not believe in evolution, he was a creationist. Cliff believed that there is a God and that this same God created everything in the universe. Cliff believed that there was a natural and a spiritual world. Cliff did not believe that there were any aliens living in star systems called Zeta Reticuli 1 & 2.

Cliff believed that God created two different types of living entities; angels and human. Angels were created first and are extremely varied in looks and purpose. Then God created humans. Cliff believed that there was a small contingent of angels who rebelled; once they found out that their purpose was to service God's- human beings. Humans were created after the angelic hosts, were created with less power than the angels, yet they held a special place in God's heart that the angels did not understand.

Cliff believed that before humans were created, God told his plan to his servants, the angels. One angel in particular named lucifer became enraged. lucifer, who was probably the first angel created, decided God had lost his mind. lucifer would never be subject to a human being- and God needed to be "impeached" for even thinking of the idea. lucifer was able to gather a third of all the angels created and convince them to rebel against the Lord of Hosts.

As a result, God banished them from His Holy Mountain. lucifer has been on a mission to rule humanity and replace God every since.

Cliff believed that the aliens humans have become so fascinated with from these far away star systems are in fact fallen angels. Cliff believes that these same angels have been conversing with our governmental leaders around the world for decades- if not longer.

Hugo told Cliff of the latest experiment gone wild. Apparently, one of these "visitors" had provided some type of genetic material that is not found here on Earth. Scientists were able to extract this genetic material and insert into a human embryo in a lab and grow a human/alien hybrid. This experiment was light years ahead of any scientist's tinkering with genetic materials. Before this, scientists had been limited to cross breeding plants, animals and human DNA, because they were limited to the materials found here on Earth. But now, something had changed and the world would never be the same.

"You have got to be kidding me Hugo."

"Sadly friend, I am not. The problem is that the experiment has gotten out of control. The human hybrid that was created exhibits evil tendencies. All it thinks of is destroying human beings and creating a new species that will take over this planet."
"Hugo, this sounds like something right out of the movies. I mean, it is possible if they have the right genetic materials, but why?"

"To build bigger and better human beings of course. They want to usher us into an age of post-humanism; humans with abilities far beyond what we know of now."

"Did it work? Does this thing have abilities?"

"Oh yes...amazing abilities. We don't even know the extent to which its abilities have grown. It is an independent entity with a highly developed mind and I think it has chosen to keep some of its abilities hidden from us. As of now we do know that it is telepathic, it has amazing strength and a certain amount of telekinesis. We don't know what else it can do yet."

"So what happened?

"About a week ago, this thing they call Shemihazah decided it was time to leave the lab. It talked about finding a woman whose DNA contained the genetic material that will support his second generation life-form. Shemihazah was talking as if he was already a god. The powers that be now consider him a threat. Shemihazah has already killed five of the original scientists that had a hand in its creation and he almost escaped the facility itself!"

"How did they stop it?"
"They didn't so much 'stop it' as 'put it to sleep'. The entity does have human DNA in it. They were able to subdue him by pumping poisonous gas into the ventilation system. The poison did not kill it, but it did work as an anesthesia of sorts. The entity was just transferred to the lowest lab at NASA, strapped down on a specially built table and continuously fed a diet of this poison."

"What are they planning to do?"

"Well, a few people are going to watch from above in the observation rooms while another group of scientist in the lab does the autopsy."

"I thought you said it is still alive."

"It is. They are going to cut into it and dismember it to see how it ticks. I guess they figure if they can see how it ticks, they will have better luck when they repeat the experiment."

"Repeat the experiment? What the hell is wrong with them, why would they want to do it again?"

"Come on Clifford, you know why. We are trying to solve problems in this world...the problems of sickness and disease. We want to overcome man's final enemy- death. If we can accomplish this perhaps man can become gods and create other universes to rule."

"You've changed Hugo. I don't know who you are anymore."

The two old friends sat in silence for the next five minutes, neither daring to break the silence until they had their emotions under wrap.

"Why am I here Hugo?"

"You are here at my request. I told them that you were the only person qualified to speak on the potential of the next experiment to be successful, if you could have a firsthand view into what is going on now."

"Hugo, you have to know I would never help them with their goals. You shouldn't have involved me."

"I had to involve you. You are the only person that is familiar enough with this topic to see the dangers. You have to come so that once this thing is dead, you can warn the world about what is being done in the name of science."

"Hugo they will kill me before I can say a word. You just put my life in danger."

"Your life was already in danger. I saw the latest 'kill list'. Once *this thing is studied and done away with, they are going to do a round of 'cleansing' of all of the people who have enough information about the process to become a thorn in their side. Your name is on that list Clifford. I convinced them to bring you in and that you would help them further their goals. Right now Clifford, you owe me your life."*

The two friends sat in the room for the next hour looking out the window in silence. They watched the people on the streets below milling about with no idea of how quickly things were changing around them. Cliff thought to himself, *"Poor suckers. They have no clue what is waiting for them at the end of this rainbow."*

Chapter 19

The next evening, Cliff was in a secret lab at NASA. This lab was like nothing he had ever seen. The lab itself was huge; the ceilings were at least four stories tall. Inside the lab was brand new, State of the Art equipment. In the center of the room was a simple cot bed with a small figure strapped on it. From the observation room which was three stories above the figure on the cot, one could barely see any details of what was happening down on the ground level. The observation room was therefore equipped with HD monitors all around- providing a close-up view of the action below. Cliff and Hugo sat alone in the observation room for a while before anyone arrived; just so Hugo would have a few more minutes to talk with his friend before the procedure.

"Do you see that closet down there in the room by the door?

"Yes Hugo, what of it?"

"From what I understand, inside that closet is a bag of supreme importance. Inside that bag is supposed to be a few items that can stop Shemihazah. I don't actually know what is in the bag. I just know it's in the cabinet. If anything goes wrong, I need you to go in there, get that bag and get out of here."

"How can I get..."
"Quiet, I'm not finished and I don't have much time. After you grab the bag in that closet, you will need to make two more stops- one in California and one in New Mexico. You will need to sneak into these facilities and grab a couple more items. In California you will be looking for a book and in New Mexico you will be looking for a necklace with a cross on it. The necklace is some type of talisman."

Just as Cliff was about to open his mouth in protest, the door to the observation deck opened and people started pouring in. There were a number of people in their full military uniforms from each branch of the military. There were men in dark suits with dark shades, and an array of businessmen- surely representing private money. Once these men began filing into the room, Hugo's demeanor changed. Hugo looked more scared than anyone Cliff had ever seen in his life. Hugo stood up and introduced Cliff.

"Gentlemen, at your request, this is Mr. Clifford Vale."

One of the gentlemen in a dark suit walked over to Cliff and stretched out his hand.

"It's a pleasure to finally meet you in person Mr. Vale. I have been following your work quite closely over the years. You have come a long way with some of your...assertions."

Cliff shook the man's hand and remembered his friend's advice to him before they arrived at NASA. *'Keep your mouth shut'*.

"I think it is time for you to go down and get things started Hugo, wouldn't you agree?"

"Yes Sir."

Cliff watches his friend as he leaves the observation deck. Hugo did not tell Cliff that he was one of the people charged with doing the autopsy. When Dr. Hugo exits the room, Cliff's new acquaintance, along with a group of five other men in dark suits and dark glasses take seats surrounding Cliff.

"This is so exciting! I can't wait to get started and to hear your thoughts Mr. Vale."

Chapter 20

Brandon is listening to Cliff's story quite intently. Although Cliff has not gotten to the point yet, Brandon is in no way rushing the story. Brandon is like a child on Christmas Eve listening to the story of Santa Claus before he is off to bed. While Brandon listens, he looks out of the window with a blank expression on his face. Once or twice through the story, Brandon turns to where his sister lies in a deep rest, and wishes that this was all a dream. But Brandon knows it is not a dream.

Brandon realizes that Cliff has stopped speaking, perhaps caught up in a morbid memory of his own...

"Continue Cliff."

Chapter 21

Shortly after Hugo leaves the observation room, Cliff watches as his friend reappears below in the room with the 'creature'. Cliff watches the monitor closely and he can see fear in his friend's face. Hugo is now in the room below with four other people. They all have on some type of bio-hazard suit with what looks like a portable oxygen tank strapped to their backs. The room is set up like an operation room; all manner of knives and other surgical tools are laid out neatly on steel trays.

As the team of scientist move in closer to their subject, Cliff fixates his gaze upon the subject on the table. The being looks like a man; an unimpressive man at that. Cliff wonders if this being is as powerful and deadly as his friend suggests he is. Right now he is just lying there on the table breathing shallowly. The gentleman sitting next to Cliff is talking to him, but Cliff is focused on the people below. Cliff is watching his friend Hugo intently, watching every move that he makes. Cliff looks into the face of the man on the table, the man Hugo called Shemihazah. How did they come up with this name and what does it mean?

As Hugo grabs the electric saw to begin the procedure by slicing into Shemihazah chest, Cliff thinks he noticed slight movement. The eyes...Cliff thought he saw the eyes open for just a moment. The gentleman sitting next to Cliff will not stop talking and it is annoying. Cliff is just about to turn towards the man to ask his to please shut up so he can watch the 'show' when he sees Shemihazah eyes flicker open, and this time a small distinct smile crosses the patient's face. Fear and dread hit Cliff in a wave and suddenly Cliff is on his feet shouting down at his friend.

"Hugo, get out of there! It's a trap! That thing is not sedated, it's fooling you!"

Everyone in the room with Cliff is now staring intently at the HD monitors to see what the fuss is about.

"Get out of there Hugo, get out of there now!"

Hugo can't hear his friend. Even if he could, it's too late.

Just as Cliff is screaming at Hugo to get out of the room, the being known as Shemihazah broke the restraints and sat up. Shemi was smiling; not at anyone in particular, just a general smile like the moment he had been waiting for finally presented itself. The doctors in the room were stunned- too stunned to move at first. Then the screaming began.

Shemihazah wheeled his legs around towards the floor and stood up. As he was standing, he grabbed one of the doctors by the neck. Shemihazah's hand grew…they actually enlarged as he reached out towards the doctor's neck. Shemi's hand had grown so large that he was able to completely surround the doctor's neck and his fingers were touching each other. Cliff was stunned; all he could think was *'this is ridiculous'*; only in a movie can a hand grow that large. But this was not a movie, it was happening right before his very eyes. As Shemi grabbed the doctors' neck, two other doctors started running for the lab door. Shemi let out a shrill laugh just before the door locked itself. If Cliff had not been watching it on the HD monitor he would not have believed it.

"Telekinesis?"

Shemi began to squeeze the neck of the doctor in his hand until the doctor's head popped off like a cherry. Blood shot everywhere. The two doctors that ran for the door turned around and looked at Shemihazah like rats trapped in a corner. The fourth doctor picked up a steel pipe from the far end of the lab and swung it with all his might at Shemihazah's head. The pipe connected with a solid "thud", but instead of the blow doing damage to Shemi, it only made him mad. Shemihazah turned towards the doctor that had struck him with the pipe and smiled.

"That must have taken guts. Speaking of guts, let's see yours."

In a flash, maybe one tenth of a second Shemi pounced on the brave doctor like a cat. The doctor fell backwards, falling over the trays holding the operating tools. In another split second Shemihazah had his hand on the electric saw that Hugo was holding moments before. With one felled swoop, the saw split open the doctors' lab suit, penetrated his abdomen and sliced him wide open. Shemihazah then stuck his hand inside the suit and inside the doctor's stomach and snatched out a handful of the doctor's intestines. After bellowing out what Cliff could only describe as a scream of victory, Shemihazah opened his mouth and stuffed the handful of intestines inside, chewing and laughing like a baby in its high chair eating spaghetti.

Across the room, Doctor Hugo pointed to the closet that he had just told Cliff about. One of the doctors understood what Hugo was implying and quickly ran to the closet to open it up. Shemihazah was not paying attention at this point, too busy eating human intestines. However, the closet door was lock as it always was. The second doctor by the door grabbed a nearby ax from off the wall and ran full speed towards Shemihazah to give the first doctor time to open the door.

Shemi was ready for the axe wielding doctor. As the doctor swung the axe, Shemi moved to the side with lightning speed. The axe missed Shemi and instead landed deep into the face of the doctor on the floor that was missing a handful of intestines. With one movement, Shemihazah turned around to face the axe wielding doctor and grabbed him by the head. Shemi brought the doctor's face close to his own face.

"That was very rude of you."

Shemi stuck out his tongue; a grotesquely shaped appendage covered with blood and a few chunks of meat, and proceeded to lick the front of the doctor's helmet. Through the HD monitor, Cliff could see the complete horror on the doctor's face. Shemi then began to squeeze the doctor's head between his hands until an audible "pop" could be heard. Shemihazah threw the doctors' body aside and went back to the body on the floor and scooped out another handful of intestines like he was grabbing a piece of cake for consumption.

The doctor by the closet was finally able to open the door. The doctor extracted a green tote bag from the closet. Once the bag was out, it seemed as if time stood still. In slow motion Shemihazah turned around and looked straight at the doctor who had retrieved the bag. Cliff could see in the monitor that Shemi's face changed... it somehow became a disfigured mass of flesh with a completely different facial impression underneath. It was hard to explain. Cliff thought of the movies he had seen like 'The Devil's Advocate', where a demon's face was revealed underneath the human face for a split second. Cliff could see some sort of ancient evil...perhaps the very source of evil itself.

As the doctor looked Shemihazah in the eyes, the temporary cement that was holding Dr. Hugo in his spot finally gave way. Hugo was able to breathe again and was able to speak...and he had to choose these words very carefully. Dr. Hugo looked right into the camera lens that was taping this entire ordeal and yelled through the microphone in his suit...

"Cliff, get the bag. The poison is in the syringe on the table. Remember everything I told you!"

Cliff stood up upon hearing this command from his friend and quickly snapped back to reality. Cliff realized he had been looking at the monitor like he was watching a blockbuster movie thriller...but this was really happening. All of the men in the room stood up as well and slowly began to move backwards and towards the door they originally came in.

Cliff continued to look at the monitor and saw his friend Hugo makes a dash towards the door of the laboratory. As Hugo ran, Shemihazah leaped off of his snack and landed in front of the doctor that had taken the bag out of the closet. Shemihazah grabbed the doctor by arms, brought him in close and bit a hole in the doctor's face…through the suit! Cliff watched as this monster's mouth grew triple its size quicker than he could blink his eyes. It was as if Shemi had another *'dimension'* of mouth hidden inside his mouth. Cliff knew that didn't make any sense when he thought about it, but there was no other way for him to describe what he saw.

Shemihazah turned towards Hugo as he ran towards the lab's door. With a grin on his bloodied face, Shemi took the doctor with the newly made hole in his face and flung his body at the door before Hugo could reach it. The body smashed through the door, taking the door off its hinges with force. Hugo stopped in his tracks and began to scream; like the best scream queen you can remember from the old days of slasher films.

The moment Hugo began to scream, so did Cliff. Cliff let out a shriek that matched his friend's in passion if not in pitch. The other men in the room with Cliff were a little less shy about running for the door of the observation room. On the lab floor, Hugo ran through the lab's door and down the long hallway to the elevator.

When Shemihazah heard the scream from upstairs, he looked up and saw Cliff, and all of the other men running out of the room as they finally negotiated the door open. And that's when Shemihazah did it. Like the comic book scientist known as *'Ant man'*, Shemihazah grew and grew…and grew! Shemi did not stop growing until his body had reached the fourth floor of the laboratory! Shemihazah reached his hand forward and smashed the glass that separated the two of them. Shemi grabbed Cliff through the glass, holding him firmly in his hands ready to squeeze him until he popped. The only words that were able to make it out of Cliff's mouth were *"Jesus please save me."*

Just as these words were uttered the last man from the group was trying to make it out of the door. In a panic, the agent took out his service revolver and started shooting at Shemihazah. The bullets struck Shemihazah six times in the face; once in the forehead, once on the cheek and twice in both eyes. Shemihazah let out a growl that shook the room, causing glass from to fall down on the hand holding Cliff.

Cliff is not sure which happened first; did Shemi drop him towards the floor and started to dematerialize or was it the other way around? All Cliff knows is that Shemi dropped him; it was about a two story fall to the floor out of Shemi's hand. Cliff grabbed onto an outstretched pole just above the floor with no problem and from there he jumped down to the floor. Cliff grabbed the green tote bag that was on the floor and picked up the syringe that was lying on the table.

Shemihazah began to dematerialize- his body turning into some type of black smoke, or black ink. There was a bit of a texture to him, but it wasn't exactly solid. The black ink went upward, since the face was already at the observation room's level. The ink enveloped the shooter, taking the body with it as it flowed out of the door and down the hallway in the direction the room full of men ran.

Hugo was standing in front of the elevator. Hugo knew that something terrible would happen tonight, he almost planned it to happen by lowering the dosage of poison being pumped into the body of Shemihazah. Hugo hated to run off and leave his friend back there, but he was tired of the charade. Hugo had been the team lead on this project and he knew that he had done a very bad thing. Now Hugo hoped his friend would have the courage and ability to correct the wrong he had committed.

While Hugo waited for the elevator, he heard a terrible sound coming from back where the laboratory was. It was almost like a crunching sound…like someone eating a bag of pork rinds. Crunch, crunch, crunch….

Cliff heard it too, that terrible crunching sound. Cliff had an idea of what the sound was but dared not think on it, afraid that the though alone would send him into paralysis. Cliff put the bag over his shoulder and began to move towards the lab door himself.

As Cliff was moving, the dark ink began to pour back into the room. As the ink solidified, it became a human again drenched in so much blood you could not see any color but red.

"Hi Cliffy. How ya doing today?"

Just then the ring of the elevator arriving could be heard down the hall.

"Why don't you hang around a bit…I'll be right back."

Just as quickly it turned back into the black ink substance and flowed out of the door and into the hallway.

Chapter 22

The elevator dinged to alert Hugo that it had arrived.

Hugo stepped into the elevator and began pressing the 'lobby' button, but the elevator didn't move. Hugo then remembered he had to go into the secret panel at the bottom and press the R-12 button first. It was a precaution to make sure no one who wasn't supposed to get out could get out. As Hugo fumbled with the keys, he looked down the hallway and could see a dark ink like substance flowing through the hall towards him. It was as if the darkness of the hallway itself was moving; like it was alive and was reaching out its dark icy hands to grab Hugo. Hugo pressed the button frantically, wishing they had created an elevator that moved via thought power or something.

As the door of the elevator ding to signal its closing, the darkness sped up, meaning not to let him escape his sentence of death. In a matter of a second or two, Shemihazah had materialized in the elevator right in front of Hugo's eyes.

"Leaving so soon papa?"

Shemi reached out his hand and pierced it right through Hugo's chest, pulling out Hugo's beating heart. With the heart pulsating in his hand, Shemihazah's mouth begins to grow and he swallowed the heart whole.

As the doors to the elevators close, Shemihazah walks out of the elevator with the doctor in tow and sits down in front of the elevator and devoured Hugo's entire body. It only took one minute. When Shemihazah was done, his body morphed into the black ink substance again and began to move back to the lab to finish off Cliff.

Chapter 23

Cliff was now standing at the lab's entrance, tote bag around his body and the syringe in his hand. As the darkness slowly moved towards Cliff, he prayed for a way out of this mess.

The beep of the elevator door rang out in the hallway again. The elevator had returned, and Cliff could see a way out. If Cliff could make it through the darkness past Shemi, maybe he could make it out of this hell-hole and back upstairs. Cliff hoped Shemihazah could not follow him and thought that if Shemi could navigate the elevator it would have gotten out long ago.

Shemihazah was ready for whatever Cliff's plan was and whistled as he came down the hall. When the elevator arrived, someone was on it, a slim woman who was pointing a gun in Shemihazah's direction. Shemi thought he would have a little more fun before he killed Cliff and the black ink began to turn and go back down the hall towards the elevator.

Cliff saw his chance. There was someone on the elevator. If he could make it to the elevator before the doors closed, maybe this person could get them out of the basement and back upstairs. The elevator rider had made it down to this level so apparently they must have a high clearance level. Cliff charged forward, syringe in front of him as he yelled to the person in the elevator,

"Don't leave me! Don't leave me down here with him!"

The syringe idea worked. Since Shemihazah was in an alternate form, the syringe did not lodge into his body, but it did cause the darkness of Shemihazah's body to clear a path for Cliff to get through.

Poison. Shemi knew what was in the syringe; its contact with him even in his alternate form was enough to sap a major portion of his power away. For the moment, Shemi was unable to materialize back into body form and he was also unable to follow Cliff into the elevator. Cliff hit the back of the elevator with a hard 'thud', barely able to turn around before the doors shut. Right before the doors did close, Cliff heard Shemihazah speak words to him that chilled his soul,

"I'll see you soon Cliffy. And tell your new friend Victoria I'm coming for a visit."

Chapter 24

When Cliff finishes his story, Brandon is still staring out of the window. One lone tear traces a path down the side of Brandon's face and falls onto his lap. Brandon is hurting; he has lost his family and all semblances of his former life. The sad part was, Brandon was not completely sure what this was all for.

"Thank you for telling me that story Cliff. It sounds crazy as hell, but no crazier than some of the things I've seen these last few weeks. If someone would have told me just a few months ago that I would be sitting here today under these circumstances, I would have called them a damn fool. Yet here I sit."

Cliff said nothing. Although Cliff did not know what to say, the choice of silence was the best thing for this moment. After what seemed like an eternity of silence, Brandon began to sob.

The truth was that Brandon didn't know what happened. All Brandon remembered was that the night Vic met Cliff was the same night that she had a terrible argument with their father. They had all gone out to dinner as a family, something they all had not done in a long time. Throughout the dinner, Vic was silent. It was obvious that Vic had something really big on her mind. At one point Vic and their dad excused themselves from the dinner table; they said they were going outside to have a talk. It didn't seem like a big deal because the two of them always found a few moments to go off somewhere and talk together. The rest of the family just dealt with it.

This time something was different. When dad returned to the table, he was visibly shaken. He mumbled something about them having an important meeting and then rushed off with wife and oldest son in tow. As they left, Vic came back into the restaurant and sat at the table. Victoria and her dad stood facing each other, both looking completely defiant; dad with his family in tow, Vic with the look of a wounded cat written all over her face. Brandon remembered their last words to each other that night; he had played the scene over and over in his mind every day since then.

"Dad, it wasn't my fault."

"That doesn't matter now Vic, can't you see that? The fact is you were there when you shouldn't have been there. You saw something you should not have seen and you got involved. You've kidnapped the man for Christ's sake."

"I didn't kidnap him, he just came with me."

"Semantics. You try telling that to them when they come looking for you. I can't protect you with this one baby girl. And now you've put us all in danger; you mother, your brothers and me."

"But what can I do? Help me make it right."

"I can't baby, I'm not supposed to know any of this. Don't you understand? This was classified. It is higher than my rank; it is higher than my pay grade. The fact that you waited until now to tell me about it has put us in further danger. Don't you know that there is a price for secrecy? Don't you know that the people who wield enough power to make this happen also wield enough power to cover up any and every loose end? We are now loose ends because we have knowledge of things we shouldn't have. We are now a danger to them. For all we know we are being monitored right now...this entire conversation. God only knows who's been listening. We have to go."

Brandon remembers watching his family walk out of the door. Brandon wanted desperately to go with them, but he could not leave Vic in her time of need. Brandon knew that if he left Vic now, she would have no one to help her, and you just don't leave family out in the cold like that.

It wasn't until the next morning that they found out what happened. The news report said that the family hit a curve too hard and the car flew off the side of a mountain, exploding below and killing everyone in the car. Vic knew that was a lie and so did Brandon. Their family was going home and there were no mountain between the restaurant and their house- it was a straight shot on the freeway. Brandon's parents and brother had been killed and a story was planted in the media to cover it up.

Brandon slumped down further in his chair and his sobs became louder. Just as Cliff began to reach out his arm to console Brandon, he was shocked to hear a voice behind him,

"Don't touch him. Leave him be."

Vic had awoken and walked up behind Cliff without his realizing it.

"Go ahead and get some sleep Cliff. We have a long travel day ahead of us tomorrow."

Cliff did in fact walk off and lie down on the makeshift pallet that Vic was using. Cliff could see Vic stretch out her arms to comfort Brandon. Brandon fell into her arms and let out his grief on her shoulder. The scene would have been tremendously touching to Cliff, had it not been for the fact that he was scared out of his mind.

As Cliff drifted off to sleep, the last thing he remembered hearing was Vic's voice saying,

"It's going to be Okay. I will make sure that we get through this...together."

Chapter 25

About two hours into the road trip and all is well.

Bobby is driving and Stormy is sitting in the front passenger seat. Bobby kept trying to start a conversation with Stormy for the last twenty miles, but Stormy was having none of it. For some reason Stormy seemed bent on not having a good time. Bobby couldn't understand why; it was a waste of time to go to a beautiful cabin in the woods with the intent purpose of having a bad time. Bobby and Stormy could have stayed at home and had a bad time.

Come to think of it, Stormy had been acting stinky for a little while now. It seemed to him the problem started soon after he moved in with Stormy. Bobby knew she was upset about him being fired from his job, but he had only told her he was fired. The truth was that Bobby had quit. Bobby had a situation arise that he did not know how to deal with.

Bobby was relatively new on his job; he had only been there a few months, but he was their golden boy. Bobby was a business major that had spent his previous summers as an intern. Bobby completed the management training program and had been placed in one of the Richmond stores. After completing his summer schedule at work, he would be given the position of store manager in the Fall. The current store manager was moving on to greener pastures. There were a few other workers that had been hoping to get the job, like the assistant store manager who had been there for the past five years. Since Bobby was a new comer to this store, some people could not understand why he had suddenly become the top pick.

The current assistant store manager was Valerie Foxx; an apt name for this beautiful twenty-eight year old woman who was smart, strong and capable. When the announcement had been made that Bobby was going to become the next store manager, some of the workers held resentment towards him. However, Valerie didn't seem to harbor any ill will towards Bobby. On the contrary, she seemed to cozy up to him at once. Bobby was a few years her junior and he was certain that she was hitting on him. Perhaps she was just cozying up to her new boss, but her mannerisms made Bobby feel a little uncomfortable. Bobby had often thought about bringing her up on sexual harassment charges, but always backed down because he thought he would end up looking like a fool. Men didn't bring women up on sexual harassment charges. What he needed to do was just talk to her…again. Bobby had to get her alone and explain to her that he was happy with his current situation and not interested in her sexually. Valarie was fine; slender body, incredible curves, great proportions and a beautiful face. Valarie could be a bit loud at times, but Bobby had a knack for ignoring people. Bobby was sure she would respect the fact that he was just not interested in her and she would respect him for being straight forward with her. Women always said they wanted honesty, so Bobby was going to be honest with her. Bobby invited Valarie to lunch so he could talk to her about the situation. As it turned out, that was not such a good idea.

When lunch time arrived, Bobby went to Valerie and asked her to lunch with him. Valerie seemed overjoyed and agreed to meet with Bobby for lunch. Bobby drove an old conversion van, which was parked outside the Home Depot store where they worked. The two of them walked out of the store together towards the van, but Bobby had forgotten to get his lunch out of the refrigerator.

"Hold on, I forgot my lunch. I'll tell you what; here are the keys to the van. Go ahead and jump in and I will be there in a minute."

Valerie gladly took the keys and walked towards the van smiling. Valerie unlocked the door and jumped in.

Bobby went back into the store and grabbed his lunch. Bobby always brought his lunch from home because he refused to eat from the roach coach that stopped by every afternoon at the store. Bobby was trying to save some money so he could have a great year with his girlfriend.

Bobby went outside and walked to the van. It was a hot day and the sun was beating down on the streets with the full force of its heat. As Bobby approached the van he heard the engine running and was pleased, thinking that Valerie had turned on the air conditioning. When Bobby got into the van, he did not see Valerie in the front passenger seat. Bobby jumped in on the driver's side and wheeled around to talk to Valerie, whom he assumed was in the back of the van eating her lunch.

When Bobby turned and saw Valerie, he was shocked. Valerie was indeed in the back of the van but she was not eating her lunch; she had removed all of her clothing and was sprawled out across one of the seats in the back- arms spread across the seat revealing two perfect breasts. Her legs were wide open too, and her cleanly shaven vagina seemed to be pulsating...inviting him to come closer for better view.

Bobby was stunned; he did not expect this. Bobby knew that she wanted him but never thought that a simply invitation to his van for lunch would end with him being invited 'in' for lunch.

"What are you doing Valerie?"

"I am trying to be subtle."

"You call this subtle?"

"No, I call this playtime...do you want to play with me?"

Bobby's mouth said no, but he never stopped looking at her naked body. Valerie slowly moved forward to the front seat and gently grabbed Bobby by the shirt and pulled him to the back of the van. Bobby moved forward as she pulled, the whole thing seeming so surreal. When they got to the back of the van, Valerie sat back down on the seat where she had been and Bobby was now on his knees on the floor in front of her; face and mouth eye level with her perfect breast. Her nipples we huge, beckoning Bobby to move in closer to lick and caress them. Before Bobby realized it, he was on them- slowly sucking those nipples like a child sucks on a candy treat after a visit to the dentist's office.

Valerie moaned slightly, giving in to the pleasure of his mouth on her. She squirmed in her seat, letting out soft moans of pleasure that enticed Bobby to continue. Valarie grabbed Bobby's face firmly, directing him from nipple to nipple as she heaved in deeply and he legs opened wider. As Valerie squirmed in her seat, she began to push Bobby's head lower and lower on her body; first to the top of her stomach, then below the belly button, until his face had finally met the waiting center of her pulsating womanhood.

Bobby had no idea he had packed a lunch for nothing; today's feast would not be the carefully made bologna and cheese sandwich he brought with him. Bobby only resisted what was happening in the initial seconds when she was pulling him towards the back. Once he had arrived in the back of the van and was nestled between her, all rational thought went out the window and there was only the animal lust of sexual conquest that remained. As Bobby's face approached her pulsating vortex, he was no longer thinking; he became a man on a mission and the mission was to indulge in this sweet treat that was moaning wantonly at the end of his tongue. Soon Bobby was eye level with the center of her womanhood; looking at the parting of her soft juicy lips, a moist mass that smelled of freshly cut flowers and was beckoning for a kiss. Bobby was all in; ravishing her with his tongue, plunging into that moist flesh like he was a starving man who had not eaten in weeks.

"No Bobby, stop. Please stop, your tongue is driving me mad...I can't do this."

The more she moaned the more turned on Bobby became; and he continued with a vigor that brought her to climax twice before he even considered taking out his '*Johnson*'. Bobby was now hard enough to cut diamonds. Valarie let out a soft moan, as her second climate sent a wave of water careening from her private part and drenching his entire face.

Bobby was beside himself; forgetting where he was, forgetting '*who*' he was doing, forgetting time itself. As he pulled out his rock hard Johnson, all he could think of was relieving himself inside her.

"No more Bobby, please. I can't take it anymore. What would your girlfriend think?"

"The hell with her, I got to have you now."

And with those words, Bobby was on top of her. Angling his body for entry and imagining the reward that lies in wait at the end of this caramel rainbow. Valerie began to push him back...

"No more Bobby, no more. Please don't kiss it anymore, don't suck me anymore. I can't take it, I didn't want this... I thought you just wanted to talk."

"No, baby, you got me going now, I need some sweet release. I want to be inside you."

As Bobby stood over her ready to plow in, she grabbed his manhood firmly and began to stroke it over and over and over, the softness of her hands quickly bringing him the release he was seeking. His juices dripped down from him onto her clothing, which was just below them on the floor of the van. Once again she pushed him away.

"No Bobby. I can't have sex with you. I didn't want to go this far. I am so ashamed, you made me cum twice."

Valerie pushed Bobby away from her and quickly began putting back on her clothes. In a matter of seconds she was completely dressed and moving towards the van door to exit.

"You've got to be kidding me Valerie, you're leaving? Now?"

"Yes Bobby. Thank you so much, that was just what I needed."

Valerie jumped out of the van and walked back to the store. Bobby was sitting in the van watching her as she walked away, wondering how all of this just happened. Bobby felt like a heel; he had cheated on Stormy and he really had not planned it…it had just happened.

A week went by before he heard from Valerie again. She had not shown up for work since their 'encounter'. Bobby didn't much care, as he thought it might be a bit uncomfortable at work now with her there. After a week he received a package in the mail. Inside the package that had no return address were two items; a SD chip and a photo. The photo was of a dress. Bobby recognized the dress; it was the one Valerie had been wearing the day they ended up in the back of his van. The dress had a few spots of it and Bobby knew what those spots were. A very bad feeling came over Bobby, a feeling of dread. Bobby rushed to the computer to see what was on the SD Chip. When he opened it he found two items on it; a Microsoft Word document and an audio file.

"Shit."

Bobby opened the Word document first and cringed as he read it.

Dear Bobby,

It has been over a week since out 'encounter' in the back of your van. The way you ate me was so delicious, I almost reach another climax when I think of it. I did not want you to see me like that; I never wanted a physical relationship. But you persistence was overwhelming. I had no idea when I accepted your lunch invitation that you would take advantage of me like that; ripping my clothes off and forcing your mouth down there, making me cum over and over. I feel ashamed. I feel betrayed. I never expected my new boss to take advantage of me like that. I don't know what to do Bobby…what do you think I should do? I asked you to stop, but you wouldn't and now I feel like something has been taken from me. What should I do Bobby? Let's talk about what happened and your unwelcomed actions when I get back to the store. I had to put

in for two weeks of vacation time immediately. I told Bill it was because my grandmother was near to death and calling for me to be by her side. I'm sorry I lied to him but I was too ashamed to tell him you raped me in the back of your van in the store parking lot.
Valerie

Wow, what the hell just happened? Bobby opened the audio file and played it. What he heard shocked him.

"No Bobby, stop. Please stop, your tongue is driving me mad...I can't do this."

...followed by more moaning...

"No more Bobby, please. I can't take it anymore. What would your girlfriend think?"

"The hell with her, I got to have you now."

...more moaning...

"No more Bobby, no more. Please don't kiss it anymore, don't suck me anymore. I can't take it, I didn't want this...I thought you just wanted to talk."

Then the audio file shut off.

Bobby was in shock. *What the hell had just happened?* Hell no, he didn't rape her...if anything, she raped him. She forced herself on him. *What was going on?*

Bobby had to quit his job at the Home Depot because Valerie knew where she could find him if he was there. Bobby needed time to think...time to sort this out. What would he do? Bobby supposed that this would end in extortion; if she was going to have him arrested for rape, he would be in jail already.

Bobby needed to regroup; he needed to find himself and reconnect with himself and with humanity. Everything would become clear soon. But first, Bobby needed to cut all the ties to the life he was living, which meant he had to quit his job. He dared not tell Stormy the real reason he was leaving so he told her that he was fired. Bobby needed to come up with a plan. Right now Bobby knew he was in a bad situation. The worst part was that he would have to wait and see what Valerie's intentions were. If Valarie's intentions were to get that store managers job, she can have it. Bobby would much rather be unemployed and free from prosecution than fight this battle and have his future decided by a jury of his '*so-called*' peers

Chapter 26

In the middle row of the mini-van, Rick and Sheena were playing a game of Rummy 500. Moon and Mimi were in the back doing God knows what. Because of the giggles coming from the back seat, no one wanted to turn around to see what was going on. To be free from the noise in the rear of the van and to stop their imaginations from running wild, Sheena decide to start a conversation.

"So what's been up with you Moon?"

"The same old same."

Moon looks out the window at the trees surrounding both sides of the car as they travel.

"Where in the hillbilly hell, are we?"

Rick replies,

"Don't worry about it. We'll be there in a couple of hours."

"Okay, Okay. I'm just saying, you didn't tell a brother we would be traveling through Boonesville."

Sheena laughs,

"Through what?"

"Boonesville. You know; no people, no lights, paved roads. I mean this is like something straight out of a horror film."

Stormy jumps into the conversation,

"What do you mean?"

"Have you ever paid attention to horror movies? Usually

something happens that strand people out in the middle of nowhere... the car go off the road, or a tire blows out. All those things that conveniently happen and get people stranded in the middle of nowhere, just so the killer can get them."

Rick turns and looks at Moon,

"Man, come on with that superstitious bullshit."

"Whoa, this is not superstition."

"The hell it ain't."

Stormy jumps back in,

"Come on guys, just stop it."

Sheena chimes in,

"Yeah, we are going to be just fine."

The van rolls on for about five more minutes in silence. Sheena turns to ask Moon the question they have all been waiting to ask.

"So Moon, what are you planning to do after this year?"

"Well if I don't get drafted, which I believe I will, I guess I'll go back home and help out my dad with his business...at least until I can get on with a team."

"Who do you want to play for?"

"New York Giants baby, I thought you knew."

Rick couldn't wait to respond,

"The Giants?"

"That's right."

"I knew you didn't have any sense. Why not go for a contender?"

"Well first of all, I don't get to pick where I go...hence the term 'drafted'."

"I know that. I'm just saying, why set your sights so low."

"Low, are you crazy Rick? New York is the bomb baby; I'm New York straight through and through. Look at it like this; the New York Knicks are the reigning NBA Champions, the New York Rangers are about to win the Championship- and you know the Yankees ain't no joke. Now it's time for me to bring the glory back to the Giants...then all will be right in the world once again."

"I'm just saying the Giants' ain't winning any more championships any time soon."

"Well when I get there, we're winning back to back championship. And you know this baby."

"You want to make a bet on that?"

"How much?"

"Fifty bucks."

"You're on baby."

Chapter 27

Cliff hated the woods.

Cliff kept pressing on, not exactly sure of where he was going. He missed traveling with Vic and Brandon. At least with them, Cliff never had to worry about where he was going or how he would get there. Vic had been so resourceful. In Chicago, they had stolen a car and Vic drove them across the State line into Indiana. From Indiana they walked a bit, keeping off the main roads and out of the prying eyes of the general public. A few times they saw their faces on news reports; it seemed that they were being hunted by the Federal Government in addition to Shemihazah.

However, with Vic and Brandon dead (Cliff was sure they were dead, he couldn't image how they could have escaped a face to face confrontation with this special version of evil); Cliff was on his own trying to remember how Vic had led them across the land. Cliff was tired; all he wanted to do was find rest, but he knew that the rest he sought would only be available to him in the form of a permanent sleep- which Shemi was sure to provide him once he caught up with him.

Cliff stopped in the woods for a moment. The sun seemed determined to beat him down until he was crawling along the ground in desperate search of his next breath. The humidity in Virginia was brutal, hovering at about eighty five percent every day. Cliff only had one pair of clothes- the clothes on his back which was now soaked through with perspiration again.

Cliff lay down on the floor of the woods, trying to make his body blend in with its surroundings. It wasn't working, but it felt so good to rest. Looking up into the sky, Cliff questioned his sanity as well as his purpose.

"What am I going to do?"

"Snap."

Cliff heard the snap of a few twigs off in the distance. Cliff shot up to a sitting position and waited…listening intently for the return of that sound that could signal someone approaching.

"Crack".

Another sound; Cliff thought someone could be following him closely and trying not to make any noise. Cliff was now on his feet and turned his entire body in the direction of the noise. A flutter of birds suddenly rose into the air and began flying high above Cliff's head in the direction Cliff had been traveling. In Cliff's mind he knew that the sound could be anything, a branch breaking because of some unseen weight, a small forest animal running for cover from stalker of its own…or it could be the sound of Shemihazah catching up to him after he dared to steal a small rest for himself.

"Snap."

Cliff looked up again and saw a raven sitting on the branch of the tree above him. There was something a bit disturbing about the raven. Cliff looked and looked at the raven to see if he could tell what was '*off*' with it. It took Cliff a few minutes but then he recognized what was wrong with the raven; *the eyes.* Cliff wasn't sure if it was his 'survival sense' that noticed it or if he was just tired and paranoid. Cliff was tired and paranoid, but he was sure there was something wrong with this raven's eyes; *they look almost human.*

As Cliff stared non-blinkingly at the raven perched over his head, he heard another,

"Snap."

With this last sound Cliff was moving fast through the woods. Cliff was certain that his death was imminent; the only question now being whether or not he would find a way to prevent the important items he carried in the green tote bag from ending up in the hands of his stalker. Too many lives have been lost and too many sacrifices made.

Cliff ran as hard as he could, not noticing that a clearing was coming up ahead and not noticing the road just beyond it. Fear had once again enveloped Cliff and as he ran, his mind went blank of all common sense. No, Cliff did not notice that he was fast approaching a road, nor did he notice the car barreling down that road at almost 65 miles per hour.

Chapter 28

While Bobby was trying to think of a way to start a conversation with Stormy, his mind was not actively engaged on driving. All types of visions were dancing through Bobby's head, making it hard for him to focus. Bobby turned his head to Stormy, who was now looking at him and smiling. Bobby thought he saw kindness in that smile, and in that split second he allowed himself to put all other thoughts out of his head and be consumed with only thoughts of her.

Stormy was indeed looking at Bobby, thinking about the things they had been through. While it was true that Stormy was infatuated with Moon, she did still like Bobby. Bobby was sweet and did seem to put her first in everything. No, he did not have a job right now and it was a strain on the household and their relationship, but Bobby was always a responsible man. Perhaps she was just judging him harshly because she saw her opportunity with Moon fading away. Moon did not like Stormy that way so they had settled into a comfortable friendship. But Stormy was a senior this year and wanted to sow her wild oats with all of the people she found attractive during her college years. Freshman year Stormy had been very shy, not willing to join in the regular fun of college through giving up her goodies to just any and everyone. Stormy had always played it safe; now she was regretting being safe. Stormy was regretting not living her life a bit more open. Now she wanted to play around, but didn't know how to talk to Bobby about it. Bobby seemed to be the one woman type of guy and that was great…for a time. But how would Bobby feel if she told him that she wanted to throw off convention and get buck wild. She wanted to *fuck*. Once, Stormy had even thought of asking Bobby to do a *ménage trio* just for the experience of it. Stormy wanted to be ravaged by two men at the same time, often imagining it in her 'alone' time. If she could get Bobby to be open to the idea, she would even consider letting him have some fun in a ménage trios as well; two girls with just him. As a matter of fact, Stormy had already figured out the girl she would invite into the bedroom.

Stormy didn't consider herself to be gay or bisexual, she was just curious. She wanted to try it once so she could look back at her college years and perhaps one day shares her dirty little secret with her bridge buddies when she was old and grey.

It was at that moment, during those thoughts, that Bobby looked over and caught her smiling in his direction. She wasn't actually smiling at him, but it was concerning him. When their eyes met there was a small moment, a quick spark that suggested this thing between the two of them could be repaired. Perhaps it could work. Stormy was sure Bobby would find another job. He was probably just taking a break from the regular routine just like she wanted to take a break from the regular routine. Besides, Stormy had a plan. It was not the best plan in the world and it was risky, but as a first step to her sexual revolution she was going to try it. Before they departed for this trip, Stormy went to one of the stores in the Southside and picked up a packet of *Spanish Fly*. People said Spanish Fly was an aphrodisiac but technically Spanish Fly was a date rape drug. Stormy also brought along her Ambien. She had even taken the time to crush up a couple of the pills into powdered form. One of these nights she would slip some Ambien into the drinks of Sheena, Mimi and Rick and wait for them to get sleepy. Once she saw that they were about to dose, she would slip some Spanish Fly into a couple of drinks and give one to Moon and one to Bobby. Whether Bobby got a drink full of Ambien or a drink of Spanish Fly would depend solely on how he acted on the drive to the cabin. If he was being cool, he would get the Spanish Fly and be invited to the fun with her and Moon. If he was an ass, he would get the Ambien cocktail and have a nice long sleep while Stormy worked off three years of sexual frustration on Moon's fine ass. Stormy was going to have a piece of Moon and there was nothing any one of them could do to stop her. Stormy smiled at Bobby as he looked at her and Bobby smiled back. So far Stormy was siding in favor of a threesome with Moon and her man Bobby. A threesome was the logical choice; this way Stormy could cross two things off of her sexual bucket-list.

When Bobby and Stormy's eyes met, Bobby of course was no

longer looking at the road. Instead, Bobby was trying to decide how and when he was going to tell Stormy that he had made a terrible mistake. All of Bobby's instincts told him to wait until they got back home. This weekend was a chance for him to put all the worries and frustrations out of his mind. Bobby just wanted this weekend to be about them; him and Stormy. He wanted to get lost in her beautiful smile, her lovely brown eyes, and her sensuous embrace. As Bobby looked into Stormy's eyes, he though he saw her soften. *"Perhaps this will work out for the best. Maybe I am worrying about nothing."* Bobby's smile widened; the longer he looked into Stormy's beautiful brown eyes, the more convinced he became that they could make it through this minor adversity. All Bobby wanted to do was continue staring into her eyes; and he did. As a result, Bobby never saw Cliff when he ran right into the middle of the road and consequently, right in front of their car.

"Bobby, look out!"

And just that quickly, moment was over.

Chapter 29

The car hit Cliff and flung him fifty feet from the point of impact.

Bobby stopped the car. The hood was bent in and the windshield had a huge crack across the center from where Cliff's head connected with the glass. The force of the impact was amazing; if the passengers in the mini-van not had their seatbelts on, they would have gone flying through the windshield. Everyone in the car sat motionless while the reality of what just happened set in. Sheena was just rocking herself back and forth repeating the same words over and over,

"Oh my God, oh my God, oh my God..."

After one or two minutes, Bobby was finally able to ask the rest of the passengers if they were alright. Smoke was billowing up from the front of the car; perhaps the radiator was smashed in.

"What the hell did we hit, a moose?"

"No Moon. I think it was a man."

The car door opened and Bobby got out of the vehicle first, followed by Rick, Stormy, Moon and Mimi. Sheena did not get out of the van right away. The students slowly walked the fifty foot stretch to where their victim laid, a mass of meat covered in blood. As the students stood around Cliff's body, Sheena finally summoned up the courage to exit the car and join them. Once she arrived by her friends, Sheena asked the obvious question...

"Is he dead?"

Moon pushes Sheena towards the body and responds...

"Why don't you go check?"

"You go check him; I'm not touching that man."

Rick pushes Moon and Sheena out of the way.

"Move. I'll check him."

Rick slowly bends down and checks Cliff's neck for a pulse. After a few seconds, Rick turns back to the group to announce his findings;

"He's still alive...barely."

The group takes a collected sigh of relief. It was still a terrible thing that they hit this man with the mini-van, but at least they were not murderers. Now they just needed to get him to a hospital.

Sheena is the first one to break the silence.

"So what are we going to do?"
Stormy speaks up immediately and voices her opinion.

"We have to take him to the hospital. No question. That's the right thing to do."

Moon squints as he joins in on the conversation.

"Well now, let's hold on a moment and think this through..."

Stormy retorts,

"Think what through Moon, you know we have to take him to the hospital. What else are we going to do, just leave him here to die?"

"I'm not saying that Stormy, I'm just saying let's just look at all the options before we rush to a decision."

"No, I'm not having that..."

"Stormy, please. You're right, okay? Taking him to the hospital is the right thing to do. He does need help. Then what? Are we just going to drop him off and then walk away? Are we going to stick around and tell them we are the ones that hit him?"

Sheena takes Stormy's side;

"But we did hit him."

"I'm just saying; let's get our story straight first."

"We don't need a story, we're telling the truth."

Moon stops talking. He knows when he is beat. Moon feels uncomfortable having his face seen, because of the media storm that will follow. Moon is all for doing the right thing, but he also realizes this could have implications for his life that translates into his pocket. This is just the type of thing that could come back to haunt him come draft time; perhaps knocking him down a couple of notches if the media gives a negative spin on it. Moon is a local football 'phenom', but he is also a young black man in the State of Virginia. Moon hated that he had to think this way, but he had learned some hard lessons along his journey.

In his freshman year of college, Moon joined a Fraternity on his campus. Moon always use the work *joined* instead of *pledged*...because of course pledging had been banned years ago. Freshmen do not normally get the opportunity to pledge their first year, but Moon came in as a highly sought recruit and that means he'd miss out on pledging during his sophomore year and could possibly leave school for the Draft his junior year. If Moon was to join, he would have to seek admission in his first year of college.

Moon made it on line and was as happy as could be. Moon was what they called the 'Tail-dog' of his line, which meant he was the last person on his line of thirteen. Moon was positive that if you asked anyone on campus, they would tell you Moon was the baddest Tail-dog of all times.

During Moon's sophomore year, he was involved in an 'incident' on campus that cost him a few games and where he learned a valuable lesson that *any publicity is not always good publicity*.

During one of the Fraternity's sponsored parties on campus, his line of thirteen had started to 'step' around the party. At that time the college still allowed their fraternity to sport their traditional 'canes' in the parties. This one particular evening, there were a number of 'townies' at the party. A townie was a derogatory term that students used to refer to people who came on campus to go to the parties, but did not go to the school- the lived in the town the school was in. As the line of thirteen *party stepped* around the party chanting their fraternity songs, one of the townies pushed Moon's line brother, Big Redd, out of the line. Big Redd jumped up and pushed the townie back…over the table and into the wall. Just as he pushed the guy, two more townies rushed Big Redd. Moon ran over and put a tackle on both of these dudes that should be shown in Hall of Fame video clips.

Suddenly, a brawl erupted! Moon and his fraternity brothers against about fifty townies. One of Moon's fraternity brothers named Big El was trying to encourage peace amongst the black men. Big El was taller than Moon and was the Tail-dog of the line that crossed the year before Moon. Big El put out his hands to stop two of his black brothers from fighting, when another of his 'black brothers' from the town snuck up behind Big El and hit him across the back of his head with a chair. All peace for his fellowman disappeared in a split second as Big El grabbed his cane, grabbed the guy who hit him with a chair and introduced wood to skull. There was fake jewelry; wood chips and jerry curl juice flying everywhere.

At the end of the matter no charges were filed against anyone, but Moon's face was everywhere. Even though Moon held his own and knocked about six townies flat on their backs, the only video footage captured on a cell phone was the moment some four foot four inch guy landed a lucky punch in Moon's nose. Moon's nose was not broken, but it did bleed a little and someone had a photo of the bleeding nose as well. Moon still has not lived this bad media down, not to mention all of the wonderful laughter it birthed everywhere he went for the rest of the year.

Moon knew that this was not the same thing and he was a bit embarrassed that the first thing he thought about was his career over a human being. *But, if Moon didn't consider his career, who would?*

Before Moon could get his entire foot in his mouth by continuing to speak, Cliff started moving and talking. His voice was barely audible, so it took all of Rick's concentration to figure out what he was saying.

"He's coming...he's coming..."

"What? Who's coming?"

"Shemi. You've got to get out of here...."

"Guys, be quiet. He's trying to talk."

"Somebody get me the bag...where's the bag?"

The other students walk over to Rick and Cliff to hear what is being said. Rick turns to the group and motions for them to stay silent so he can hear what Cliff is trying to tell him.

"Where's the bag..."

"Moon, he's talking about a bag. Take a look around and see if you find some type of bag he may have been carrying."

Moon immediately moves out, happy to have a mission to accomplish that would keep him out of the way. Although Moon loved to be seen as a leader and he wanted to be looked up to, Moon knew that he was a much better follower than leader. Moon liked to complete tasks; he wanted to do the heavy lifting that was required to obtain the goal. He didn't really like the added pressure of coming up with the goal.

"What's in the bag can stop him..."

"Stop who?"

"Listen to me. He is evil. A creation that should not be here. An abomination among the human race. You have to stop him..."

After these words, Cliff seemed to fall off into a sleep.

Rick stands up and motions for the group to follow him away from Cliff's body. The group follows Rick and form a semi-circle about forty feet from Cliff's outstretched body. Sheena is the first to speak...

"What did he say?"

"I don't know what he was talking about exactly. He was mumbling something about us having to stop someone. Someone evil. He said the items in the bag could stop him"

"Did he say who this 'someone' is and why they need to be stopped?"

"No. What do you guys think?"

Stormy remains adamant...

"I think he needs to go to the hospital. We need to take him."

Moon comes back to the group with a green bag in hand.

"I found the bag you were talking about. You want me to check and see what's in it Rick?"

"In a minute. First we need to decide what we are going to do.

Let's have a vote. I vote that we take him to the hospital. We already know what Stormy's vote is. Sheena, I assume you are siding with Stormy to take him to the hospital?"

"Yep."

"Okay. How about you Bobby?"

Bobby looked around the circle at the rest of the gang. His eyes finally rested on Stormy. Stormy was looking intently at Bobby, as if his answer weighed heavily on their future together...

"*I vote taking him to the hospital.*"

Stormy give's a slight smile and adds one point to the '*yes*' column for Bobby.

"*Okay, how about you Mimi?*"
"*Hospital.*"

"*That's five out of six. How about you Moon?*"

"*It doesn't much matter what I vote at this point. The majority decision is already made.*"

"*But we want to hear what you have to say anyway Moon.*"

Moon was torn. He didn't want to go along with the plan, but he knew he was outvoted. None of them knew where the hospital was; hell, they didn't even know where they were since Bobby had taken that short cut forty-five minutes back. Since they had been on this road they had seen nothing; no cars, no houses, no people. For all Moon could tell, they had crossed over a portal leading them deeper into the Twilight Zone. Moon chuckled and thought to himself '*man, I got to cool out with this crazy imagination.*'

"*I vote with everybody else. If you want to take him to the hospital, I'm in. I just hope no one gets mad at me when I stay outside near the car. Is that Okay?"*

"Yes Moon. Okay, so it is unanimous, to the hospital we will go."

Now that the decision was made, they all turned back around to get Cliff's body and put him into the van. When they looked at the spot Cliff had been, he was gone. All that was in the spot was a black raven, standing where Cliff's body lay not more than three minutes ago. Rick walked over to the spot Cliff was just in, looking around like his car was moved from the spot he knew he had parked it in. The raven flew up into a tree as Cliff approached.

"What the hell? Where did he go? Did anyone see him leave?"

"How could he have left? He was an inch from death's door. What the hell is going on?"

There was no trace of Cliff, just the raven in the tree *starring* at the group. Rick had to look around to see their mini-van just to make sure there was really an accident and he was not part of some sort of mass delusion. Cliff really was gone- and there was nothing to show for it but the dented car and the stunned looks on everyone's face as they tried to piece together what had just happened. Since there was no body to take to the hospital, the crisis was averted.

Moon was relieved.

"Well, let's go. There is nothing left for us here."

All of the students begin to walk back to the car except for Sheena. *"So wait. We are just going to walk away? We're not going to do anything?"*

Moon turns back to Sheena annoyed. Perhaps she didn't know what 'crisis averted' meant.

"Come on Sheena, let's go."

"No Moon. We just hit a man and almost killed him. Now everybody just wants to walk away like nothing happened?"

"Well what the hell would you like us to do Sheena? It's obvious that we didn't kill him and that he didn't want to go to the hospital because he got the hell up and moved the hell on..."

"Don't talk to me like I'm stupid Moon..."

"Then stop saying stupid shit..."

"The hell with you Moon, you get on my nerves. You don't talk to me like that..."

"I'll say anything I want..."

"Not to me..."

Rick once again steps between Sheena and Moon. Rick knew that these two were the best of friends but they get along like cats and dogs.

"Both of you just chill out. Sheena, Moon is right. We voted to take the guy to the hospital but he left. He's gone now. Moon, be a little more understanding man. Don't be an asshole all of the time."

They all stood in silence. Slowly they begin to walk back to the van and pile inside. Rick walked back over to where Cliff's body had lain. The raven in the tree with the peculiar eyes was staring at Rick. Rick felt uneasy about the raven so he picked up a rock and threw it at the bird. The raven, perhaps knowing that this human meant him physical harm flew onto a branch of a different tree. The raven was still staring at Rick; almost as if to make sure Rick knew that the raven knew Rick could do it no harm. After the raven flew into the nearby tree, Rick moved on towards the van.

The van was a mess; the front was dented all the way to the radiator, the window was cracked and caked with blood and there was smoke coming from under the hood. However, no one mentioned the obvious. They all just piled into the van, buckled their seatbelts and waited for Bobby to pull off and get them the rest of the way to the cabin...hopefully in complete silence.

Once in the car, Bobby turns the key in the ignition but nothing happened. The engine did not turn over and the car did not start. Bobby tried three more times to start the car, but nothing happened.

"Great. Just great."

The men got out of the car and Rick lifted the hood. Just like clockwork, Moon followed him to remind him that he didn't know anything about cars.

"What are you looking for Rick?

Rick understood completely what Moon was suggesting and closed the hood back.

"What's the plan now Rick?"

Rick paused for a minute to collect his thoughts.

"Where's the map Moon?"

Moon disappeared back in the car to retrieve the map. As Moon studied the map, the women started to exit the van and join in the discussion.

"So what do you see Moon"

"Well, when Bobby got off the road about an hour ago, that put us on this road. We should be somewhere around here...right in the middle of East Boonesville, USA."

'*Here*' on the map referred to an area where there appeared to be nothing but road. According to the map, they were in the middle of a stretch of road with no exits on either side for at least forty miles.

"Can anyone get a signal out here?"

Out of six people using four different cell phone service providers, not one of them could get a signal.

Taking its cue from Moon's 'Boonesville' declaration, a pack of wolves started howling somewhere off in the woods. Sheena was getting visibly disturbed...all of the women were. Stormy moved close to Moon and grabbed his arm for support. Mimi didn't like what Stormy was doing and pulled Moon in the direction of the car and away from Stormy.

After a few minutes of brain storming, the decision was that the women would walk next to the van while the men pushed it in the direction they were heading. It was further agreed that if the women saw anything they thought could attack them, they would get inside the mini-van while the guys pushed. The group already knew there was nothing behind them or they would have seen it when they passed. The hope was that there was something in front of them. Maybe there was a house or a business that was not shown on the map; somewhere they could stop and use a phone. It would be dark soon and they would lose all the light. They all agreed that the last thing they wanted was to be caught out in the woods of Virginia.

"What did you do with that bag Moon?"

"I tossed it in the back of the van under the seat. It's safe...safer than I feel right now."

Chapter 30

After six rings, Frank hangs up his phone.

"Damn."

Frank has been trying to reach his daughter by cell phone for the past twenty-four hours. Frank called four times yesterday and this was his second call today. Even though Frank was on his way to a crime scene, his mind was racing. Usually Frank's daughter would pick the phone up right away when he called. Frank was probably the only person that Sheena would always answer the phone for, and Frank knew it.

"This is not good"

Frank was a single parent; he had been since his daughter was three years old. Frank's late wife was the only woman that Frank ever loved- and in the end, Frank could not save her life. It was exactly eighteen years ago that Frank walked into his house and found that they were being robbed. What's worse than being robbed was the bloody mess that Frank found in the house that night.

At that time in his career, Frank had already been an officer for twenty-two years. Frank loved being an officer of the law; it was his destiny. Frank's father had been a highly decorated police officer, his grandfather had been a Virginia State Trooper and his great grandfather had worked his way up from district attorney to become the Mayor of the City of Richmond. Frank had uncles who served on the bench and his aunt on his father's side was the first woman Judge in the State of Virginia. Frank grew up listening to all kinds of stories during family gatherings; but his favorite stories were the ones that his father told him. Frank and his father, Bill White, would go fishing or camping or on any one of their many 'men trips'. Bill would tell Frank countless stories of his ventures in law enforcement. Now that Frank thought back over the stories his father told him, he doubted that all of the stories were true. However, the truth in those stories didn't matter to Frank. What mattered to Frank was that his father believed in what he was doing; he believed that he made a positive difference in people's lives every single day. Frank's father knew that he was on the front lines of the fight against evil in this world, and he took that responsibility seriously. Frank's father always projected strength, confidence and a level head. Frank entered law enforcement to follow in the footsteps of his father; Frank too wanted to make a difference in this world. Over the years Frank had made a few bad decisions and everything did not work out the way Frank had planned them, but Frank never stopped believing that he could and would make a difference in the lives of the people he came into contact with.

When Frank arrived at the warehouse on Leigh Street, there were officers everywhere. Frank hardly spoke as he walked past the initial barricade, into the warehouse and up to the second floor.

It was a mess. There were blood and body parts everywhere. Whatever happened here was a level of violence that Frank had not seen since the day he walked into his home eighteen years ago. Eighteen years ago...Frank could still remember the moment he walked into his home and his life changed forever. That gruesome night, Frank lost a bit of his humanity...

The day was July tenth. It was abnormally humid that day. Frank had been on the police force for two years, following in the footsteps of his father. The entire police force knew Frank as an honest, light-hearted man who believed in what he did. Frank was tough but fair; when Frank was on duty the people he came in contact with were guaranteed to be treated with respect and dignity. Frank did not resort to violence as a first measure, but make no mistake and take his kindness for weakness. Although Frank would not resort to violence as a first measure, you were also guaranteed to get a first class beat down if you went too far.

Frank was one of the lucky ones; he had met and married the

woman he loved...his soul mate. While most of Frank's friends were living it up on the dating scene and the party scene, Frank chose to end his search and surrender to what he knew was good. Kimberly was the one; the only one Frank would ever love. Sure there were millions of women that he had never met, but Frank didn't care.

Kimberly was beautiful, smart and fun to be with. She did come from a large family, three sisters and five brothers, but Frank didn't hold it against her. Frank often felt like he got the only sane person in that family. Kimberly was a partner in her law firm and had just made local history for a successful lawsuit against the tobacco industry. The $875 million settlement on behalf of her clients is the largest settlement on record in the State.

Frank and Kimberly were married and just like clockwork, Sheena was born about a year later. Both parents adored their baby girl. Frank was only an officer back then, but he was on the fast track to leadership. It's true that Frank's family legacy would play a part in his rapid ascension, but the real truth is that Frank was good at what he did. Frank communicated with people very well and that was the difference. Frank communicated in a way that allowed individuals to give their opinions and points of view in a situation. Some people were surprised at how many deadly situations Frank diffused just with communication. Frank's father had shared with him long ago the secrets to longevity on the streets and it has served Frank well over the years.

A month after Sheena turned two years old, Frank had been promoted again. Frank didn't even realize he was up for a promotion. Frank called his father to tell him the news and then called Kimberly. Both were happier for Frank than he was for himself. Frank's father Bill White invited him out for drinks that evening and Kimberly said she would drop Sheena off at her mom's house so they could celebrate when he got home. Frank was on cloud nine, it was turning out to be the best day of his life.
When Frank finished his shift he walked over to the Silver Bullet, a bar on the West End in Henrico. The Silver Bullet was owned by

a former police officer turned businessman. William Wilson had been a cop with a questionable history on the force, who took a bullet in the back during a routine traffic stop in a bad part of town. Some of the local criminals on the streets that night claim that Officer Williams was there shaking down the area drug dealers when he was shot, but the investigation showed no wrong doing on Wilson's part. Wilson retired from the force soon after with full benefits and this profitable business. Perhaps there was more to it than that, but Frank did not care to know.

Frank and his dad had a great time that evening. Bill told Frank how proud of him he was and paid for the appetizers and drinks. Bill wanted to have dinner but Frank explained that he was taking Kim out for dinner when they left to celebrate his promotion. Frank's father was happy to hear it and encouraged his son to have a great evening. Bill offered Frank a ride home and Frank accepted since Kim had dropped him off at work today because his car was in the shop.

Bill pulled up to his son's house that evening around 8:30 pm. After a few more words between them, Frank exited the car and walked up his driveway to his front door. Frank's dad honked the horn as he pulled off and disappeared down the tree lined street. Frank walked to the door, pulling out his keys and smiling because of what he knows is waiting for him behind this door…the most beautiful woman in the world who loved only him.

When Frank approached the door, it was open. As Frank reached out to push the door open, he noticed that the lock had been busted. It looked like someone had busted their way through the door. Frank pulled his service revolver and opened the door a little further to see what was behind the door.

From the front door, Frank could see the living-room. In the back of the room was the door that led to the kitchen and on the right was a staircase leading up to the second floor. The living room looked a bit messy; there had obviously been a struggle or fight of some sort. Frank walked further into the room slowly, trying not to make any sounds to alert an intruder that he was now in the house. Frank eased his way further into the room, deciding to pass the staircase and check the kitchen first. As Frank walked pass the staircase, he heard a noise from upstairs that sounded like a muffled thud. Frank quickly made it across the living-room and through the kitchen door; he had to check the kitchen to make sure there was not another criminal waiting to sneak up behind him once he hit the stairs.

No one was in the kitchen. Frank could see a few pots on the stove with steam coming out of them and realized that Kim was probably in the house because Kim had to have been back from dropping off Sheena at her mother's house- she would never leave the house with the stove turned on. While Frank was thinking over this information, he could hear another muffled thud and then a noise that sounded like a body hitting the floor.

"Kimberly!"

Frank moved quickly out of the kitchen and to the stairs. Frank could hear more movement and he took the stairs quickly. On the second floor of the house there were four doors- one door for the bathroom and three bedroom doors. The sounds he heard downstairs in the kitchen had come from the master bedroom above the kitchen. Frank snuck over to the bedroom door and peeked around the corner. What he saw stunned him. The sound he heard and thought was a body hitting the floor was actually a *body part* hitting the floor. There was a madman in the room and there was blood everywhere.

For a moment, Frank watched as this intruder pulled and pushed a saw across his wife's body. The intruder had already sawed off most of her limbs; the arms, legs, hands and feet. It looked as if the intruder had sawed off the pieces and flung them carelessly around the room. Blood covered the bed and the floor and the walls and the drapes. Frank resisted the urge to vomit as he watched the intruder place the saw across his wife's neck and prepare to saw her head off. Frank looked at his Kimberly's face, covered in blood. His wife's eyes looked like it still had life in them; she had suffered through this horror alone. She probably called out his name over and over to no avail because no aide would come to her. The very thought of it made Frank sick to his stomach. Just before the masked intruder rolled the saw across Kimberly's neck to separate head from body, Frank stepped into the doorway with his gun drawn. For Frank, time was moving in slow motion. Frank watched as the intruder looked up from his work and noticed Frank standing in the door with his gun pointed. Frank watched as something like recognition seemed to take over the intruder's body; Frank could not see the intruder's eyes or face, but Frank thought that the intruder's body told a quick story of recognition and revenge. Frank was sure that he could even see a smile come across the intruder's face underneath the mask, a smile that spoke of joy and elation at this heinous crime he was performing right this moment.

"Don't make another move or I will shoot you dead."

The intruder's smile widened as he summoned his strength for one last pull of the saw. With one powerful pull of the saw her head would be separated from neck. The very thought gave the masked intruder a hard-on. Frank could see the moment the intruder decided to pull the saw across his wife's neck...and he shot. Frank squeezed the trigger and almost cheered as the bullet left the chamber and struck the intruder. Frank would have loved for the bullet to pierce through the intruder's head, blowing a big chunk off and splattering brains against the wall behind. However, death was too quick; this man needed to suffer. Frank wanted to personally see that this man suffer for the rest of his life. Frank did squeeze the trigger of his service revolver and he did hit the intruder, but it was not in the head. Frank's bullet tore through the intruder's shoulder; knocking him back against the wall, off the bed and onto his back on the floor. The intruder tried to get up and Frank shot him twice again- this time in the meaty part of both legs. With the intruder down and bleeding, Frank walked over to the bed where his wife laid. Kimberly looked a mess and Frank could see nothing but here eyes. Frank watched as the final moments of life drained out of his wife's eyes; there was a split second of recognition, then fear then relief as the light of her life was extinguished.

Frank was enraged. As Frank walked over to where the intruder laid smiling, all Frank could see was red. Frank stood over the intruder, his mind racing with possibilities of harm. Frank bent down and removed the mask from the intruder's face- he wanted to look into the face of the attacker that killed his wife. Frank pulled off the mask and saw the intruder was Marcus Wells. Marcus Wells was a career criminal that Frank had put in jail three years ago. Armed robbery was the charge. Was this a revenge killing? Did this man really come into Frank's home and upend his life purposely? Frank had a chance to kill this man the last time he arrested him and chose to respect this man's rights. Could Kimberly's death be place at Frank's feet now? If Frank had killed this intruder three years ago, Kimberly would be alive right now.

These thoughts and many others swirled through Frank's mind as he stood over the intruder. Frank didn't even realize that he was pointing the gun at the intruder's head.

Chapter 31

Bill had just dropped Frank off that evening and was going home to his own wife. Bill was Frank's partner and Bill was just as proud as could be of Frank. Frank had made a good life for himself; he had a great career, beautiful wife and was viewed as a man of integrity. Every time Bill thought of his son, the biggest smile would come across his face. Bill White was probably the only person who was happier than Frank was about his son's life. While sitting at the stop sign around the corner from dropping off his son, Bill picked up his phone and gave his own wife a call.

"Hi sweetheart, how are you?"

"Hi Bill, how did drinks go with Frank?"

"It was great. I am so proud of that boy. The family is good and he loves that new promotion he received. I would say that life is very good for them right now."

"How are you doing? Is life good for you right now?"

"Life couldn't be better my love. Is our granddaughter doing ok?"

"I just put her to bed; she fell asleep on the couch again. I'll tell you, Sheena is the cutest grandbaby in the world."

"I know it. I'm on my way home. Do you want me to pick up anything?"

"No dear, we have everything we need...providing you brought me that punch bowl from Kim's house like I asked you."

"Aw, I forgot to get it. I just dropped Frank off and kept it moving. How bad do you need it? Can we pick it up when we take Sheena back?"

"No Bill. I need that punchbowl for my meeting in the morning. I guess you are just going to have to turn back around and pick it up."

'Fine. I will see you in a bit."

Bill turned the car around and went back to his son's house. Truth be told, he didn't mind at all. Going back to his son's house will give him a chance to see his beautiful daughter-in-law...and a chance to get a cold brew out of the refrigerator for his trip home.

Bill pulled up to his son's house and immediately noticed the front door was open. Thinking nothing of it, Bill walked up the to the door to go inside. Bill had just reached the steps to the house when he heard a gunshot. Bill ducked down and looked around him. The gunshot came from inside the house.

"Frank! What's going on in there Frank?"

Bill pulled out his gun and rushed in the house. He heard two more gunshots and looked upstairs where the shots rang out. Bill ran up the steps and saw the door to the master bedroom open. Bill moved to the side of the open door and peeked in. Bill saw blood and body parts all around the room. In the center of the room at the foot of the bed, Bill saw his daughter's torso lying on the floor. Next to Kimberly's torso was a man lying on the floor with Frank standing over him, service pistol pointed directly at the man's head.

"Frank!"

Frank looked at his father for a split second and Bill could see the whole story in his son's eyes. This was an intruder; and the intruder had come into his house and caused mayhem. Kimberly had been viciously murdered and Frank was standing over his wife's murderer with a gun pointed at his head. These were vital seconds. Bill did not want his son to become a murderer; he didn't want that type of stress added to his son's life, which would be hard enough from this point forward. Bill called out Frank's name one more time, trying to break through the fuzz that was certainly clouding Frank's thought process at this moment. Bill could see murder in his son's eyes…and emptiness.

"Frank, don't do it. Let the law handle this."

Too late. One final gunshot rang out in the night. Frank shot the intruder in the center of the head.

Chapter 32

Frank arrived at the crime scene on Leigh Street and made his way up to the second floor of the warehouse. This floor of the warehouse was a direct reminder of the day he lost his wife at the hands of a brutal murderer. There was blood everywhere in the warehouse; on the walls, on the boxes, on the furniture…everywhere you looked. Body parts were strewn across the room like dirty clothes in a teenager's room; legs, arms and appendages. There had to be at least two bodies if not three lying around the room.

"What do we have?"

"Hello chief. Not a good scene. There seems to have been some type of battle here, but we are a little stumped about exactly what happened. We have body parts suggesting that at least two people were killed. There are bullet shells all over this part of the room, suggesting that the intruder came in from that way, and was immediately attacked. We are guessing that a number of the bullets in the room had to have hit the intruder because we cannot find enough bullets to account for all of the shells. The body parts around the room seem to have been cut off by some type of sword or large knife. The separations of the limbs from the body are clean. We are not exactly sure what weapon was used."

"Did you I.D the victims yet?"

"Not yet sir. It's a bit hard. We can't find their heads."

Frank took a minute to process this information. The first thing Frank thought of was the conversation he had with the agent from D.C. *Strange killings…with missing body parts.* Two missing heads from victims that were sliced to pieces did fall under the agent's definition of *strange* murders.

"What else you got?"

"Well, there was at least one other person in the room at the time that may have gotten away. You remember that mess of glass and boxes you saw on the ground outside the warehouse?"

"What about it?"

"Well, it looks as if someone jumped through this window over here and landed on those boxes to get away."

"Did they get away?"

"We believe they did. We can't find a body outside and no one has called in a body, so we are thinking that this person got away and is still somewhere out on the streets."

"If that's the case, then this is probably not over. I'm going outside to make a couple of calls. You know what to do in here."

"Yes sir."

Frank walked out of the warehouse to his car. Once Frank got into the car, he made two phone calls. The first phone call was to a friend that Frank has known for many years now. The phone rings on the other side two times and Frank hangs up, then calls right back. On the second ring Frank hangs up again and calls right back. This time Frank lets the phone ring three times before it is answered.

"Hello Frank."

"I need to talk with you. I have an important task that I need completed."

"When?"

"Tonight at midnight."

"Same place?"

"No. This time I want you to meet me in the shed behind my house. Make sure no one sees you."

"Don't I always?"

With that, Frank hangs up the phone and calls his daughter's phone again. Frank lets the phone ring five times before he hangs up.

"Damn girl, where are you?"

Gripping the steering wheel with both hands, Franks pulls off into the night.

Chapter 33

"How about a dance?"

"Not right now, maybe later."

"You mean you came to a strip club and don't want a dance?"

"I may or may not get a dance tonight...I don't know yet. What I can tell you is that I am not ready for a dance right now."

"Bitch ass. Get the fuck out of here then."

Shemihazah stared at the woman in front of him straight in the eyes. Shemi was only in here taking a look, to see if the woman he was searching for was in here. Shemihazah was more than human, but it still had human in him. The human part of Shemi's was strong enough to make him want to go inside 'The Candy Bar' and see what was happening. *'Naked women, alcohol, darkness and desperation...a nice blend indeed'.* Shemi was not pleased with this woman's attitude though-and he thought she needed to be taught a lesson.

"Come on now, don't be like that."

Shemihazah took a wad of cash out of his pockets. The stripper he was talking with, Nikki, saw the knot of hundred dollar bills and changed her attitude. Money was king in this establishment.

"I'm listening."

Shemihazah peeled off the top two hundred dollar bills, folded them and slid the bills down the front of Nikki's thong. Nikki's brightened up quickly.

"I'm sorry. I didn't mean no disrespect. It's just that a lot of these guys come to take a peek, but don't want to spend any money. I just

thought you were one of them too."

"No apologies necessary."

"You want your dance now? Follow me."

"Well, I want to wait a little while; have a few drinks, listen to some music. What time do you get off tonight?"

"Actually I get off in about an hour. Why, you got something on your mind?"

"I was thinking we could go for a drink when you get off. I still have a pocket full of money and would be happy to transfer more of it into your pocket for a pleasurable evening."

Nikki looked at the man standing in front of her and sighed deeply. Normally Nikki did not do business outside of the club. Yet this was a difficult time in her life; Nikki needed to make as much money as she could right now. Rent was due, daycare was due, the light bill was due…there were a number of reasons that Nikki could think of to break her rule and make some money tonight. Prostitution was not Nikki's business of choice, but tonight was going to be a bit different.

An hour later Nikki was getting off of work. Nikki changed into her street clothes, packed her small suitcase and made her way towards the door. Nikki looked around the club but didn't see Shemihazah anywhere. To tell the truth, Nikki was a bit disappointed.

"Oh well, I guess I'll just roll with the two hundred then."

Nikki walked out of the club and into the brisk air of the night. Her car was parked in the back next to the tall street light. Nikki took out her phone as she walked to her car, planning to call her mother and let her know she had just gotten off of work. Nikki always picked her daughter up straight from work. Tonight would have been different if the stranger had stayed until the end of her shift, but since he left she had nothing to stick around for.

Nikki took a pack of cigarettes out of her jacket pocket and put one in her mouth to smoke. She stopped in the middle of the parking lot looking for her lighter, the one she bought in the Dominican Republic last month on vacation. Searching for the lighter, Nikki did not hear Shemihazah as he approached her from behind.

"*Boo.*"

Nikki screamed in fear and dropped her cigarette as she almost fell over.

"*What the fuck?*"

"*I'm sorry. I didn't mean to scare you.*"

"*You didn't mean to scare me? Then why the hell are you jumping out of shadows screaming 'boo'? What did you think would happen?*"

Shemi couldn't contain his laughter.

"*Oh, this is funny to you, huh?*"

"*No it's not. I'm sorry. I was hoping we could still spend a little time together tonight.*"

Nikki paused before she answered, looking at Shemihazah from head to toe. He was not really Nikki's type; kind of short, not remarkably handsome and he looked a bit frail under that leather jacket. But Shemihazah did have one thing that Nikki found very attractive…a roll of hundred dollar bills.

"*I do have plans tonight, but I guess I can hang out a bit. What would you like to do Mr.....?*"

"Shemi. My name is Shemi."

"Shemi? I've never heard that name before, what kind of name is it?"

"I was named after my father."

"Is your father Jewish or something?"

"No, my father is not from around here, he is from far away. My mother was an American."

"Ok...Shemi. What did you have in mind?"

"Well, I know a beautiful place not more than fifteen minutes from here. It is close to downtown, going towards the Church Hill area. It is a nice spot overlooking the City."

"Ok, I think I know the area you are talking about. You want to go somewhere outside? I thought you wanted to do something that would take a little more privacy. I thought this was going to be a business meeting of sorts."

"Well it is Nikki. But we can be a little creative about it, can't we?

Shemihazah dug his hand into the inside pocket of his jacket and pulled out a zip lock bag with an ounce of marijuana in it. As Nikki gazed at the bag of weed; she could smell it the moment he pulled it out of his pocket. Shemi also pulled out that wad of hundred dollar bills.

"I was thinking maybe we go over there, look out over the City, smoke a little bud, and then see where that leads us. If you are interested, the Jefferson Hotel is only a few minute's drive from the overlook."

As Shemi spoke, he took three hundred dollar bills off of the roll of money and placed them gently inside her bra. Nikki loved the feel of cash on her body. She was beginning to like Shemi more and more...at least Nikki did like the fact that Shemi wasn't scared to spends some money. Nikki definitely had the skills to pay the bills and she planned on paying a bunch of bills by the time this evening was over.

"Ok, we can do that. Do you have a car?"

"No I don't. I can call a cab for us unless you have a car. When we leave from overlooking the City, we can stop off at the Jefferson if you are game."

The Jefferson Hotel. Nikki had lived in the City of Richmond her whole life and had never been in the Jefferson. It was a very upscale Hotel in Downtown Richmond. Although Nikki made enough money to spend a night in the hotel if she wanted, Nikki chose to use her money a different way. Nikki was saving her money to buy a house...for cash. Nikki wanted to give her daughter the best that life had to offer, which meant she would forego some of today's pleasures for tomorrow's security. Nikki was all in...intrigued even. She was not sure of exactly who this stranger was, but he was rolling in dough and willing to spend it on her tonight. Let's have a party indeed.

Nikki led Shemi to her car in the back of the parking lot under the light. Nikki's car was an old beat-up Nissan Sentra. Nikki had owned this Nissan for about three years now- the entire time she had been working at the club. Nikki had plenty of money to buy herself a new car- a luxury car even. However, Nikki thought that would be a waste of money. 'Cars depreciate, property appreciates'. What was important was buying a house and making sure her daughter had everything she needed.

Chapter 34

Nikki and Shemi drove off from the strip club's parking lot and down East Broad Street towards their destination. When they arrived at the overlook, it was beautiful. While Nikki marveled at the lights of the city, Shemihazah rolled up a huge joint that would get Nikki higher than high. Shemihazah did not smoke marijuana himself, but he was happy to provide it to those that he came in contact with.

Inside the car, Shemi asked questions that would force Nikki to talk and reveal things about herself. Shemi was on a hunt; he was looking for a woman who could provide something that no other woman could provide...an acceptable match for his DNA sequence. Shemi's ultimate plan was to create second generation versions of himself; a completely Earth born being that could devour the Earth. Shemihazah wanted to do the same thing his 'father' had done thousands of years ago; create a new race of beings in his own image- something that God had not created and never intended. Shemihazah smiled at the thought and began rolling a huge joint for the evening's festivities.

Once Nikki and Shemi made it to the place where they could overlook the City without being disturbed, they got out of the car and sat on a bench. The view was spectacular. Shemi let Nikki light the joint as she talked on and on about her life. When Nikki passed Shemi the joint, Shemi pretended to smoke with his back to her. After a few fake tokes of the joint, Shemi would pass it back to Nikki who looked to be thoroughly enjoying the weed and her company. An hour later they were still outside; Nikki was as high as a kite and Shemi was sober and still on the prowl.

Now was the time. Shemi moved in closer to Nikki as she sat on the bench smoking and watching the city below. Shemi put his arms around her on the back of the bench and signed deeply. Nikki did not see Shemi's hand as the pinky finger on his hand grew to twice its size...the fingernail included. Shemi quickly brushed the fingernail of his pinky across Nikki's back, slicing skin and drawing blood.

"Ouch. What the hell was that?"

"I'm sorry Nikki. I think one of the rings on my fingers may have nicked you by mistake. Let me take a look at it."

Nikki moved her body forward as Shemihazah surveyed her back, exposing the paper thin cut he made across her flesh. With one finger, Shemi wiped up the blood that had trickled from the cut and tasted it. It was warm and full of iron, sweet to the taste. However, Nikki was not the woman he was looking for. Shemi knew that she was not the one, he could tell by the taste of her blood. Shemi knew, as he told the doctors that 'created' him that the life is in the blood. Nikki's blood revealed that she did not have the genetic make-up to carry his children to term.

"What a waste."

Nikki turned around and looked at Shemi in the eyes...

"What's a waste?"

"It such a waste that a beautiful woman like you does not have everything you need in this life."

"I know; that's what I've been saying for years!"

"I can make it better."

"How? You're going to be my sugar daddy?"

"You're what?"

"My sugar daddy...you want to be my sponsor don't you...yeah, you want to take care of me, I can tell."

"I do want to take care of you Nikki. I want to take care of you right now."

"Okay, for the five hundred dollars you gave me so far, I guess I can take care of you first. Let's go to the car."

Nikki rubbed her hand across Shemi's chest and down his stomach. Nikki leaned over and kissed Shemi gently on the neck. Shemi had not had an experience like this and let her continue on. As Nikki's hands explored Shemi's body, she moved her hand downward to his genitals. After a second, Nikki stopped and looked Shemi in the eyes...

"Let's go to the car."

Shemi and Nikki walked back to the parked Sentra and Nikki opened the back door. Nikki pushed Shemi into the back seat and got in with him. Nikki unbuckled his belt, unzipped his pants and pulled out his throbbing penis.

"Jackpot."

Shemi relaxed as Nikki explored his throbbing penis with her mouth. Shemi had never known this experience; actually he had never experienced sex at all.

Chapter 35

Shemi was born in a lab and cut off from almost all human activity. He had grown at an accelerated rate; they said he aged five human years for every one year he was in existence. Shemi had just turned six years old when he busted out of the lab and started his adventure to fulfill his destiny. Destiny for Shemi was a fancy word that described the path he was on. No one told Shemi this, but he knew that he didn't have much time in this world. He had to find a way to pro-create. That was his mission…he had seen it in his dreams. In Shemi's dreams, his true father appeared to him and talked with him. Shemi's father told him of things to come should Shemi accomplish the mission he was created for. Shemi was promised Godhood…and that his children should start a new chapter of history in the known and unknown universe. All Shemi had to do was find his genetic match and create three children.

So Shemi studied human nature. He studied by way of movies. Shemi would request his 'caretakers' bring him all sorts of movies. Shemi particularly liked Action Movies. Anything with crime, mobsters or any other type of violent theme was Shemi's favorites. Shemi learned about sex too, all from the movies. The movies had shown Shemi what to do and how to do it. Although he had never had sex, Shemi knew that one day he would have to partake in this human ritual in order to create the children that his future depended on.

In most of the crime movies that Shemi watched, he noticed that almost all of the movies had these 'strip club' scenes. The strip club seemed to be where all of the women that were willing to show their naked bodies and more times than not, negotiate deals to sell their bodies for man-made paper hung out. Even the scientists that worked in the lab with him consistently planned to go 'hang-out' after work at various strip clubs. Shemi decided that when he made it out of the prison he was trapped in he too would make his way to one of these strip clubs.

In the back of that Nissan Sentra with Nikki, Shemi allows himself to drift off…back to the day he escaped the lab. Shemi acknowledged that life had finally begun the day he escaped. Sure, there were loose ends to tie up; he had to find Cliff, kill him and retrieve that bag. The contents in that back are dangerous. Shemi's life and possibly his death are connected to the green tote bag that was stolen.

Cliff had escaped from the lab with the green tote bag, helped by some woman Shemi had never seen before. Inside the bag were four simple items; a book that told the story of the Watchers; angels that were punished for their crime of creating mixed breeds in the Earth. The book told the story of Shemi's father and how he convinced a group of about 200 angels entrusted with watching over the creation, to come down to rape, pillage and destroy what was in their charge.

That book contained both history and future. Shemi also knew that inside the pages of that book was all the foundational information that led to the Trans-humanist Agenda; the movement to justify creating 'super-humans'. The movement that will see some incredible human/animal/plant/computer hybrids beings created. The information is contained in Shemi's DNA and the methods are contained in that book.

In addition to the book, there is a syringe of the only compound on earth that can stop Shemi. By stop he means paralyze; hand-cuff or otherwise immobilize Shemi. It is the formula humans created that attacks Shemi's DNA. It stops him from moving in his physical form…and if Shemi is in his 'ink' form it stops him from shifting back to human form. That is dangerous because Shemi's DNA is not stable in the 'ink' form and can easily be manipulated. No threat has presented itself to Shemi in the lab, but this is a big world…Shemi knows that he will have to always be on guard. Some of these humans are quite crafty.

There was also a necklace with a special 'gem' hanging on it that has a few special powers and a vial of blood. The gem that hangs on the jewel is similar to a spiritual tracking device. It let's Shemi or its possessors know when they are in the presence of man-made hybrids and extra-terrestrials and their hybrids. It is quite a handy necklace to have. The blood in the tote bag is 'blessed blood'. Shemi heard the story of how some quack pot scientist that was also a Christian took some of Shemi's original blood samples and had it blessed by a priest. Shemi didn't think he had anything to worry about with the blessed blood, mainly because most 'spiritual leaders' have already made a pact with satan in exchange for worldwide ministries and millions of tax-free dollars. How many real blessings can a miss-guided spiritual leader bestow on others?

Chapter 36

'Oh my..."

Shemi had never felt a sensation like this. Nikki had covered his penis with her mouth and went at it like it was the 'Lollipop of Eternal Life'. After a short while Shemi could feel some of his essence go out of him, as well as a bit of his strength. This was the greatest thing ever!

Once Nikki relieved Shemi of some of his 'angst', she removed her underwear and sat on his still hardened penis. She moved up and down as Shemi groaned and stared at her wide-eyed, while lying on his back. Shemi had no idea he had more essence to give; he thought he had given it all a few minutes ago. When Shemi invited Nikki to hang out with him, he did not expect it to go like this; he expected it to be like all of his other 'dates' since he had been out. All of his dates thus far had been quite comical...until the killing began. With Nikki, there was no kicking and screaming...she had went on the offensive from the start and Shemi did not expect that. Now he was feeling quite good...thinking of a cigarette and some sleep. Shemi started to contemplate giving Nikki an unexpected gift for a job well done...her life. Never before had Shemi changed his mind on killing a human- it was something he did so very well. But tonight was a momentous occasion; Shemi had his first sexual experience. All is well in the world; live and let live and all that jive.

By the time Nikki dismounted, Shemihazah had decided to let her live. So far Shemi had left a trail of blood and body parts everywhere he went. His travels have seen him cross four different States to date; searching for Cliff and his 'posse'. Shemi knew that the woman from the elevator...'Vic'... had joined Cliff in his run across the States. The day Shemi killed Vic's parents he also found out that Vic's baby brother was traveling with them as well. Three deaths...Shemi could arrange that. After all, Shemi had been getting plenty of practice since he left the lab. Shemi had cut people, ripped out entrails and feasted- separated body parts and strewn them around to create fear in those who investigated the crimes. Tonight, he planned to either find a DNA match from the heft selection at the Candy Bar, or leave a trail of blood like no one has seen. Fortunately for the rest of the girls, Nikki had presented herself a willing target for Shemi's blood lust, so he left the others alone and played the cards he had now.

However, when Nikki went on the offensive and offered Shemi a chance to experience sexual relations, she was granted a *'pass'*. *Sex is a powerful thing*, Shemi thought; as he pulled his pants back up and moved to exit the car. Nikki was happy to simply bask in the thoughts of what she had just experienced…never had she had three orgasms before. Most of the men she dated talked a big game but were barely able to give her one orgasm.

Nikki shifted her body as Shemi put on his pants and exited the car. She reached over and grabbed the half of joint left that she put in her jacket pocket. *Man, this is the best stuff I've ever had.* Nikki lit the joint and puffed away, feeling as carefree as a newborn tot.

Then, things began to change…

The first thing Nikki noticed was her stomach beginning to hurt. She put the joint down and tried to burp. Shemihazah was standing outside of the car watching. He was curious himself about what would happen should he have sex with a woman who was not the DNA match for his bloodline. Shemi knew that if the woman was a match, she would be successfully impregnated and a healthy offspring would be born to him six months later. It would only take six months because he too would be on a slightly accelerated growth schedule. It would then be up to the offspring to repeat the process until the aging factor turned in reverse. It was Shemi's estimation that it would only take five generations of propagating to create his 'godlike' offspring, which would live human lives of more than five hundred years.

In the car Nikki became more and more agitated. Shemi watched as she moaned and groaned, holding her stomach. Shemi watched Nikki's as a drop of blood first appeared and made its dark trail down her face. As she wiped the blood away, Nikki screamed suddenly and grabbed her head, as if grabbing it on both sides was keeping it from exploding. The blood that first trailed out of her nose now became a gush of blood running from her nose. You could see blood exiting from the corners of her eyes and her ears.

Nikki's screams were now silent; as if here very vocal chords had declared mutiny and simply stopped working. Her eyes were sunken and black; her hair seemed to go white in mere moments. Nikki's body had rejected the semen that she took into her body both vaginally and orally. It was as if the cells in her body began to break down once the foreign DNA patterns in Shemi's semen came in contact with her. Shemi marveled at the result of what he was looking at. '*I got some powerful stuff*'. At that, Shemi burst out in laughter. Shemi took out a pack of cigarettes, 'Lucky Strikes', and grabbed one for his walk in the night air. Shemi knew that this little venture set him back time wise, but it was ok. All work and no play started to be a bit boring. Shemi had a mission; he needed to find Cliff again and get that bag back. He also needed to find a woman and complete his propagation mission. Shemi knew that the world was waiting on him...godhood was waiting on him...the disembodied spirits of all of the murdered offspring of "The Watchers" were waiting on him. Shemi was the chosen one, chosen to change the course of all things. Shemi would remake the entire world in *his* image...and then rule it with an iron fist.

As Nikki finished choking on her own blood in the back of her Nissan Sentra, Shemihazah turned his back to the car and walked away. There was no one on the streets. If someone was looking at him through their window, they better not let Shemi find out. Shemi had a knack for evil and an appetite for murder.

Shemi fixed his collar, brushed off his jacket and walked into the night once again, whistling as he walked. This time the tune was, Welcome to the Hotel California.

Chapter 37

Frank was almost home.

Those days after Frank's wife died were the hardest of his life. Becoming a single parent was not the biggest change; Frank knew that tens of millions of people in the United States alone were single parents. Frank missed his wife. She was his best friend, his light, his guide. There have been many times that Frank teetered on the edge of sanity in his job, but Kimberly was always able to bring him back to reality. Without his wife, Frank knew that he had to pay special attention to himself; he was able to fly off the deep end at a moment's notice. He had done it several times; never with his baby girl, but in the streets where violence happens.

After leaving the crime scene at the warehouse, Frank decided to stop by Sheena's apartment before he went home. Since he was not able to get in touch with her by phone, Frank decided to take the more direct approach.

Sheena was not there when he arrived. From outside of the apartment you could see that all of the lights were off, except for a slight illumination in the living room window. Frank knew that it was a night light that had that faint shine in the back of the room. Every since Sheena was a child, she had to have a nightlight on in her room.

Frank had a key to Sheena's apartment. She had given it to him a few years ago when she first moved in. It was not because she was scared, but because she was her father's child and safety was paramount.

Frank used the key and entered his daughter's apartment. Nothing seemed out of place, everything was where it would usually be. Frank walked through the house to the bedroom. In the bedroom he saw the closet door open and a few shirts on the bed. Looking at the impression on the bed, it looks like something large and rectangular had been placed on it...a suitcase perhaps. She probably packed a suitcase and went on a short trip for the weekend. Rick. She was probably with Rick. Frank knew that Sheena and Rick were an item these days, and had been for a while. She tried to hide it from him, but Frank was an excellent detective and even better father. Frank always joked that his 20/40 vision allowed his to see through bullshit.

Frank decided he would track down Rick or his family and confirm that Sheena was with him. Then maybe he could find out why she didn't tell him she was going away for the weekend. Frank knew that Sheena was grown now, but she was still his baby girl.

Frank left Sheena's apartment and was home in twenty minutes. His house was at the end of a cul-de-sac in Eastern Henrico. Frank had lived here with his wife and daughter since the day they got married. Frank pulled in and turned off the car. It was dark and the motion lights did not come on when he pulled up. Frank looked around his landscape intently; checking for any signs of danger or anything out of place. Frank stepped out of the car and walked towards the back of the house instead of going in the front door.

Walking around the back, Frank noticed that none of the side motion lights on the house lit up as he walked. *Curious.* Frank instinctively put his hand on his service revolver. There was no shame in being ready.

Frank owned a three bedroom house. It was about 1400 square feet and had a shed in the back that Frank kept locked up for himself. No one was ever allowed in the shed. Approaching the shed, Frank noticed that the lock was off the door. Someone had broken inside. Frank put his service revolver back in the holster. Frank knew who was inside; Frank had just called him and said to meet him at his house in the shed.

Chapter 38

"Evening Frank."

"I've asked you to stop breaking into my house and my shed. I could have shot you thinking you were a burglar."

"Shoot me Frank? Now why would you want to do that? As useful as I have been to you."

"Yeah, well...just stop breaking into my house. Are you the one that disconnected my motion lights?"

"You called me Frank."

"Why the motion lights? Couldn't you get back here without triggering the lights?"

"You certainly are asking a lot of questions tonight Frank. Is something wrong? You called me and asked me to meet you here, remember?"

Frank sighed and walked over the chair across from the couch that Dave was sitting in. For a shed, the room was nicely furnished; a solid oak desk with chairs, a bookshelf, a couch, two comfortable and ergonomically designed chairs and a nice coffee table between the couch and chairs. Everything was neatly arranged and recently cleaned. Dave doubted that he would ever find any dust in this room; this was Franks personal 'Bat Cave'.
Dave was already sitting comfortably on the couch. He had a cigar lit and a glass of brandy on the coffee table in front of him. Frank walked over to the bookshelf where he kept his scotch, and poured him a glass. Frank took a large swig of the scotch;

"Ahhh"

Frank finished the glass and poured another. He took his drink and walked over to his desk to pull out a fresh cigar from his wooden cigar case. Frank walked to the chair directly in front of Dave, sat his glass on the coffee table and slowly sat down. After lighting his cigar, Frank took another swig of the scotch and settled back in his chair to begin the meeting.

"So what is this about Frank?"

"My daughter. I'm looking for her."

"And...?"

"And I need your help."

"Come on Frank. You know I don't do kid work. I don't even do missing persons. You know what I do Frank."

"Yes I know what you do."

"Then why am I here?"

"Because I need your help."

Dave fidgets uncomfortably in his chair. He could tell right away that he was being called to do a freebie. Frank knew that he was an assassin; probably the top assassin on the East Coast. Frank knew it because Frank had used his services before. Frank and Dave grew up together. Actually, it was Dave's assistance that helped Frank get the Chief of Police job. The interview process had narrowed it down to two candidates; Frank and another cop named Sully. Sully had more everything; more seniority, more friends, more favors owed…more, more, more. Frank didn't think he would get the appointment and mentioned it to his old pal Dave. Two days later, Sully was dead. It looked like a suicide. With Sully gone, the job was Frank's. Frank always did have his suspicions that it was Dave doing him a solid that got him his job as Chief of Police, but of course Dave denied any knowledge.

Over the years, Frank and Dave have had a strange relationship. Before Kimberly died, Frank was a straight laced cop with a chip on his shoulder. Frank was hard, but fair. He went in hard on criminals, but he would give the shirt off his back when it counted. After Kimberly was murdered Frank changed, he seemed lost. Frank became a dark soul; short tempered with a violent streak. Frank was not only willing to walk the line, but also cross said line when the occasion called for it. It was after Kimberly died that Frank started using Dave's *'professional services'*.

"So what is it Frank?"

"Sheena's gone."

"And..."

"And I'm worried about her. She's not answering her phone and neither is her boyfriend. I think they went on a weekend trip, but I am not positive and I don't know where. I want you to find them."

"You know Frank, just because Sheena went away for a minute and didn't tell you, that is not unusual. Sheena is a young adult trying to have some college fun. I don't doubt she wanted to keep some of that away from her Chief of Police father."

"Perhaps. But I have a gut feeling she may be in danger. We have a psychopath on the loose and I don't want her to get caught up in this mess."

"Come on Frank, don't be paranoid. What are the odds of her getting caught up in something crazy?"

"About the same as me coming home one day and finding an intruder in my house killing my wife."

"Touché. So where do I start?"

"Well, she has two girlfriends and two male friends that she would

probably talk to if she were planning a trip. I wrote their names down on this paper. I think the psychopath that is on the loose is the one responsible for the murder at the warehouse down on Leigh Street. Go over to the address and have a look around. You'll have to wait until about two in the morning, after all of my people clear out. Maybe you can find some information over there to make sure this maniac and my daughter are one two different paths right now.'

Dave takes the paper with the names of Sheena's friends and the address to the warehouse on Leigh Street.

"Okay, now to address the elephant in the room. How do we work this out? This job seems to be personal in nature. What do I get out of this?"

"This is my daughter Dave!"

"I understand that. I am just saying that people do what they do. You know what I do and you know my services are not free. So again I ask you, what do I get out of this?"

"What do you need?"

"I don't need anything. But there is something you could do for me."

"What?"

"My niece's son is a real dick head. Last week he robbed a convenience store over on Midlothian Turnpike for some beer. It was a dumb prank and I know he is very sorry. They have him at the lock-up downtown. Perhaps there is a leniency program that you have for first-time offenders."

"I'll work it out."

"Thank you Frank. And with that our business here is concluded. I

will give you a call as soon as I get a heading on where to look."

Dave stands and walks towards Frank who seems engrossed in a thought of his own. Dave walks past Frank and towards the door to the shed. Dave turns before he leaves and catches a glimpse of Frank's face from the side. Dave has known Frank for over forty years and he thought he saw something in the profile of Frank's face that he has never seen before; fear. Frank is afraid of something. Dave couldn't help but wonder what it was that could place fear in the heart of a man who has been in five serious gunfights? Whatever it was, Dave was happy that it was not his problem. Yes, he would find his friend's daughter. Actually, that was a rather easy assignment. Dave contemplated that he might not have to kill anyone. Dave didn't mind the killing, it was the occasional cleaning up afterwards that Dave didn't cherish.

"Okay Frank."

Frank does not respond as Dave walks out of the shed door.

Chapter 39

Dreams no more.

One of the benefits to being in the lab was the poison that they pumped into Shemi's veins. Shemi was not sure what the concoction was made of, but somehow it could affect his blood to the point that it paralyzed him. Shemi remembers lying on those cold steel tables while person after person poked, prodded and assaulted him at their whims. He remembered the tubes that ran throughout his body; tubes into his nose, tubes into his mouth, tubes up his anus. Actually, Shemi thought that the man who shoved the tube up his anus liked his job a bit too much. Shemi can remember watching the man grin as he approached him with those clear tubes…

"Who's been a bad boy today?"

If Shemi had not had an IV tube in his arm pumping in that green poison, he would have shown this pervert exactly how bad a boy he could be. Shemi wouldn't worry about shoving a tube up this man's butt; he would probably like that. If Shemi were to shove something up the man's butt, he would probably opt for that flat screen television mounted on the wall.

The reason Shemi saw a benefit to lying on a cold steel experimental table and allowing the green poison to be injected into his body was that it afforded him time to dream. Ever since Shemi left the lab, he has not had one dream, at least not that he remembers. Part of being human is that he is bound by some of the human laws. As a human, at first Shemi could only use ten percent of his brain's function. He could not change the nature of his human DNA. However, as Shemi was pumped full of poison, it allowed him to dream. In those dreams Shemi was given information that helped him unlock some of his special talents. Through his dreams he saw who he was, how he came to be and what he was to do. Shemi's dreams were powerful. The scientists thought they were harming him and imprisoning him but they were doing the exact opposite; they were freeing him to see beyond human reality. He existed inside and outside of a dimension where time did not exist as a linear thing. Shemi learned some truths about the nature of reality on earth. One movie the staff brought him that was a good reflection of nature was "The Matrix". Everyone was plugged into the matrix, but in his dreams Shemi could see the Matrix itself. Shemi had come to change the nature of the Matrix to something else.

It was in this space that Shemi learned to change the form of his body from solid to a living liquid substance. It was in this place between dimensions that Shemi learned to challenge the physical laws. Shemi found that he could use the power of the life in his blood to do some amazing things; one of which he is about to do right now.

It is Thursday night and he is in the City; Downtown Richmond, Shockoe Bottom. There are people everywhere, the clubs and the streets are full. The women are out in full force. Shemi begins to focus a bit to see if his woman of choice is around, but it is hard to focus…Shemi wants to have some fun. He wants the streets to run red with blood. But first he has to keep his mission intact; find Cliff and find the bag- then there will be nothing that can stop him from fulfilling his mission. Nothing.

Shemihazah continues walking down the packed streets of Richmond and suddenly stops. He can feel the vibe he was hoping for. It was a vibration that let him know someone who dabbles in occult practices is in the area. Not merely a dabbler, but someone of knowledge. Shemi continues to walk up the street, using his senses as a 'divining rod'. Soon, Shemi stands in front of a nondescript, two story building. The upstairs is completely dark but the downstairs has a light on somewhere inside. Shemi could not see it directly, but he knew it was there. There were no markings on the door or the building to say exactly what type of business resided downstairs, but Shemi found one written word on the mailbox next to the front window. The word written on the box was one that made him smile; it read simply,

Seer.

Shemi would go inside and talk with this seer. If they were halfway decent with the skills, he would be able to use them to help locate Cliff. Shemi had a bit of Cliff's blood from their previous encounter at the lab. With Cliff's blood, Shemi could use the seer to transport Cliff from wherever he is to them in that room. Shemi would be able to lay his hands on Cliff finally and move on with his work. *'This is almost too easy'*. The seer would not make it thought the ritual; blood had to be sacrificed to make this happen. But that is the cost of power.

Shemi walks to the door and turns the knob. The door opens easily. The shop is still open for business. Shemi walks inside to see what the seer can see.

Chapter 40

Three miles is a long way.

The guys had been pushing the car for about three miles. Bobby, Rick and Moon were full of sweat, as they pushed the weight of the van along with the three women who were now inside the van.

"That must be what the kings of old felt like, sitting in a shaded room while tons of slaves carried him around the lands. But I'll tell you what, this is not the move."

"I agree Moon. Whose idea was this anyway?"

"I do believe it was your Rick."

Rick, Moon and Bobby continued to push, not knowing how long they would be pushing this van before they saw a place to stop or before a motorist comes along and helps them out. It did not seem like a motorist would be the one to save them; they had been on this road and pushing this van for at least two hours and they has seen no motorists as of yet.

After another thirty minutes of pushing Moon stops to wipe the sweat off of his brow. While standing still, Moon surveyed the land around him; nothing but trees and nature. Moon looked on the left side of the road and saw what he thought was the roof of a structure not more than three hundred feet from where they were now.

"Rick, do you see that?"

"See what?"

"Look over there."

Rick stopped pushing the van and looked in the direction that

Moon was pointing. Rick saw the roof that Moon was referring to. Rick turned to Bobby, who was the smallest and quickest of the three men, and pointed out the roof that he and Moon had been looking at in the distance.

"Bobby, run over there and see what that structure is real quick."

Bobby ran in the direction of the structure. In about five minutes, Bobby was back at the van with news.

"It is a building, a hotel."

"Really?"

"Well, yes. But it is an old building; it looks like it might be abandoned. But the grass has been cut recently and the front door looks like it is operational. I guess there might be someone in there and they might be open for business."

"Is it worth pushing our car all the way over there?"

"I think so...there may be someone inside the office. Even if there is no one there, it is a place where we can get off the road for a few minutes and plan our next move before it gets dark."

After a few minutes of talking, the men decided it would be best if they got off the road and checked out the hotel. The men started pushing the van towards the hotel in hopes that this would be their lucky day.

Chapter 41

After ten or fifteen minutes, the men, women and van arrived in the parking lot of the hotel. As soon as the men pushed the van into a parking space in front of one of the hotel's room, the men collapsed on the ground breathing hard. When the van came to a stop, the three women got out of the van. Moon is the first to speak, always ready with a quick whip…

"Damn, now that was a workout. You ladies are going to have to lay off the kit kats, snickers and Bon Bons."

Stormy is not happy with the weight reference…

"Oh no, Mimi, you need to check your man. He needs to get it together."

"You got that right."

Mimi gives Moon the evil eye look to back up her words. Moon shrugs it off and wipes the sweat from his face.

The rest of the women get out of the van and start looking around at the hotel. It is not very welcoming. The building itself is old; perhaps built in the early 1900's. The shutters have fallen off most of the room windows. The building itself is worn; the paint is faded, the doors are old and splintered and there is dirt and cobwebs everywhere outside of the building. There are even a few thorn bushes around the building. As the students gather in a circle to discuss what they are seeing, Sheena starts the conversation.

"So what's the plan?"

Bobby takes the lead and responds,

"Well we're going to go into the office, use the phone and call someone out to fix the van."

"What about the guy we hit?"

Moon sighs deeply,

"Oh please don't start that shit again..."

"What do you mean don't start that shit again..."

"Come on, you already know what happened..."

"Screw you Moon, don't talk to me like that..."

"I am talking to you like that, what you gonna do about it..."

Moon and Sheena get back into their typical arguing mode until Booby interrupts,

"Come on you two, look; we did hit the guy, but he got up and walked away. If he's hurt he'll go and get himself checked out. Now we are going to go into the office over there, use the phone get the van fixed and be at the cabin by morning.

"Now that's what I'm talking about."

Stormy rejects the idea,

"Wait, this is where we have to stay?"

Rick looks around at the hotel,

"Sure, what's wrong with this place?"

Sheena is uncomfortable with this hotel also. As Sheena looks around the property, she voices her discoveries.

"If this place is open, then where are all the cars?"

"Cars?"

"Yes cars...vehicles...like the one we arrived in. It looks like we're the only ones to stop at this motel in the last five years. Is it even open?"

"Well fellas, I do have to admit, that is kinda weird."

"Oh, listen to the superstitious football player over here...you still sleep with a teddy bear before every football game..."

"Rick! Come on man, why you trying to out me in front of company? It's not a teddy bear, it's a grizzly bear. And it helps me focus my subconscious...you know that Rick."

"All I'm saying is that it's fuzzy and it's pink..."

"Really Moon, a teddy bear?"

"It was bleached in the washing machine, you know this..."

Moon tries to grab Rick by the shirt, but Rick is fast and moves out of the way. Moon chases Rick around the van as he laughs."

"Boys will be boys."

Stormy walks off a bit from the rest of the group. She is looking around the property when Bobby walks up behind her and puts his hands on her shoulder. The move makes Stormy jump.

"What's wrong Stormy, are you nervous about something?"

"This dirty, stinky place. Why do we have to stay here tonight? Why can't we go someplace else? This place is deserted."

"Who cares if anybody else is here? That's even better. That means we'll have this whole place to ourselves, you know what I'm saying?"

Bobby grabs Stormy by the waist and leans in for a kiss.

"I know you don't thing you getting no loving...not in this dirty, stinky place."

"Don't be like that baby. It's for one night tops. We are going to go into this office, use the phone and get the van fixed. We'll be at the cabin first thing in the morning."

"I'm sleeping in my clothes tonight. Maybe even my coat."

"Come on baby, don't be like that."

Bobby pulls her in close again and kisses her on the neck. Even though Stormy was not in the mood to be touched, her neck was her excitement spot and Bobby knew it. A few quick kisses on the neck and Stormy could be mad no more. Mimi was on the other side of the car watching their interaction. When Bobby started kissing Stormy on the neck, Mimi had to let them know what she thought;

"Ewww. Get a room you two."

Bobby agreed,

"That sounds like a great idea. Moon?"

"I'm on it."

Moon walks over to Mimi and holds out his bended arm. Mimi hooks her arm into his and they both walk off towards the front door of the hotel establishment.

No one noticed the raven sitting on the roof of the van. If anyone had investigated it, they would have noticed that this raven had the weirdest eyes they'd ever seen; its eyes looked like human eyes.

165

Chapter 42

The door to the hotel office is unlocked so Moon and Mimi walk into the office. Moon announces their arrival,

"Hello..."

Moon and Mimi walk further into the office. As they do, Mimi lets go of Moon's hand to inspect the other side of the room. As Mimi walks to the other side of the room, Moon is given a great view of Mimi's 'assets'. All Moon can think to say is,

"Damn, I am a blessed man...Hello? Is anyone here?"

"Moon, come here..."

Moon walks over to Mimi who is looking though a basket on the desk and finds a movie in its original brand new box. The movie has never been opened.

"What is it?"

"Some movie I never heard of. It's called Unborn Sins. You ever heard of it?

"Not off hand, but I will make sure to look it up on my phone when I get back home."

As Mimi and Moon look through the basket, they had no idea that they were being watched.

Chapter 43

"Oooh, now dat is an ass on dat dere dark meat right dere! Good Christmas."

Jake is the proprietor of this hotel establishment. The hotel was still standing, but it was seldom occupied. Jake was the third generation owner of the hotel, which sits off the main road on a little known stretch of highway. Jake was here by himself now; his parents had long been dead and his siblings ran as far away as they could as soon as they got their hands on their inheritance money. You would think they worked hard for that death benefit the way they talked about seeing the world and no more working by the sweat of their brow. Yes, Jake's two sisters and his brother couldn't wait to bail; but Jake would not hear of leaving. This was all Jake had known his whole life. He lived on a stretch of undeveloped land in the midst of nothing but trees. It was clean out here. No littering of arrogant city folks, no constant pollution from factories, no sexual diseases from those fast hip hop dancing teens. *'No sir, this was a beautiful place'*. Jake was quick to give up his share of the million dollar payout from the life insurance company in exchange for full ownership of the hotel…and his siblings were very happy to oblige. Not one of them had any plans on staying in Virginia…hell, none of them planned to stay in the United States. They were all off gallivanting around the world.

Jake knew better. Jake had been on the internet…he knew about the world. Jake knew that the things out there to spend all of your money on were useless in the long run. They were just things, shiny things…and Jake was not deceived. He would not spend all his parents' hard earned insurance money on trips and clothes and soap and such. Jake would remain true to the land. He would raise his own food and operate this Hotel. Jake was convinced that he was the one to bring this Hotel back to prominence. Jake would save the business and then he would be the smart one; he would be the business savvy one. Jake would finally be respected and everyone would stop calling him 'special'.

Jake was in the back office with the lights out, looking at the internet. Before he got the internet installed on the computer at his Hotel, Jake spent his days watching television. Now that the internet had arrived, Jake was learning so much. Jake researched everything from music lessons on the flute to UFO's and alien abductions. He always wondered what happened to his cousin who said the aliens kidnapped him and took him to their mother ship and did weird experiments on him. At first Jake laughed; hell even Jake did not believe in aliens. But after Jake got the internet, he knew aliens existed; he had seen their spaceships. Hell, in one video, Jake saw an alien being autopsied. Can you imagine?

Today, Jake was on the internet looking at pornography. Jake was amazed at how many women were inside the computer showing off all their God given goodies to anyone who wanted to see. Jake was not a regular pornography person; he did not spend all of his money downloading porn off of the computer. That was pathetic…especially because you could watch so much of it for free. Jake didn't need long movies, a two to three minute video worked just fine, thank you very much. Jake had gone online and downloaded a number of video for his personal collection. Out here in these parts, every storm that rolled through seemed to interrupt the internet service. The storm that rolled through last night had not only taken the internet out, but also killed the phone lines in the area. Jake found that out this morning when he tried to call his cousin Wilbur to pick him up from work tonight so they could go out drinking.

Since there was no internet service, Jake searched through his downloaded video collection and found a video of a black woman giving herself an orgasm with one of those magic bullet things he had seen on another site. This woman was amazing; not only could she make herself orgasm multiple times, but every time she did orgasm, her juices would shoot out like a geyser. The woman was not really black; she was more like a caramel. Just as the woman reached an orgasm for the third time, Jake was about to orgasm himself. Jake had all of the tools to make sure he wouldn't get too messy; he had a wad of tissue paper from the bathroom and an old tee-shirt next to him to wipe up any mistakes. Just as Jake was coming to his own climax, he heard the bell on the front door to the hotel ring. Someone had come in…he had customers.

Jake quickly stopped his activity and threw the tissue paper in the garbage. He wiped up with the shirt and buttoned his pants back. Since Jake was still stiff, he pulled his shirt outside his pants and let it hang over to cover up the evidence of his activities. Jake looked out the peephole of his office door. The peephole allowed him to see who was at the desk without alerting them that they were being watch. Jake was not positive, but the woman who walked into the office looked just like the woman from the video! Jake stared at her for a few moments trying to judge whether this was indeed the woman from the video. He wasn't positive, but she certainly did look like the video girl. There was only one way to find out if it was her; the girl in the video had a butterfly tattoo on the back of her right shoulder. If he could get her to reveal her shoulder somehow, he could find out if that was her or not. If it was, Jake had a celebrity in the hotel!

Jake straightened up his clothes, blew a breath of air into his cupped hand and winced a bit.

"Damn beef jerky smell don't ever leave."

Jake opened up his draw and took out a can of warm beer to use as a mouthwash. Jake swished the beer around in his mouth and then spit it out into the trash can.

"Oh what the hell."

Jake took a long swallow of beer. That one chug cleared the can of almost half its contents. Jake blew into his cupped hand once again…

"Ah, that's better."

Chapter 44

Mimi and Moon were standing by the desk as Jake enters the room. Jake is five foot ten inches tall. He wore a white pull-over shirt that was hanging down over a pair of blue jeans. If Moon were to guess who Jake reminded him of most, Moon would say a young Norman Bates. Moon wondered if this guy had a dead mother taunting him upstairs. Moon watched too many movies.

As Moon moved towards the desk to meet the attendant, Mimi began to move around the room. Jake watched her intently ignoring Moon all together, much to Moon's displeasure. Moon watched the man as he stared at Mimi like he was picturing her naked. At first he was furious, and then Moon thought, *"I'm not keeping her, why should I get mad? Let the little geek enjoy himself for a minute."*

Moon continued to watch Jake watch Mimi and tried to guess what was running through the man's mind. The attendant seemed to lose all sense of consciousness; he was no longer mentally in the room.

Chapter 45

Jake was watching Mimi as she walked around the room.

To Jake, it seemed like she was toying with him. She knew he was watching her as she explored the room; she even knew Jake was exploring her body as she slowly moved about the room. But she didn't seem to mind and even went out of her way to make it pleasurable for Jake. The way she walked slowly across the room so that her butt checks moved in perfect rhythm. The way she turned her body as she walked; just enough so that her bosom would play hide and seek. First appearing with its straight forward salute and then hiding again as her hips twisted to the other side, allowing her shapely back hide the vision of breasts. Jake looked up and down every inch of her body and imagined himself reaching out to touch her soft caramel body....

"I know you hear me talking to you!"

Jake snapped back to reality. While he was lost in la la land, four more people had walked into the office; two men and two women. That was not to count the big black dude that was standing at the desk staring at Jake like he was crazy. Jake knew he was not crazy...his parents had him tested.

It was Stormy that snapped Jake out of his daydream. She had walked in with the others and noticed the man's sleazy eyes all over Mimi's body...*and it seemed as if Mimi knew it and was toying with him!* Stormy looked at Moon who was looking at the man looking at Mimi. Stormy wasn't sure, but she thought that was a sign that Moon was beginning to lose his interest in Mimi. Stormy had known Moon a few years now and she had never known Moon to be the type to be disrespected. Stormy certainly thought this whole scene she walked in on was disrespectful, and she didn't even like Mimi.

Stormy walked straight into the room, assessed the situation and decided to stop it. She walked over to the desk and addressed the man.

"Excuse me…"

"Excuse me…"

Stormy slammed her hand down on the front desk,

"I know you hear me talking to you!"

The man snapped out of his daydream.

Stormy shook her head and quoted a line out of one of her favorite movies, The Color Purple,

"A girl child just ain't safe in a world of men."

"May I help you?"

Sheena, who was also watching the attendant, chimed in..,

"It looks like you were helping yourself."

Rick didn't want to upset the attendant so he changed the focus of the confrontation,

"We need to use your phone."

Jake responds to Rick,

"Excuse me?"

Sheena responds and begins to motion with sign language,

"We need to use your phone."

Jake knew when he was being treated like an idiot. Jake motioned his answer right back to Sheena, looking her angrily in the eyes...

"There is no phone."

Moon moves between Jake and Sheena,

"Why the hell not?"

"A storm came through last night and knocked the lines out."

"Are they fixing it?"

"I'm sure somebody is out there working on it right now."

Rick was still the level head,

"How long do you think it will take?"

"I am sure I don't know."

The group gives a pause and look around at each other. Stormy looked maddest of all of them. Moon addresses the attendant,

   "Well, can we at least get a few rooms in the meanwhile?"

"Only one room available."

"Only one room? How can you say there's only one room? What about all these other rooms I see?"

"All the other rooms are occupied."

"By who?"

Mimi starts losing her patience,

"Yeah right, there ain't nobody else here."

Sheena starts thinking of alternatives for them to consider.

"Well how far is the next hotel from here?"

"Thirty miles east of here."

Rick knows that would not be a good plan,

"That would be going back the way we came. Let's think about this for a second."

The group walks away from the desk and form a semi-circle around Rick as he makes a suggestion on how to proceed.

"Okay guys, I have an idea. Why don't we go ahead and rent this room for now."

The group begins to protest, but Rick continues…

"Look, we unpack a few things, relax and have a little party tonight. We can make this a good time. We'll take the room."

"Ok then, I just need someone to fill out these forms."

Moon approaches the desk to fill out the forms. It is obvious that the girls do not want to stay here, but the group has no choice. Moon takes out a pen and writes in the book that Jake provides as he questions Jake further.
"So tell me, do you have any mechanics around here?"

"What type of car?"

"American."

"Yeah, I know a mechanic."

"Cool. Can you give him a call and have him come take a look at our car?"

"No phone lines."

"Damn. Do you have a car?"

"No. I get picked up and dropped off every day."

"When do you get off?"

"Later."

"Later like when? What time?"

"Ten o'clock."

"Okay. When you get off do you think you can stop by and talk with him then? Tell him about our van and have him come up and fix it for us?"

"I can do that."

"There you go. Thank you man, we really appreciate that. So let me ask you, are the sheets in there clean?"

As the women hear Moon, they once again begin to protest. There was no way the six of them was staying in one room and anybody getting any sexual treatment tonight…no way. All of the women agreed on that point and it didn't take a meeting for them to agree.

As Moon fills out the paperwork and the rest of the gang talk amongst themselves, Jake is staring at Sheena and begins to drift off...

Jake is at the beach. He is standing in the shade of a banana tree when Sheena walks past. She is wearing a see through lingerie top with matching panties. The material is red lace and caresses her body tightly. You can see her firm, small nipples poking through the lace. There is a small tattoo above her right nipple on the left breast. As Jake watches, Sheena spreads her legs and reveals the see through material just above her split. It is lightly shaven and look like the loveliest shade of brown hair Jake has ever seen. Sheena must be a tease, because now she was turning around to reveal that ample backside view. She slowly put both of her hands on the wall and spread her legs completely; as if a police officer Jake had yelled out the command to 'assume the position'. Sheena then dropped her flower…where she got the flower Jake had no idea. Sheena dropped the flower and turned to Jake, covering her mouth as if embarrassed. Sheena then turned back around and began to bend over to pick up the flower. As she bent over, she kept her knees unbent and the promises of her treasures were about to reveal itself as she bent further…further…further…

"What the hell is wrong with you man?"

Stormy had slammed her hand down on the desk again to get Jake's attention.

"What room are we in?"

"Six. You're in room six."

"Can we have the key please?"

"I knew you were going to be coming here today."

"Really? How did you know? Are you psychic or something?"

"Actually I am a bit like that. I can sometime get a picture of different people."

Stormy was sick of Jake already,

"Oh can you now? What picture are you getting of us?"

"Well, I did get a picture of that lady right there."

Jake was pointing at Mimi. He was positive that Mimi was the girl in the video. Mimi walks over to the desk and looks Jake in the eyes...

"Really. You got a picture of me, huh? What picture did you get?"

"I saw you...dancing to music. You had a power tool or something with you. Every time you started working with the power tool, the fountain behind you would start working again and a big geyser would shoot up into the sky."

Mimi paused for a minute and looked at Jake. She nervously looked around the room and saw everyone else had a puzzled look on their faces as well. Mimi laughed it off, which caused the others to laugh too. She started walking towards the office door, but stopped and turned to Jake one final time.

"And how did you know this picture you saw was me?"

"Because of the blue butterfly tattoo on your shoulder."

Jake handed Rick the keys as Moon finished up the paperwork. Stormy, still feeling a bit uneasy, took another shot at Jake...

"I hope there ain't no cameras hidden in that room, is there?"
"No mamm, no cameras in the room."

Under his breath, Jake finished the sentence...

"I wouldn't put a camera in your room anyway...you are safe."

All of the students walked out of the office except for Moon who was still finishing up the transaction.

"So how much for the room?"

"Let's say seventy five dollars."

"Seventy-five dollars! Are you serious?

"Well, you have six people in one room. That is against the code violations right there. But for seventy-five dollars in rental rate for one night, I suppose I can bend the rules just this once."

Moon knew it was robbery and he hated to be robbed. What's more is Moon hated to be suckered by someone whom he didn't think was his intellectual equal. Moon would be the first to admit he wasn't the smartest guy in the world, but at least he had options. This guy was probably doing the most he will ever do in his life right here, selling rooms in a place no one visits.

Moon finished the paperwork, paid for the room and left the office. Once Moon left, Jake came from behind the counter and sprayed the places where they stood with Lysol. Jake went back into his office and turned on the computer monitor on the desk behind him. Jake turned the television to channel six, which corresponded with the room key he had given them. As it turned out, Jake was pretty nifty at computer networking and was able to install a network of cameras in every room in his hotel.

Chapter 46

When Moon exited the office, he saw the rest of the group standing by the car talking, so he joined them.

Rick is the first to address Moon,

"So what's the deal Moon?"

"Man I tried, but I couldn't get any more rooms."

Mimi was visibly upset by now.

"I don't see why we couldn't have another room. There ain't nobody here."

"I know. But why don't we do this. Let's take a few of our bags inside, unpack, have a little party and enjoy the evening until we can get the van fixed."

Rick remembered the stash he had brought with him.

"I got some snacks, but I don't think we have any water."

"I brought some water."

"You did Sheena? See, that's another reason why I love this girl. So we got snacks and water."

Moon had a special stash though,

"And I got the sticky icky..."

Sheena was waiting for a chance to give Moon a jab.

"Of course you do."

"That's right. So Rick, have you checked the room already?"

"Yeah"

"What do you think?"

"Well, it's a bit small for the six of us, but we can make it work."

"Well, don't worry about it. Let's take some of the bags in. Hopefully we can get some bathroom time with all these women around here."

Mimi responds,

"Keep talking and that's not all you won't get."

"Baby damn...let's not be getting all excited or nothing. Them just jokes."

Stormy turns to go to the room.

"You boys stay here. We're going inside and freshen up."

"Whoa, whoa, whoa...and what are we supposed to do while you're freshening up?"

"You got your sticky icky to keep you company."

The women laugh and walk off to the room. Moon and the guys look through the van to get the bags they need for an overnight stay at Hotel Hell. Moon decided to take out the weed and role a nice spliff. *'Might as well get the party started'*.

Chapter 47

Dave left no stone unturned looking for Sheena.

Dave didn't understand why his old pal wanted to find Sheena so desperately that he would call him in to search for her. She probably went away for the weekend to screw her boyfriend's brains out; without worrying about her father sneaking into her house with the key while they were '*doing it*'.

That is exactly what Dave would be doing if he was thirty years younger and Sheena was his girlfriend. Dave was by no means a pervert and he was not interested in Sheena, she was young enough to be his daughter. But she was not his daughter and he could acknowledge that she was fine. Sheena had grown into a beautiful, smart and physically devastating young lady.

Once Dave left Frank's house with his assignment, his first stop was to the club scene. Dave knew that Sheena liked the clubs and that she was a dancing maniac. Sheena had been dancing her whole life. Ballet, jazz, tap, modern…she even learned a bit of African Dance and Capoeira.

Dave searched every club in the city, but he found no sign of Sheena. Frank told him that he had already checked Sheena's apartment, so Dave guessed he would check with her boyfriend's apartment and his family. If that didn't work he would try her friends and their parents. After that he would regroup and look at his options again. But first, he would go back to Sheena's house and look for clues again. It was possible that even the great Frank White could have missed something because he is too close to this situation, with the potential of becoming too emotional when it comes to his baby girl.

Dave arrived at Sheena's apartment and let himself in. He did not have a key, but he didn't need one. Dave had been in the business for a long time and a door lock was the least of things that would keep him out of a place he wanted to enter. Once inside the apartment, he found it unremarkable. Dave went to the bedroom and looked around. Nothing out of place. In the bedroom he saw the impression on the bed that Frank told him about. Dave went to the closet and it did look like some items had been pulled off the hanger in a hurry. Dave checked a few of her dresser drawers and thought it looked like some items would be missing. Dave was convinced that Sheena had gone on a trip...but where?

Dave looked around the room some more and found Sheena's computer under her bed. He turned it on and perused through her files. In the pictures folder there was another folder marked 'private'. Dave opened that folder and, *'oh Lord...Sheena likes to take naked pictures'*. Dave was ashamed for opening the folder, but now since it was opened he might as well have a look see. *"Lord have mercy, I was right...she is beautiful."* Dave quickly shut the folder back as his little man start to stir awake at the sight of Sheena's naked body.

Dave closed the computer and put it back under the bed. Dave turned and sat down on Sheena's bed to gather his thoughts while he looked about the room. Dave noticed a calendar on the wall beside her dresser. Dave got up and approached the calendar. He looked under today's date and found his first clue. The entire weekend was circled with a note; "Party with the crew". Dave finally had something. Sheena had indeed gone away for the weekend and she was with her crew- which ever people she hung with the most, At the bottom of the calendar, she had written something else; Blue Ridge Mountains. Perhaps that is where they went. Dave remembered the Blue Ridge Mountains. He had been there once, many years ago, to do a job he was hired for. It all made perfect sense to him. Dave decided to call Frank and let him in on the info.

"Hello Frank..."

"You know better than to call me on this line."

"Just thought you wanted to know; you did miss a few clues over at her house. Calendar in the bedroom suggests she went away for the weekend to the Blue Ridge Mountains."

"Will you go find her for me old friend? Make sure she is ok and keep an eye on her until she comes back."

"You want me to stay there for the weekend?"

"It would mean a lot to me Dave."

After a brief pause, Dave agreed,

"I'll do it for you Frank, but it's going to cost you a little more than helping my idiot niece's son."

"This is my baby girl. Don't worry about the cost."

"You got it Frank."

Dave hung up the phone. He would go out to the Blue Ridge Mountains and find Frank's precious Sheena. Not a problem, Dave could use a few days away from the hustle and bustle of the city. He didn't need to pack a bag so he would leave now. Dave took out the map he always carried in his back right-hand pocket out and began to plot his course. Dave judged the route he would take by putting himself in their shoes…

"Okay. Six young adults and at least one of them smokes marijuana, maybe more, one of them is a local football star…I'm guessing they're not taking the highway. Bobby is probably driving so I am sure he took one of the back roads. Judging from the map, I guess they would have gone this way."

As Dave continued to plan his route, he went into the kitchen to plan it on a full stomach. Dave made himself a sandwich, grabbed a beer and turned on the television. When he finished he cleaned up his mess, wiped down his fingerprints and preceded on his way to the Blue Ridge Mountains.

Chapter 48

Another dead body…another missing head.

Frank was beside himself. This was the seventh body that he has personally visited in the last twenty-four hours. Frank did not normally go to crime scenes; but since his meeting with the man in black at the sushi place, Frank thought it would be good idea to take more of a personal interest in the crimes happening in his City. The agent had warned Frank to look out for 'odd' killings…missing body parts, body parts that had been chewed on or perhaps even rearranged and sewed back on. The descriptions Frank got from his D.C visitor made Frank curious. He knew that a call from the President and a visit from an unnamed man with card-blanche meant a potential controversy; life & death situations and an opportunity for rapid advancement if Frank could get control of this thing.

As Frank entered the crime scene, he halted for a second and stood frozen in fear. 'Red shoes." Frank was looking at a pair of red shoes lying on the floor of the living room. They looked just like the shoes that Sheena had tricked him into buying her a month ago. Frank didn't know what the name brands of the shoes were; he just knew that the shoes cost five hundred dollars. Frank normally would never spend that amount of money on a pair of shoes, but this time he had been conned. His beautiful daughter, with whom no evil could flow had lied to him about that purchase…Frank though he was giving her money to buy four pairs of shoes. When he insisted on taking Sheena to the store that morning to pick them up (apparently they had to be flown in from Madrid or something), that is when he found out there was only one pair of shoes in the bag for five hundred dollars. What's worse, there was nothing else given for the five hundred dollar pair of shoes…no gold pin, no dinner for two coupon, no buy one get one free ice cream cone at Sweet Frog…nothing. Five hundred dollars just got you the shoes and the box they came in. Hell, Frank had to make the woman behind the cash register give him a store bag to carry them out in.

These same pair of shoes was lying on the floor of this victim's apartment. Not the same pair, but a pair just like them. The woman on the floor who owned the shoes, or at least used to own the shoes, was in bad shape. Apparently she had been attacked in her home and murdered. The door wasn't broken nor was any of the windows, so at first glance it looked like she might have known her assailant. The photos in frames on the mantle suggest that she has at least two children who apparently aren't home tonight. The two wine glasses on the coffee table confirmed that she probably knew her attacker or at least was getting to know them.

The woman who now lay on the floor dead was either Puerto Rican or Dominican. It was a bit hard to tell without the head being attached to the body. It was an educated guess based on the photographs and the decoration in the apartment. Frank would guess Puerto Rican because of all of the candles and catholic memorabilia. Frank was told that Dominicans in this area lean more toward Voodoo as a religion. Frank was not sure if that was true or not and for the most part, he didn't care.

These seven bodies they found were a bit outside the norm. Usually the bodies they found around the City were victims of gunshot wounds or stabbings. Perhaps a body hit by a car or even a jumper from a rooftop. But these were different. This killing suggested the perpetrator is anti-law, anti-humanity with no semblance of a soul. Frank couldn't see how you could be human and bite the faces off of people, down to the bone and gristle. How could you decapitate a person's head and then try to shove it in their rear? Why would the missing head of one body show up at the crime scene of another body? These crimes were heinous… unbelievably evil.

Frank decided to leave this crime scene and go home to plan his next move when his phone rang. It was Dave on the other line telling him what he had found out over at Sheena's apartment. Frank told Dave not to bother going over there; that he had gone over and found no clues whatsoever. When Dave mentioned that he had found clues and a destination, Frank just closed his eyes and shook his head. Frank knew. Frank knew that he could become so stressed that it was possible for him to miss something; to disregard something important as being trivial. Frank knew that with the stress of what happened to his wife always looming in the back of his mind, just the thought of foul play with his baby girl would send him whirling. That's why he called in Dave to help out. Dave was a criminal but he was also a friend...a friend that knew Frank's darkest secrets. Frank had secrets that he never mentioned to the love of his life, his departed wife.

Frank called Dave because he knew Dave would be discreet. Dave was a cold blooded killer. His scruples were limited and his morals were a bit fuzzy, but his loyalty was solid. Frank knew that if Dave said he was in, nothing but death could keep him from completing his mission. Frank also knew that Dave loved Sheena too. He had know Sheena all of her life; Dave was there on her first day of school, he made it out to all the cheerleading events, bake sales, school plays...whatever the event was Dave was there. Dave would even make Frank record it so he could watch it again later.

Dave was on the case. He had found their destination, had an idea of who was with her and he was on his way to put physical eyes on Frank's daughter. That is a true friend; someone you can trust and count on. You don't get many people like that to enter your circle, but when one does and you recognize it, it is a wonderful thing.
Frank is on his way home after yet another crime scene to figure everything out; what to do about this case and what to do about his daughter. Frank decides to have a shower and a hot cup of tea when he gets home and mull it over. Everything will work itself out. Everything will be okay, Frank was positive of it.

Chapter 49

For the past few months, Shemi was afforded the chance to see much more of the United States than he ever imagined. Chasing down Cliff, Vic and Brandon was at times exhilarating- even if it was annoying. Every time Shemi got close to capturing the trio, something outlandish would happen that would set him back. It was as if they were getting some kind of unseen help. Shemi's father had warned him about this in one of his dreams before he left the lab.

In his dream, Shemi was standing on top of a huge mountain with nothing around him but the smoke that billowed out of it. Inside the mountain was a valley covered in complete pitch black darkness. The darkness was moving, as if it were alive. It was a black, ink like substance and it moved around the floor of the valley. Even with the tough winds that were moving all throughout the valley itself- the black ink like substance never left the floor of the valley.

Before Shemi knew it he was sliding down *inside* the mountain. He could not stop the slide. Shemi slid closer and closer to the bottom. He was enveloped by the dark ink that moved around the valley. As Shemi slid further to the bottom of the mountain, the black ink seemed to be going *through* him; it felt like it was becoming *a part* of him. Shemihazah slid all the way down until he landed on the hard valley floor.

As Shemi looked around, he could see nothing but he heard a voice come to him. The voice of one in the darkness but could not be seen through the darkness. The voice spoke to Shemi;

"My son, you have been created with a special purpose in mind. You are born of spirit and flesh although you exist in the flesh. You were created, special. It is yours to propagate and create a new world. That which is born from your seed receives dual citizenship in both the natural and the spiritual. We can then create a new

heaven and a new earth, devoid of our enemy."

"Who are you?"

"I am you father, the chief watcher that lead astray. You are my son, you are Chaos. From your loins shall spring forth the Assyrian. We shall make war."

Shemihazah was born for war. The killings he had done over the last few weeks were only an appetizer to whet his whistle. Shemi was just learning his trade and practicing the many ways he could deliver death to the earth.

Shemi had already learned the finer lessons of the 'arts' and he loved it! During his brief travels Shemi had come across several fortune tellers, psychics and diviners. Some had talent; some were dabbling in it for financial gain.

One woman in particular, Mama Rose, had been of great help. Shemi met Mama Rose in New Orleans a month ago. She had a house deep in the bayou, beyond the river's bend. Mama Rose was known throughout the land as a woman of power. So Shemihazah visited her at her home.

Mama Rose was indeed knowledgeable. She had supplied Shemi with books and with information that helped Shemi immensely. Mama Rose taught him charms and other magic he could use to help him on his journey. Shemi doubted that Mama Rose knew who he really was, which Shemi found interesting since she reportedly knew so many things. Perhaps she knew and did not care. It was Mama Rose's disconnect to the idea of what was about to happen that made Shemi decide to leave her alive. She simply did not care; she considered herself such an outsider to this life that she had no cares about it one way or another.

It was Mama Rose who helped Shemi get a fix on where he could find Cliff. The problem was that when Shemi found Cliff and summoned his body, the tote bag was not with him. Shemi knew this because he had sent out a familiar to help him find Cliff. The familiar that Shemi sent after Cliff was a raven- a black raven. Shemi had learned how to employ the assistance of a familiar during one of his dream. Shemi was always amazed at his dreams; they seemed so real that they trumped the information he received in his waken moments. The raven has been following Cliff for about a day now, helping Shemi get a fix on where Cliff was. Shemi didn't know the local geography of each State, which is why the visual information Shemi received from the raven was so important. With this information, Shemi could find Cliff in a matter of hours as opposed to days.

Cliff had obviously met someone on the way and given them the bag. Now Shemi had to perform the ritual that Mama Rose taught him again in order to get an approximate fix on who had the bag. Now Shemi had run into Cliff at the lab and gotten a sample of Cliff's DNA during their meeting. That is why the spell he cast was so effective on Cliff. Whomever Cliff gave the bag to had a little more protection from Shemi because he did not have a sample of their blood to make the connection.

Earlier this evening, while Shemi was at the hotel alone in his room, he did the ritual that Mama Rose had taught him. The ritual was for finding a person who doesn't want to be found. Shemi drew the appropriate symbols he needed to draw on the floor of the room, along with the correct number of candles and incenses burning. Shemi repeated the chant that he had been taught; same word inflections, same vocal pitch, same pauses and speed. He had been doing it for about an hour before he was about to quit. Right before Shemi stopped chanting, something like a portal opened up in the middle of the circle he had drawn. He could see Cliff. Cliff was standing in the middle of a wooded area.

Shemi had not performed this ritual before, of course. He had Mama Rose write it down for him to perform later. So as Shemi stared at the image of Cliff that was materializing in the midst of the circle he had drawn, his concentration kept going in and out. As a result, Cliff seemed to be aware of something strange around him, in the vision of Cliff in the circle. Shemi supposed that Cliff was hearing branches break or some other sound that was causing him alarm. Shemi reached out his hand towards the image of Cliff, intending to snatch him right out of the woods and into the room with him. As Shemi's hands got close to the image, something spooked Cliff and he set off running. Cliff was running as hard as he could and Shemi was following the image in the circle. Suddenly Cliff ran out of the woods and into a road. Just as Cliff ran into the road, a car was coming and hit Cliff so hard that the impact send Cliff flying in the air. The suddenness of the car hitting Cliff along with the violence of the impact was enough to cause Shemi to lose his concentration. The image in the circle disappeared and now Shemi had to try and get it back before he lost touch with Cliff all together.

It must have taken Shemi quite a bit of time to get the image in the circle back. By the time he found Cliff, he was a mess. Cliff was laid out on the ground and covered in blood from head to toe. There was no one around his body so Shemi took action; he reached into the image and grabbed Cliff from out of that road into the room he was in. To anyone looking at Cliff on the other side it would seem as though Cliff's body disappeared into thin air- gone without a trace. Yet here Cliff was; now lying on the floor of Shemi's hotel room, covered in blood from head to toe.

Shemi had a very active evening. Since Cliff was already close to death, Shemi would have to work quick and hard to get the information he wanted; *'where was the bag'?* Shemi employed several tactics that his father taught him in his dreams. His father had taught him how to bring a human within an inch of death through the most agonizing pain, and then bring him completely back to life for another round. Shemi knew how to cause agonizing pain at the cellular level to make a person talk. And then there were the teeth...Shemihazah's razor sharp, double row, growing, bone-crushing teeth. Several victims had felt the power of those teeth, but they are no longer alive to witness to others about the excruciating pain those teeth can cause.

Before Shemi *ate* Cliff; before he consumed Cliff piece by piece, Shemi found out that the bag was with a group of kids that hit Cliff with a car on the road. They were headed west, towards the mountains. If Shemi hurried and didn't stop for any 'fun', he could catch up with them by early evening. That sounded plausible, but it would be hard. Shemi was so enjoying meeting the common folks. The bright lights of the City had been fun and the action was intoxicating; but the people were the true prize. So many lost souls living in fear from moment to moment makes for a juicy selection of possibilities. Murder, death, destruction and general mayhem…oh happy days indeed!

Once Shemi shoveled the very last piece of Cliff into his belly, he let his mouth decrease to normal human size again, put on his burgundy leather jacket and his faded cowboy hat and happily made his way towards the exit. Shemi was smiling; he had not been this excited since the day he first left the lab. Shemi now knew the very last place Cliff had been and he knew that the van that hit Cliff was disabled. That means they can't be far from the place Shemi grabbed Cliff's body from. Shemi would have them in his grasp by nightfall. First, he would change to his ink substance, where he could travel his miles un-hindered in a fraction of the time. Shemi would likely have the bag in his possession in an hour or two. This thought brought a huge smile to Shemi's face, exposing his sharp blood stained teeth…

"I see you. Ready or not, here I come…"

Chapter 50

The group of students was finally having fun.

Since the room was too small for the six of them, they moved their party to the parking area in front of their room. No other car was in the parking lot yet and the students doubted that any would show up tonight. But that was old news; the news right now is that they were sitting around as couples and were indeed having a relaxing evening. Moon rolled two blunts of something he called 'white widow'. The cell phones could not get a signal out here, but Ricky had some music saved to his phone and was able to play that. As the sunlight started to fade the students laughed, joked and smoked. Eventually Rick's playlist played the song, "Before I Let Go" by Frankie Beverly and Maze and the six of them formed a Soul Train line and danced until they erupted in laughter.

Moon sat with Mimi, taking in the pleasurable smoke from the blunt he had rolled. After inhaling a massive amount of smoke, Moon noticed a raven sitting on top of the van staring at them. Moon watched the raven and the raven watched him. Moon felt a bit uneasy about the raven...there was something '*off*' about that bird.

Moon continued to toke on the blunt, getting higher and higher. When he finally passed the blunt to Mimi, he thought he could finally figure out what the problem with the raven was.

"Hey Rick...Rick"

"What Moon?"

"Take a look at that raven over there."

Rick looked around and did not spot the raven.

"Where is it?"

"On top of the van."

Rick looked at the raven on top of the van and the raven looked back at Rick.

"So?"

"Don't you see something weird about that bird?"

Rick surveyed the bird, but he didn't notice what Moon was talking about.

"Hey everybody, Moon wants you to look at that bird on the van."

Everyone began to stare at the raven sitting on the van.

"What about it Moon?"

Embarrassed, Moon replied,

"Aw nothing, I'm just tripping."

Rick doesn't let Moon off the hook that easily.

"No, what is it Moon? What is so strange about that bird? Tell us."

"Look at its eyes. Don't its eyes look strange to you?"

The students looked at the raven.

"What do you think it is?"

"I don't know...there's something about the eyes that seem strange.

Moon slowly grabbed a nice size stone that was lying on the ground by his feet and palmed it while he stood. Moon walked towards the raven, which surprisingly did not move. The raven only stared at Moon like he was a curiosity the world had never seen.

Moon stopped moving twenty feet from where the raven stood on the roof of the van. Moon raised his arm slowly like he was doing a slow stretch. Just as Moon's arm reached its apex, Moon revealed the stone in his hand.

The raven must have known what Moon intended with that stone. The raven's eyes widened, knowing it was in danger. It had allowed him to get too close. The raven's eyes widened and now they did look like human eyes; dark black human eyes. The raven spread its wings to take flight.

But it was too late. By the time the raven realized the danger that was present; Moon flung the rock in his hand with all of his strength. Moon was not a quarterback but in that moment it did not matter. The stone struck its intended target with a loud *'crack'*. It sounded like the stone had not only connected with the raven but actually cracked its small skull on impact. The raven flew backwards, spinning head over heels until it hit the ground lifeless; with blood pouring out of its head.

Moon was proud of his throw, but his new nemesis was not. Sheena screamed at the top of her lungs…

"You killed it, you killed it! Bird murderer!"

Moon turned to Sheena and gave her a smile…

"Next up…all chicken heads. I don't want to point anyone out so I will just look at the intended subject and whistle…"

Moon looked Sheena in the eyes and whistled.

Sheena lunged at Moon and Moon began a comical *"dance"* with Sheena. Sheena tried her very best to scratch Moon's eyes out while Moon ran around dodging her grabs and taunting her at the same time. Moon is the only one of the two having fun...Sheena really is trying to scratch Moon's eyes out.

Chapter 51

"This is one of the easier jobs he's given me."

Dave is on the side of the road in his non-descript 1997 Oldsmobile Cutlass Supreme. It is the classic dark blue with grey cloth interior. Dave only has two friends in this world, and they both tell him that his car looks pitiful.

"Why don't you get a car made in the 21st century?"

"Yeah, that car is older than my marriage!"

Ha, ha, ha. Very funny. Dave had a different outlook on things. First, Dave has never been the flashy type. Although he always had money, Dave didn't spend his money on fast cars and fast women. Dave didn't spend his money on tablets, jewelry or smart phones either. Dave was a throwback to the days before technology connected us to the world. Dave grew up in a time when java meant a cup of coffee, 'do you have rubbers' meant do you have rubber boots and there were no phones that were smarter than people- well, most people.

Dave only invested his money in things that appreciated in value- or at least didn't fluctuate very much. To Dave, the only good investments were land, diamonds, gold and silver. Stocks were not for Dave. The stock market usually fluctuated wildly and every few years it would *'correct itself'* as they say. *'Correct itself'* is another way of saying the average person will lose a big chunk of their damn money. The only people really making money in the stock market are the big boys that hold so much stock that when they fart, the market changes. Those few people in the 'know' are the ones that control the volatility of the stock market and the ones making big bucks. That's why people go to jail over insider information in the stock trade…the big boys don't want to lose their upper hand on who makes money off of their money.

As Dave sat on the side of the road, he actually wished that he did buy a newer car. His Cutlass finally wore down. Dave turned on his flip cell phone and dialed Frank's number. Dave paused momentarily to watch a bug walking across the windshield of his Cutlass. He watched as the bug stopped walking and just sat on the windshield of the car right in front of him; staring at him…almost seeming to smirk and point,

"Look at the weird guy in the car. What you staring at?"

Dave stuck his upper body in the car, switched on the windshield wipers and watched as the bug was dragged and squashed all over the windshield. Dave didn't turn off the windshield wipers until the blood of the bug covered a large area of the glass. It was so messy that Dave had to use the windshield washer fluid and clean the windshield.

Dave pressed the 'send' button and let his phone call fly. After three rings, Frank did not pick up the phone. Dave was relieved; he hated checking in constantly anyway.

"Just let me do my damn job."

Dave was a professional; he had a one hundred percent success rate over the last twenty five years. Who else could say that? There was one botched job in his early years, the first job he ever did. But he learned, Dave learned and never made a mistake again.

Five rings. The answering service picked up,

"This is Frank. Leave a message. Beep…"

"Frank. I found their trail. It's hot. I'll call you later."

Better that he didn't speak with Frank right now. Dave's car was done, *kaput* and he still had to find these damn kids. Right now Dave really wasn't in the mood to talk. He needed to find another car and continue on his quest.

As if the heavens were answering his personal prayer, a car could be seen in the distance barreling down the road towards Dave. Dave had not quite made up his mind on whether he would take this persons car and kill them or just take the car, put the person in the trunk and decide later. Killing was much better; it offered a more permanent solution. But you had to do away with the body which could be tricky sometimes. If he just took the car and threw them in the trunk, maybe he could dump the car somewhere and leave them in the trunk. Dave didn't mind killing innocent bystanders; he just didn't like to kill them for free.

Chapter 52

Frank heard his phone ring, but did not answer it. He did take the time out to see who was calling. It was Dave. He was probably calling with some good news about Sheena.

Frank would love some good news right about now. There seems to be an up-tick in the number of vicious homicides in his City. Frank was just leaving another crime scene, this time the victim was a young girl. From what they found in the car, she was probably a local stripper who came out to the Overlook to smoke some drugs and get busy in the car. Frank was not sure that this was the work of the same serial killer that had been involved in the previous murders. In this case the victim wasn't bitten, chewed, decapitated or ripped apart. It looks like something caused all of her inner organs to burst at the same time. However, Frank was counting this as a murder because he had no recollection of anything like this ever happening in all his years on the force. Frank's gut told him that his serial killer was at the heart of this death too. If Frank knew anything after his many years of service and his experience with his wife, *'God bless her soul'*, he knew that no one was safe

Frank had to find his daughter.

After the initial investigation was done and the forensic team had departed, a weary Chief of Police went back to his car to listen to his email from Dave.

"You have one message..."

"Frank. I found their trail. It's hot. I'll call you later."

Good news indeed. His baby girl was still alive. Frank would make sure he did not miss the next call from his ace in the hole. Frank's personal relationship with Dave over the years has benefitted both parties, but Frank had to admit that he had give Dave an *'above the law'* status. Frank had permitted Dave to operate in the City of Richmond with impunity. Murders, extortion, kidnapping…these were just a few of the things that Frank was aware that Dave has committed and/or orchestrated. However, Dave has been an invaluable part of Frank's own rise to power…and he kept some very special secrets entrusted to him from Frank. Frank would never betray Dave and believed that Dave would never betray him. Frank sometimes referred to Dave as a 'friend' but in truth he was more like a nemesis. Frank needed Dave to be Dave in order for him to be Chief of Police. The two of them were on opposite sides of the law, yet so intertwined that if one should fall by the wayside, the other would feel the pain.

Frank tried to dial Dave back, but his phone went directly to voicemail. The phone was turned off. All Frank could do now was wait until Dave returned his phone call.

Frank used his phone to dial another number. It was a confidant of his from the department.

"Hello Carol?"

"Hi Chief, how are you?"

"I'm good. How is Carl Jr.?"

"He's doing so much better. That natural medicine you suggested worked wonder for his pain. He's feeling better and doesn't have all those awful side effects."

"I'm glad to hear it. Listen Carol, I need you to do something for me."

"Anything Chief."

"I need you to take down this phone number and keep tabs on it. As soon as it is turned on, I need you to tell me where it is located. Also, check my daughter's cell phone. If you get any signal on it,

call me right away."

"Is everything ok Chief?"

"It will be. Probably just an over-worked father. I want to know where my baby girl is...its past curfew."

Carol and Franks laughed over this last assertion. Carol did know Frank to be an over-protective father; he had done the best he could after his wife was murdered. Lord knows there were plenty of gals around damn near throwing their panties at him when he walked by. But Frank always kept it professional and under control. Carol was not sure what Frank's type was, but if she wasn't married, she would give Frank a run for his money.

"Will do. Anything else?"

"That's it. Thank you Carol, I appreciate it."

"You know I got your back Chief."

"Ok. Talk with you later Carol. Bye."

Frank knew that Carol was now on the case. She would stay on it until there was something to report and then call Frank the moment she knew something. Carol was good people. She had no idea; if she wasn't married, Frank would give her a run for her money.

Chapter 53

Puff, puff, and pass.

Almost an hour had gone by and spliffs were still being passed around the circle. It seemed like every time Rick passed Moon a spliff, Sheena was passing one right back to him. Moon must have put twelve spliffs in the rotation...and now he was lighting another one. Rick tried to keep up, but he had almost coughed up a lung on that last one he smoked on. Moon joked him for being a lightweight...

"Okay, okay. Hold your arms up...baby steps young man, baby steps."

Moon would laugh at every one of his own jokes like it came from Chris Rock.

Moon lights another spliff and hands it to Mimi to put into rotation. Mimi takes the spliff and coughs a bit. Moon hands her a can of beer to wash back her cough. Mimi drinks the beer, steady's her breathing and looks back at Moon...

"It figures. The only thing the athlete brings to drink is beer."

Moon is quick to retort,

"But you're glad I got it, ain't you?
"Yeah..."

"That's right. You see, I have priorities."

Sheena and Moon have been good friends for years. That's why they can argue and fight and still walk away friends. However, every chance that Sheena gets she tries to deliver a gut-punch to Moon.

"I thought athletes weren't supposed to drink and smoke."

"Girl, let me tell you something. Everybody has a vice...whether its prescription drugs, illegal drugs or little altar boys in white robes, everybody has a vice."

"That's not what I asked you."

"I know."

Perhaps it was the weed, but Moon and Sheena burst out laughing at Moon's response. After a few moments of laughter, Mimi starts squinting towards the hotel office. The length of her squint causes Moon to look at her are ask about her with concern...

"What's wrong Mimi? Are you ok?"

"I think I see something..."

"Don't worry about that, that's just the chronic..."

"Mimi hits Moon on the arm playfully.

"No silly, at the office door. I think I see a man coming towards us."

The whole gang looked and true enough, there was a man walking towards them.

"Moon, put that out... kill the weed..."

The man walking towards the group was wearing a burgundy leather jacket, pull over black shirt, a pair of worn blue jeans, colorful boot and a worn out old cowboy hat. The man was short, but he had a gait that spoke of confidence to spare. As the man walked pass the van, he looked down at the ground and stopped at the body of the dead raven lying on the ground. The man paused for a moment, like he was speaking words of condolence to a dear family member. Suddenly the man started walking again, putting the image of the dead bird from his mind and smiling at the group he was approaching. The group watched as the man walked closer and closer towards them...

"Rick, who do you think he is?"

"How should I know Stormy? Maybe he's one of the people the guy says rented a room."

The man walks pass the rooms and right over to where the group was sitting.

"Hey...how ya'll doing? I was over there checking myself into room number six and I saw ya'll. I said to myself, 'go on over and see what these fine people are up to." It looked like ya'll were having a good time so I thought I'd come on over and introduce myself. My name is Henry...how ya'll doing?"

Rick stands up to formally meet their guest.

"Hi Henry, good to meet you. I'm Rick. This is Sheena, that's Moon and Mimi and over there that's Bobby and Stormy."

Everyone including Shemi could see that Moon was agitated with Rick giving out their names. Moon thought Rick was way too trusting of people. Rick thought that people were basically good with a few bad tendencies. Moon knew better; Moon knew that people were basically bad with the potential to be a terror.

"Damn Rick, why don't you give him my last name too?"

Shemi ignored Moon's comments and went around the circle to shake hands. He was not sure if this was the group that had his green tote bag, but he would find out in due time. Why rush things? Shemi heard one of the lab scientist say once, *'It's all about the journey.'*

Shemi shook Rick's hand. *'Firm handshake.'* Shemi thought that he might kill Rick first. Rick wasn't as physically big as the Moon guy, but Rick seemed solid as a rock and might not go down easily. Best to surprise this one and kill him with the element of surprise. That should give Shemi a few moments to get the drop on Moon. The Bobby one was small. As one of the scientists from the lab would say, *"he's a little light in the ass. I'll beat him like he stole something."*

When Shemi took Sheena's hand, he was instantly sidetracked. There was a spark…the spark he was looking for! Sheena was the one, the one who had a compatible DNA sequence hidden in her genes that would allow his special fetus to grow in her belly. Shemi had done it! His father will be so proud. Shemi tried to ease his hand away from Sheena so no one would notice the excitement he had just touching her. To make it look good, Shemi would shake hands with the other two females as well.

Shemi stretched out his hand to Mimi. Mimi took his hand and immediately there was a spark, there was even a small visible charge that went between their hands. It was a small spark; Shemi saw it and he was convinced that Mimi saw it too because she gave a small smile. Shemi could have built a world of conversation off of that reaction, but the big Moon guy was sitting right next to Mimi and his look says he didn't like the momentary exchange between the two of them. Shemi quickly moved on to Stormy.

Stormy had been watching Henry's interaction with the group. Stormy was not as trusting of Shemi because she had an uneasy feeling about him; truth be told, *he scared her.* She saw Sheena jump a bit when he touched her hand. *'Could have been an electric shock, that's all.'* She saw what Mimi did when she touched his hand, *'But Mimi is hot in the ass anyway, who's to say what I saw with her.'*

Stormy let Henry take her hand. Just like she thought, there was an exchange. As soon as Shemi took her hand, Stormy felt overcome with dread; like there was no tomorrow. Shemi looked her in the eyes, she got lost in his glare; his eyes seemed to dance from brown to pitch black to red. Stormy was sure this was the effects of whatever exotic weed Moon had been passing around. *'Eyes don't dance like that'*. Stormy was relieved when Henry let go of her hand. Stormy didn't like Henry and if the group decided to let him hang out with them she was going in the room.

When Shemi shook Stormy's hand, it was like nothing he had ever experienced before. It reminded him of the night before when he had been with the stripper girl in her Sentra. She had made his essence shoot out of him twice and the sensation that he felt when it burst through was phenomenal. When Shemi touched Stormy's hand he felt that same rush of fluid. Shemi made a little wince in his throat as it came forth. Since he was not very experienced in the sexual relation department, he was having a little trouble containing what he felt.

And it felt oh so good.

By the time Shemi released Stormy's hand he knew a couple of things. Shemi knew in which order he would kill the men; Rick then Moon then Bobby. Shemi knew that Sheena, Mimi and Stormy, particularly Stormy, were all able to carry his seed to term. Shemi decided he would impregnate all three of the women, just in case there was a complication with one or two of their pregnancies. Plus, he would get to feel that rush of fluids three more time you can't beat that.

Sheena was thinking just like her father taught her; *'always contact me if something goes wrong'*.

"Excuse me Henry. You wouldn't happen to have a phone on you, do you?"

"No, unfortunately not…I don't really like carrying cell phones on me."

"Really, why's that?"

"Well it's kind of an inconvenience, you know what I mean? Yeah they always ringing all the time, you know what I mean. So uh, so you guys from around this area?"

Moon takes the lead. He is ready to have Henry move on so they can continue their evening...

"Nah man, we're just passing through."

"I know what you mean. Yeah, me too...I'm just passing through too."

Sheena asks,

"Where are you on your way to?"

"Well, uh, I guess you could say I'm on a mission...of sorts."

"What kind of mission, if you don't mind me asking?"

"Well...I guess you can say I'm on a mission to find me some women."

Moon is taking a gulp of his beer and upon hearing the *find me some women* line from their guest, he spits up beer all over himself.

"Find you some women huh? Okay, well good luck with that. What type of women are you looking for?"

Shemi looks around the group...

"Well, I'll know them when I see them. Don't you worry about that. So ah, do you guys mind if I join your party here?"

"Well to tell you the truth, I don't think that will be possible. You see, this is a private celebration of sorts. You understand."

"Sure I do. It's a celebration right?"

Shemi digs into his jacket pocket and pulls out a clear zip lock bag filled half way with what looks like marijuana.

"Well what if old Shemihazah brought a little something to the party?"

Shemi tosses the bag to Moon who catches it with one hand.

"See that catch...skills to pay the bills boys."

Moon opens the Ziploc bag and smells the contents.

"Damn, what the hell is this?"

Moon takes out a couple of the buds. The bud is purple with white frosting all over it. Just touching the buds made Moon's hand sticky and smelly. Moon puts the buds back in the Ziploc bag and looks around the group.

"Somebody get this man a chair."

"No, no need for a chair. I'm not too proud to sit down on old mother earth right here."

"Damn, now this shit smells potent as hell. What is it?"

"That there is something I grew myself. I call it 'Purple Poison'."

Stormy laughs,

"Sounds like something you find under a sink. Why did you refer to yourself as Shemihazah? I thought you said your name is Henry."

"Well, Shemihazah is a hard name for some, so I usually use my middle name which is Henry."

Moon is still very impressed with the contraband.

"Purple Poison, huh?"

"That's right."

Bobby, who doesn't even smoke weed called himself jumping into the conversation.

"Purple poison, it looks more like some 'Bobby Brown'.

"Nah Bobby. As a self proclaimed ganja connoisseur, I can attest that this is the real deal. Where did you get this from?"

"That? Why I grew that myself."

"Really?"

"Yeah, oh yeah. As a matter of fact, that strain there is old...real old. My sources say that strain right there is what got Adam and Eve kicked out of the Garden of Eden."

"What?!"

"It's true. That is the culprit right there."

"Come on man, stop it with that bullshit. Everybody knows that Adam and Eve got thrown out of the Garden of Eden for eating apples."

"No, it wasn't apples. Everybody's wrong. That's what it was right there...a little bit of cannabis."

"Yeah right. You mean to tell me that God kicked Adam and Eve out of the Garden of Eden for getting their buzz on? Man you got to be crazy, get out of here with that."

"Why, is that so hard to believe?"

"Look, I've smoked weed from all around the world; indica, sativa, hybrids...it don't make me no difference. Talking about some Garden of Eden...this probably ain't nothing but some Durban Poison from over there in Africa."

Moon looks around with the excitement of a little boy at Christmas time. Ready for that new bicycle...

"So what do you say peoples? Let's get this party started...quickly, right..."

Chapter 54

"Can I get a ride with you up a ways?"

"Sure, jump in."

Dave got into the car; it was a 2003 Toyota Avalon, green with beige leather interior.

"Nice car."

The man who stopped and picked Dave up did not respond to Dave's comment. This man seemed distracted; he seemed to be in the midst of a conversation in his head.

"I'm gonna make it. And you better be right when I get there."

Dave watched the man as his eyes focused on the road and the imaginary person he was talking to in his head. The man looked like a maniac; unkempt hair and beard, dirty white shirt, camouflage pants and combat boots. A certifiable nut case. Dave needed to feel him out a bit. If it wasn't right, Dave needed to put a bullet in his gut and keep it moving.

"So how far can you take me friend?"

The man looked over at him from the driver's seat...

"You look just like him."

"Just like who?"

"You look just like the scum bag that's sleeping with my wife?"

"I am not him. I am not the guy sleeping with your wife."

The man looked at Dave and grunted,

"You dress like him."

"How does he dress?"

"I imagine he dresses just like you."

"You've never seen him?"

"No."

"How do you know your wife is cheating on you? Did you catch her in the act?"

"No. I've been in prison. She was visiting me for the first year, and then I didn't see her no more. She stops accepting my phone calls and my man wrote me and told me she lost weight. What she losing all that weight for? Wasn't nobody paying her no attention when she was big as all outdoors, but now she losing weight...going to the gym? Probably paying some girl named Victoria to tell her some secrets. I don't know what the hell she's doing, but I'm not having it. If I get there and another man is in my house, I'm gonna kill everybody!"

'*Okay, we have a meathead here.*' Dave started rethinking his plan. He might have to kill this man now before he freaks out and thinks he's his wife.

Just as Dave began considering where he would get the man to pull off so he could kill him, he saw steam streaming out of the hood of the car.

"Shit. I got to pull over."

The man pulled the car over to the side of the road. The man angrily got out of the car and slammed the door behind him. He stormed over to the hood and opened it up.

Dave changed his plan again. He decided to let the man work on his car. Dave would walk up a ways and if the man got his car fixed and drove up he would flag him down, kill him, dump his body off somewhere in these woods and keep on trucking to catch up with Sheena and her gang. Good plan. In the meanwhile, if someone else comes driving along, Dave would catch a ride with them. No need killing this guy now, if he had to leave the car behind too.

Dave got out of the car and walked to the hood.

"Any idea what's going on under there?"

The man grunted and looks at Dave,

"Yeah I know, you damn right I know. She knew I was getting out today and decided to stay in bed with her boyfriend. She never came to pick me up. I had to call a cab, jump out and kill some guy to get this car. See now she fucking with my freedom. Why she got to be like that? I told her I'm gonna get the ring."

"I'm sorry; you haven't given your wife the ring?"

"She's not my wife yet okay! I had just told her I loved her. She said she couldn't be with me because I didn't have no money. I told her I would get her a big ass ring, bigger than that Beyonce chick. She didn't believe me so that night I robbed the Jewelry store before they closed. I stole the biggest ring they had, and a few other trinkets. I hid them in the apartment. When she got home I was just about to tell her I loved her and go get her the ring when the police kicked in the door. They come arresting me like I was a criminal or something. I spent the last eight years in jail. She came and saw me for the first year and I told her I hid the jewels somewhere in the apartment where nobody could find them. After a while, she stopped coming to visit. I just heard some things from my boy over the years, but he got shot while I was in. About six years ago he told me she started losing weight. I think she found my stash and spent in on her boyfriend. Now I got to go set the record straight."

Dave stood there amazed at the story this man had just told him. No words, just amazement. Dave wondered how this idiot lasted on the streets this long. Dave began to walk away from the man and down the road.

Chapter 55

Puff, puff, and pass.

The weed was the best Moon ever tasted. It got him so high; and he kept getting higher! It was like eating a good weed brownie and staying high for hours. Moon didn't think he could ever come down...what is that, a cloud?

Shemihazah watched the kids as they all *'partook of the fruit'*. Shemihazah smiled because he knew what was coming soon enough. Shemi knew he had to find the group with the green tote bag, but that could wait until morning. Right now he had in his clutches three women who could bear him children...and one of them was probably the queen mother of them all. Yes, he would have them tonight, just let the *'weed'* do their work...

Since Bobby and Stormy were not really smokers, they stopped after a few hits and were now both tired. Stormy knew she had a plan of her own with Moon, but maybe tonight wasn't the night to pursue it. It would be too tricky. Best to keep that under wraps until they get to the cabin. Stormy was sure she could whip up the perfect spot. She had decided not to let Bobby in on the fun. She wanted all of Moon's attention. She could have the threesome another day if there was some of the Spanish Fly left.

"I'm going to lie down for a little while. I'll see you guys later."

A few seconds later, Bobby stretched his arms and proceeded to yawn.

"Okay, I'm gonna go lay down too."

Moon laughed,

"I bet you are. Just do me a favor, don't get the sheets all messy, I want to sleep in the bed too."

"Sheena looks at Moon with *the yuck* face and Mimi hits Moon on the arm.

"What?"

"You can be so crass Moon."

Shemi watched them act as if he wasn't there. They might have truly tuned him out. Shemi waited. Shemi knew that very shortly all of them would be sleeping soundly. All Shemi needed to do now was give each a little bite when he was ready to have them…just a nip at the carotid artery so he could inject some of his blood while taking in a bit of hers. The life is in the blood. This act would cause their DNA to have *'intercourse'* through the mixing of their two genes. Then as their bodies mixed and he released his essence into each one of them, the magic would have begun. Who knows how many children Shemi would have from this one night?
"Father, I will complete my task."

Shemi waited…waited until they fell asleep one by one. There goes Moon…there goes Sheena…goodnight Mimi and there goes Rick. Shemi is certain the two in the room are sleep as well. Shemi stands and surveys the group. He looks around the landscape. Not a car or a person in sight. Shemi could not have picked a more perfect spot if he tried.

Before Shemi had his fun, he wanted to make sure there were no peeping toms. *"The man in the hotel office…now he looked like a peeping tom. Best to go eliminate him first. Yes, kill the man in the office, lock the door and put a note on it that says, 'sleeping in back, do not disturb."*

Chapter 56

Time for the Shemi special. Shemihazah walks over to the sleeping students.

"Now for the moment you've all been waiting for."

Shemi went to Mimi first. She was arguably the curviest of the group. Shemi sat down next to Mimi and slid her shirt off revealing soft subtle skin that smelled of apples. Shemi took off her pants and she now lay across his lap in nothing but her lace bra and matching red panties. Even sleeping she was so very inviting.

Shemi removed Mimi's bra revealing the soft perky breast of a twenty year old. They stood up firm and erect, the very sight of her young nipples made Shemi's manhood rise. Shemi took off her panties which covered a soft mound of hair that was brown in the fading light. Shemi laid Mimi down on the ground for a moment so he too could remove his clothing; his jacket, shirt, pants and underwear. Shemi sat back down on the ground and grab Mimi's body, placing her directly on top of him. Once in position, Shemi bit down on Mimi with his teeth and Mimi came to life. Mimi was not fully conscious; she was very much under the effects of the substance that she smoked. While not actually marijuana, it did have the mind altering effects that were similar to marijuana…at first. There was much more to this drug than just getting high.
When Shemi bite Mimi and drew just a small amount of blood, she felt invigorated. As more of Shemi's blood mixed with hers, Mimi felt like a lioness; a sexy, sexual lioness. Mimi slid herself onto Shemi's waiting shaft, and had the most physically tiring sex she would ever have. In the end, Mimi cried out loud two times before falling limp over Shemi's naked body.

Shemi placed Mimi back in the beach chair she was in. He put the blanket that was covering her back on top of Mimi. Shemi didn't do this because he was concerned Mimi, but she now had his seed in her so she had to be protected. He would always protect her...until she was no longer able to bear him children.

After securing Mimi back in her chair, Shemi made his way over to Sheena. Sheena was a pretty girl; *stacked* as some would call her. She was short, but her proportions were just right. Her body was smooth and blemish free, just asking for Shemi to step inside and get comfortable.

Shemi lifted Sheena off of the beach chair she was sitting in and carried her over to the van. He stood her up against the van and took off all of her clothes. Shemi lifted her in his hands by the thighs, placing her back on the door of the car and her legs wide open to receive him. Shemi bit down on Sheena, causing her to moan a bit as she jerked awake. As soon as she was awake, Shemi entered her; creating instant wetness as he moved further and further inside of her. Sheena moaned in rhythm to his movements; louder and louder until in a frantic tizzy Sheena screamed out into the night air. Birds lifted from their nests, bushes moved and small animals ran out into the night. Sheena screamed as he released into her. She kept screaming, making Shemi more excited than ever. Shemi pumped and pumped until sweat was dripping off of his brow. As the sweat trickled down his face and onto the ground below, Shemi began to slow down and then stop; knowing that he had to keep some of himself intact as he went into the room for the final portion of tonight's menu. Sheena eventually stopped screaming and fell limply back into his arms. Shemi proceeded to place Sheena back into her chair and prepare himself for the coup de *gras*. There was no need to worry about these two. As long as Shemi had his way with them while they were sleep, they would have no particular memory of the event. They will think it must have been a dream. The only time there could be a problem is if Shemi took them while they were awake or without giving them some of the '*weed concoction'*. These two ladies made his job ever so much easier on him. Shemi would hate to have to kill any of the few people on earth that could carry his seed to term.

Chapter 57

"What's that?"

Stormy jerked awake on the bed, sending Bobby's arm shooting off and slamming against the wall.

"What the hell?"

Stormy sat up in bed completely; she was drenched in sweat. She though she must have had a bad dream.

"Move."

Stormy got up off the bed. She was in her bra and panties; Stormy really wanted to be naked, but because of the other guests in the room, she settled for semi-naked. As Stormy stood up, Bobby took a good long look at her body; the slender physic, the cleanly shaven legs, the way her cheeks fought to escape the fabric of her panties with every step she took. Bobby was ready. It was not often lately that he had a chance to make love to Stormy. He once told his friend who had commented on how beautiful his girlfriend was; *"Her beauty doesn't matter a lick if you can't touch her."*

Stormy knew that Bobby was watching her and she even knew what he was thinking. Stormy liked the attention. She had not gotten much attention from men in her life until recently when the braces came out and she worked out to get her curves and that butt. Now she can get a few looks when she goes out, but it's never from the people she wants it to be from.

"Do me a favor. Go to the Van and grab some snacks and a bottle of water. I'm going to clean up a bit. Maybe I'll have a surprise for you when you get back."

"Hot damn."

Bobby threw on his shirt and pants and rushed out the door at once.

Chapter 58

At first, Bobby didn't notice anything out of order when he rushed outside. He went straight for the van and started fiddling around in the bag. Bobby emerged with a bag of Potato Chips and a bottle of water. He was running back towards the room door when he noticed Shemi standing in the middle of his sleeping friends butt naked. Shemi looked back at Bobby.

"What the fuck...what the hell are you doing?"

Shemihazah stretched out his arm towards Bobby and squeezed his hands. Bobby stopped moving in his tracks and raised his arms to his throat. The air was constricted in his throat; he could not move, he could not breathe. All Bobby could do was clutch his hands around his throat and try to pull off the imaginary hands that were squeezing the air out of his passageways. When Shemi saw he had Bobby in his clutches, he squeezed harder...

"You want to save them, don't you?"

Shemi slowly walked towards Bobby as he squeezed his hands tighter.

"Look at you. You are pathetic; a worthless waste of breath. You don't deserve to exist. Humans...my father was created first. We were created with more power. Yet He expects me to bow do to you? Me, Shemihazah; son of the first watcher created in the light and ruled over those that kept the order of the Earth. Now my heirs will rule this place by the power of my might. And you...yes you-you will die."

Chapter 59

Stormy is in the bathroom washing her face. She had not expected this hiccup in the trip. No worries though, they will be at the cabin tomorrow and then the fun will begin.

Stormy stood in the mirror admiring her body. She did remember to bring her pocket rocket with her, but now was not the time. She was positive that when Bobby came back in the room with those snacks, he would want some kind of reward. Like going to the car to get some popcorn was deserving of some booty. '*Nevertheless…*" she sighed, '*a girl does have needs.*'

Stormy had to laugh at herself in the mirror. She had been such a good girl up until this part of her life. She studied hard, worked her part-time job and never gave herself away cheaply. To tell the truth, besides Bobby, she had only been with one other man in her whole life. It was her first love; a ruggedly handsome, top-notch athlete and scholar. His name was Elliott. Every time she thought of him for more than five seconds, she got a tingly sensation deep in her loins. Stormy laughed out loud…'*I be thinking some real bullshit sometimes*', and this thought made her laugh even harder.

While Stormy amused herself in the bathroom mirror, she heard the room door open. '*Good, I'm ready for a snack and to be a snack. Maybe I'll let him snack on me while I snack on some Cheteeos'*. This thought sent Stormy into another round of laughter as she removed her bra and draped the towel over her shoulders letting it hang down to cover her hardened nipples.

Stormy walked out of the bathroom expecting to see Bobby standing in the middle of the room waiting with mouth open to see her walk sexily from out of the bathroom. Stormy sauntered out of the bathroom and was surprised to see that it was not Bobby standing there; it wasn't even Moon as she would have hoped…it was the guy from earlier. Henry, or Shemihazah or whatever he referred to himself as being. Not only that but he was naked from head to toe except for that stupid faded cowboy hat he was wearing.

"Now before you say anything I just want to tell you one thing..."

Stormy was stunned silent. She was with five other people; a football player, two girlfriends, an ex-vagrant and her own boyfriend, yet here she stood just about naked in a room all of them shared, and she was about to be rapped...or worse.

"I know, I know, this is highly irregular...but let me tell you, these are irregular times Miss Lady. Now this is gonna happen; you can't stop this. It's bigger than the both of us. But I'm gonna give you a choice since you are gonna be the mother of my children..."

Stormy was frozen stiff. She could not move. Never in her wildest imaginations, her most creative stories or the worse movies she had seen could she have been prepared for this. All she could think of to do was to run. If she could make it past this guy and out of the room, she would be okay. The others must not know he was in here. She had to make it past him now.

Stormy mustered up all of her courage and made a mad dash towards the door. Shemi seemed to know exactly what she was going to do. He stepped to the side with the grace of a ballet dancer and grabbed Stormy by the back of the hair. Shemi flung Stormy around and she bounced off the wall and landed on the bed. Stormy's nose was bloodied already. Surely the sight of blood all over her face would gross out her attacker.

It did not. Shemi walked over to the bed and stood over Stormy. He put his finger to his mouth to warn her to be quite. Shemi shook his head and waited for her to shake her head in agreement. Once she did, Shemi reached down and removed her panties. Stormy began to cry. Shemi touched her check gently and looked into Stormy's lovely eyes and whispered,

"You should have taken the drugs. This gets a bit painful for you

when you're awake."

Stormy finally found her voice…

…and she screamed to the top of her lungs.

Chapter 60

"On the road again..."

Dave is still walking down the side of the road waiting for either his former driver or another unlucky driver to come barreling down the road.

"Shit."

It had been at least an hour since he checked back in with Frank. Frank was probably blowing his top right about now. Dave guessed he should go ahead and make the call, before Frank sent the whole police force to find him and Sheena.

Dave took out his cell phone and turned it on. He didn't like leaving his cell phone on. Dave knew the power it held. He remembered being one of the last hold outs in getting a cell phone...he had just gotten used to his sky-pager. Dave estimates that he purchased his flip phone in 2001. He never upgraded his phone and refused to get a smart phone. When asked why he did not like cell phones Dave would respond, "Y*eah, like I want a CIA tracking device in my pocket with my profession."*

Once the phone turned on, Dave dialed the number to his old friend...

"Ring..."

"Where the hell have you been?"

"Hello Frank."

"I'm sorry about that, but I'm going crazy over here. Any news?"

"This is what I got so far. It seems to me like Sheena and a few of her friends went on a weekend trip to the mountains. You were

right *about her packing a suitcase on her bed. I talked to her boyfriend's sister and she said that Rick took her up to a cabin. They also took a couple of Rick's friends and their girlfriends; a guy named Bobby and that college football star Elgin 'Moon' Pittman. They in turn took two girls; one named Melinda 'Mimi; Stubbs and Taryn 'Stormy' Mitchells. It seems that they took some sort of scenic route through a stretch of road off the main highway. Maybe their car got caught up in some brush or something; you know how those side paths can be through the country. I'm walking towards them now. The brush looks kind of thick, I'll probably lose cell phone signal soon."*

"*You're walking? What the hell happened to your car?*"

"*Don't worry about it; I'll get the job done.*"

"*Keep me posted. I want to know everything from now on. Check back with me in an hour.*"
"*You got it Chief.*"

There was a slight pause and then Frank hung up. Dave smirked to himself; he knew just how to gut punch Frank.

"*Just in time.*"

Dave could see headlights coming down the road towards him. He stepped up to the road, not too far as to be a target. The car came down the road and started to slow down just a hair.

"*How lucky can one man be?*"

Chapter 61

T.J was driving recklessly now. After T.J had blown his top earlier, his car had given out on him. He had picked up a hitchhiker and was having a pleasant conversation and *blam*; his car just started spitting out smoke and stopped. T.J got out of the car and before he knew it, his passenger just jumped out and started walking. No warning, no gas money- not even a solid goodbye. Just turned his back to him and walked off in the sunset like Billy the Fucking Kid. As a matter of fact, maybe he was the one who sabotaged his car. *Why not?* His car was running fine until he picked up Billy the Kid. He was dressed just like one of those guys that be sneaking around with other peoples wives who are in prison but are ready to make it right. Oh, that just made him so mad!

Once the car stopped and Billy the Kid left, T.J sat on the side of the road for a minute to pray. He wanted to make sure he was on the right path. After twenty-two seconds of praying, T.J went to the trunk of the car and got out the Jack Daniels. Straight to the head.

In a little while he took another look at the car and saw there was no water in the radiator. He had a couple of jugs of water in the trunk that he put there for just this type of emergency situation and poured them in the radiator and on the engine. He then sat by the side of the car, drinking Jack Daniels and waiting for the engine to cool off enough to drive the car again.

Now T.J was barreling down the road again, on his way to see his wife. *'Let's see how much you miss me'*. T.J looked down the road and saw a guy waving his arms looking for a ride. T.J could use a companion for a while; that Jack Daniels made him want to talk with somebody. T.J had just started to slow down the car and prepare to stop when he realized it was the jerk from earlier…it was Billy the Fucking Kid, the one who was banging his wife and sabotaged his car. In a flash T.J. sped up the car and ran him over. Dave's head hit the windshield with a solid thud, hard enough to crack the entire windshield. Dave's body flew off the car and down in the side of the road underneath the overgrowth.

"Serves him right. He should have given me some gas money, he knew I was broke."

T.J drove on, grabbing the bottle of Jack Daniels from the back seat and having himself a sip.

T.J never once looked back to see the damage he had caused. Dave lay on the side of the road with a cracked skull, a broken neck and was bleeding profusely. In a matter of minutes, Dave was dead... his cell phone's light blazing brightly on the side of the dark road.

Chapter 62

"Its morning...and we slept the night away..."

That was the song ringing in Mimi's ears as she woke up. It was still a bit dark outside. Mimi gave a long stretch and yawn. She felt great; actually, she felt better than she had in a long time. She felt like she could run five miles right now without breaking a sweat. How did this happen from sleeping outside in a beach chair?

As Mimi stretched, she let the wind gently flow over her face...through her hair...over her breast...

Over her breast? Mimi looked down and discovered that she was naked under the small blanket that she had grabbed out of the van. She panicked; Mimi looked around to see her surroundings. Everyone was outside with her except for Bobby and Stormy. They were all sleep, but they were here with her.

Mimi looked around and saw that her clothes were on the ground near her chair. She grabbed them quickly and put on her clothing under the blanket. She tried to make as little noise as possible so she would not wake the others. She would hate to have everyone see her '*ass out*'. When she finished getting on her clothes, Mimi tried to remember why they were off in the first place. All she can remember is smoking some weed and that's it. Mimi turned to Sheena to see if she could fill in some blanks and noticed Sheen's clothing on the ground next to her chair.

"I wonder if we've been raped."

Mimi slowly got up out of her chair, trying not to make a sound. She moved slowly over to Sheena and whispered in her ear...

"Sheena...."

Mimi placed her hand on Sheena's shoulder and gave her a little shake.

"Sheena..."

The third time Mimi called her name she gave her a sharp smack to help jolt her to life.

"Sheena!"

"Ow!"

Sheena sat straight up in her chair; the blanket thrown over her body fell off, revealing her bare breast for all to see.

"Oh my God. Why am I naked?"

Mimi was handing Sheena her clothes as she spoke and helped keep the blanket around her as she dressed.
"I don't know what happened girl. Do you remember anything?"

Sheena tried hard to remember. She remembered meeting a new guy called Henry or Shemi or something like that. She can remember smoking with everybody else and even having fun. That's when everything goes blank. Sheena looks like another thought just crossed her mind. She thought she remembers having a wet dream; it must have been a sex dream because she was still a bit wet down there. But it couldn't have been real because she thought she remembered it being brain tingling good. That didn't describe Rick and she didn't have sex with anybody else...did she?

While Sheena was putting on her clothing, Rick and Moon started waking up. Rick wiped the sleep out of his eyes and saw Sheena putting on her clothes under a blanket that Mimi was holding.
"Uh, Sheena..."

"Yeah."

"What are you doing?"

"What does it look like I'm doing?"

"It looks like you're getting dressed. But I am wondering why you are undressed in the first place?"

Sheena was not about to answer that question because she didn't know the answer. But she had to say something. A non-answer would only bring more questions that she couldn't answer. Hell, she had a bunch of her own questions that she couldn't answer. Sheena opened her mouth to answer until Moon and broke the moment for her. Moon stood up, stretched his arms, scratched his butt and yelled out,

"Damn...now that was some good ass weed. I got to get me some of that shit."

With those words, Bobby began to open his eyes. Bobby jumped up like he had been sitting in a fire pit. He ran to the room door and inside, letting the door slam shut behind him. Moon looked at Bobby like he was acting crazy as hell...

"Crack heads."

Chapter 63

The door slammed behind Bobby as he entered the room. He paused for a moment and locked the door behind him.

Bobby immediately put his head in his hands. His worse fears were coming to the surface; something had happened to Stormy and he wasn't here to protect her. First he got tricked into cheating on Stormy, and then he is blackmailed into quitting his job or being prosecuted for rape. Now this, Stormy is violated on a trip that he took her on, promising to protect her.

Bobby thought, *'perhaps it's not as bad as I'm thinking'*. After all, he had just entered the room. Stormy was laying on the bed, awake- staring into the void, but she looked intact. She was sporting a blackened eye and there was caked up blood on her upper lip, but she look conscious and she was wrapped up in the sheets.

Bobby walked over to the bed and bent down to look Stormy in the eyes...

"Baby, baby. What happened?"

Upon hearing the question out loud, Stormy slowly turned her head towards Bobby and started crying. She started clutching the sheets she was wrapped in as the tears streamed down her face.
As Stormy clutched the sheets tighter and tighter, Bobby noticed a lot of red on the sheet covering her lower body. Bobby reached out and grabbed the sheets so he could steady his mind on the area, but he already knew what it was- blood; lots and lots of blood. Bobby looked at the blood and tried to make sense of it, Stormy's eyes followed his and she saw the blood on the sheet…lots and lots of blood. She went into shock and started to convulse. Bobby grabbed her by the head, took a pen out of his pocket and put it in her mouth. He was trying to prevent her from biting off her tongue. He heard about doing that in some book he read or some movie he

watched. Bobby rocked her back and forth while stroking her hair. It took maybe two or three minutes before Stormy's body stopped its involuntary movements, and another couple of minutes before she got her senses back. Bobby held her tightly until the tears dried up and she had a sense of her surroundings. But true to form, Bobby opened his mouth and said something that made it worse.

"Are you okay?"

Stormy looked at him with pure hatred in her eyes. True, he had asked an obviously dumb question at the wrong moment. He knew she was not okay. If looks could kill, Bobby would be dead at this very moment.

Stormy stood up and kept the sheet around her. She moved over to the second queen sized bed that was in the room. She was now seated directly across from Bobby, on the side of the room where the light was not as bright. She could only imagine what her face must look like at this very moment. She looked into Bobby's eye and she could see his shame, she could see that he wanted to apologize until the cows came home. But she did not care. She did not want to make him feel better. She had been raped and she remembered ever moment of this heinous action. She remembered how his skin felt and how his breath smelled. She could remember him hitting her over and over and the pain- the searing pain with him smiling and laughing all the while. Stormy had been violated in the worse way and in every way; he had even taken the time to draw symbols on her body and write Latin word on her body with the blood he collected as he bit different areas of her body. Some areas no one could readily detect. Stormy was victimized; she was mad and she was hurting and she was scared...and she didn't want this punk sitting in front of him to say one damn word about him being '*sorry*'.

"Do you want to call the police?"

Bobby could sense he was treading on thin ice. He wanted to help Stormy but he didn't know what to do. He did know that the rest of the group would be coming to the door soon to get inside. They had to come up with a plan and quickly.

"I hate to have to say this, but the others will be in here soon. You want to go in the bathroom for a little bit? Maybe check yourself out, clean yourself up?"

Stormy said nothing. She just sat there staring at Bobby, seething with anger.

"Just tell me how you want to handle this. I will make sure that guy pays."

Stormy slowly stands up and Bobby does also. She walks towards the bathroom without saying a word. After taking five steps towards the bathroom, she stops and turns back towards Bobby. Thinking that she was about to tell him what she wanted to do and how she wanted to handle this situation with the others, Bobby ran up too her and stood close in case her voice was but a whisper. Stormy reached back…way way back and swung her arm forward. As she did, she boiled her hand into the tightest fist she could. When her arm came completely forward, her fist connected with Bobby's left eye and it felt to her like she broke her hand on his face. Bobby winced in pain, grabbed his eye and dropped to the floor like a ton of bricks. While Bobby lay on the floor clutching his eye, Stormy stood over him giving him the look of death.

"I told you I didn't want to stay at this hotel. Get me out of her now!"

Stormy went into the bathroom and left him lying on the floor.

As Stormy made it into the bathroom and the door closed behind her, Bobby could hear the knob to the room door turning. Someone was trying to get into the room. Bobby got up off of the floor. Now there was a knock at the door. Bobby moved over to the room window and took a look out. The first thing he saw was Moon's big ugly face.

"Open the door. I know you can see me because I can see you. Catch that yellow bus of yours and have it stop at the room door. Unlock it and let us in."

Chapter 64

"You know something Moon; sometimes you can be such an asshole."

As the group walked into the room, they brought plenty of noise with them. Sheena and Moon were going at it again. *'They're like damn children'*, Bobby thought to himself. Bobby knew Moon was destined for greatness as long as he didn't get hurt. Bobby and Moon were tight, had been for years. But Sheena was still right; sometimes Moon could be a giant asshole.

Mimi chimed in with Sheena,

"You are so right girl."

None of this phased Moon. Moon was good at speaking his mind whenever he felt like it. Bobby thought this was a good thing in the long run. He guessed it was this freedom Moon acted on that made him the type of person who could lay it all on the line and live each minute to its fullest. Bobby sure knew he was not that type. Between his work life and his home life, things were not looking good.

"So Bobby, tell me...did you get it popping last night? Did you ride the pony, do the horizontal tango, test the bed springs, bring it around town, put the lime in the coconut and shake it all about?"

Moon's jokes were met with silence. The silence had gotten so thick that Moon stopped and looked around the room as if he didn't know the people in the room.

"What?"

Sheena was happy to respond.

"Such an asshole."

"Alright now girl, I ain't going to be too many more assholes tonight."

Moon started jumping up and down throwing jabs at Sheena like a boxer. Sheena just gave him the ugly face.

Bobby was standing in his spot, lost in his own thoughts. While Moon was doing his boxing routine, Bobby was about to break down and had to get out of the room before he spilled the beans. Booby needed air. Bobby ran past Moon for the room door; pushing past Moon hard enough to knock him off balance and send him flying into the wall. Rick saw Bobby bolting for the front door and yelled out to Moon,

"Stop him."

But Moon was too late. Bobby shot past him and made it out the door. Moon rebounded off the wall and went after him, just as Rick jumped off the bed and went out the door too.

Chapter 65

When Rick and Moon ran outside, they saw Bobby moving quickly towards one of the other hotel rooms. Bobby started banging on one door- room number six. Bobby began screaming at the top of his lungs;

"Open this damn door right now!"

Moon caught up to Bobby and grabbed his arm to pull him back. Bobby violently jerked his arm out of Moons hands…

"Get the fuck off me Moon."

Bobby and Moon stood there and stared at each other. Moon can see that Bobby is upset and something is wrong, but Moon will be damned if he is manhandled by this little chump. Moon really had to collect himself or Bobby would have had a face full of fist.

Booby turns back towards the door just as Rick approaches him and grabs him.

"Bobby, whoa man, slow down. What's going on?"

Bobby stops for a moment and looks Rick in the eyes. Bobby sighs and then tries to wriggle out of Rick's grasp. Rick see's him trying to get out, so he continues to grab Bobby so he cannot get away from him.

"Come on Bobby, we are not the enemy. Stop and tell us what's going on."

Moon is paying attention but decides not to grab Bobby right now. If he did grab Bobby, it would be with a headlock.

Just then, Mimi and Sheena walk out of the room to see where the men are. Sheena looks right and spots them at the door of another room.

"What's wrong?"

"Sheena, take Mimi and go back in the room."

"Why Rick? What's happening?"

"Take Mimi and go back in the room. We'll be there in a minute."

"I want to know what...

"Sheena!"

Sheena stands there and stares at Rick for a few moments. Sheena usually does not allow people to talk to her any kind of way, but she also knew that Rick would never talk to her like that unless there was something serious going on. Sheena decided to give Rick a pass...for the moment. They would talk about this, but not now. Sheena turns to Mimi,

"Let's go back in before I have to curse this man out like I don't know him."

"He's been hanging out with Moon too long girl."

"You go that right...assholes, the both of them."

Sheena and Mimi walk back into the room.

Bobby is still standing relaxed. Bobby seems to be off in his own thoughts, not paying attention to anything in particular. This change in attitude convinces Rick to loosen his grip.

"Bobby, it's me man. What's going on?"

As soon as Rick loosens his grip on Bobby, Bobby runs to the door again, pounding and screaming...

"Open this damn door!"

Rick and Moon grab Bobby and wrestle him to the ground. It's amazing how much strength anger can give a person. It takes a bit of doing to get Bobby on the ground and immobilized. After a few minutes of wrestling against Rick and Moon, Bobby finally gives up and goes limp. Rick notices that Bobby's body is convulsing and turns him on his back in fear that they may be suffocating or something.

When Rick gets Bobby on his back, he sees that Bobby is not convulsing…he is crying. Tears are streaming down his face. Rick nods to Moon, who is also witnessing the tears. Both Moon and Rick let go of Bobby and help him back to his feet. Rick uses the most calming voice he can to appeal to Bobby to trust them with whatever this problem is.

"Bobby, you know we are here for you man. Tell us what's going on…so we can help."

Bobby stood there facing his two best friends in the world, and he was ashamed to admit what the problem was. Bobby thought he might be having a nervous breakdown, with all the recent events that has happened to him. This was just one more thing in a long list of things that would break him down. Bobby stood there looking at his longtime friends with tears in his eyes. He did not want to share; he did not want to tell them what had happened. He didn't want them to know that Stormy had been raped last night and that in the end Bobby was too weak to stop it. Bobby did not want to mention that he was choked within an inch of his life by a pair of invisible hands clutching his windpipe…an invisible hand controlled by the same person who raped his girlfriend. But in the end, Bobby knew he had to talk.

"What's going on is, I'm going into that room and I'm going to literally kill that man with my bare hands. So what's up Moon, ya'll with me?"

"Look B, you know we got your back anytime, anywhere. But you got to tell us what's going on. This seems just a bit out of character for you."

"Fine."

Bobby leaves them and heads to the van. Moon and Rick look at each other because they have no idea what is going on with Bobby. After searching through the van, Bobby finds what he is looking for- the steel tire iron. Bobby hits the iron against his palm one time and decided he had a good weapon. Bobby fixates his eyes back on room number six and heads towards it.

Rick and Bobby see what is happening and react in an instant. The two wrestle Bobby back to the ground and take the tire iron from him. They lift Bobby's entire body off the ground and carry him to the side of the hotel building, away from the hotel room door. When they set Bobby down he tries to walk away, but Moon makes it clear that playtime is over and he will seriously restrain Bobby if he does not calm down; Moon makes it very clear with the expression on his face. Bobby gets the message and truly calms down this time; no fuss, no tricks. Rick walks up to Bobby gingerly and tries to calm him further.

"That's it Bobby. That's it. Calm down brother. Now tell us, what's the problem?"

Bobby stands defiant. Rick and Moon can see he doesn't want to talk, but it's too late for that. They don't rush Bobby to talk, they give Bobby all the time in the world to collect himself and begin to tell them his story.

"Man, I think Stormy was raped last night."

Both Rick and Moon respond at the same time,

"What?"

"She's in the bathroom checking herself out now."

Rick seems even more upset than Moon...

"Is she going to report it?"

"I don't know yet."

Moon has had enough,

"Man, what the fuck are we waiting for?"

Moon brushes past the two of them and starts banging on the door,

"Man get your perverted ass out here right now!"

Rick runs over to Moon to dissuade his actions...

"Moon come on man, wait."

"Wait for what Rick?"

"I don't think he's in there."

"How do you know?"

"The lights are off. Plus he would have at least come to the window by now with all of this noise."

Moon thinks about this statement and decides Rick is right. Moon tries to peak through the window of the room, but the thick curtains block his view.

"So what do you suggest Rick?"

"Well first, let's go to the office and talk to that guy behind the desk. Maybe he can give us some information on this dude before we rush in. I'm sure they have some information on him in the *office. Then we can either make him come to the door or at least get that attendant to open the door so we can check this out. Then we'll ask Stormy how she wants to handle this."*

"No, no, no, no…"

"What's the problem now Bobby?"

"You got to act like you don't know about this.

"What? Act like we don't know about this? Why the fuck are we playing these games?

"Moon, I said you got to act like you don't know. That's how it's going down right now, alright? Agreed? Rick?

"If you say so man."

"Moon?"

Moon pauses before he speaks. Moon is a '*confront your problems*' type of person. Moon is not one known for patience or lying low, but he does see the pain in Bobby's face. Moon has no intentions on letting this man get away with raping his friend, but he knows he can't let on to it.

"Ok, it's your world. So, what you want to do now Bobby?"

"I agree with Rick. I want to get some info on this guy. Let's go in the office, find out who this guy is and then we can go from there. But I want in this room…you hear me? I want in this room. We agreed?"

Rick and Moon look at each other then back at Bobby. This is a serious matter and it is true that they need to be together on this. Both men agree.

"Sure Bobby."

"Agreed."

Chapter 66

"Such an asshole."

Sheena and Mimi went back into the room after being ushered off sternly by Rick. Sheena had her feelings about the situation, but she also had her suspicions that whatever was happening had something to do with Stormy also. Stormy has been held up in that bathroom every since they woke up a little while ago. When Sheena and the others walked back into the room, Stormy was in the bathroom. Sheena watched Mimi as they came back in the room to see if she knew anything that was happening- a trick she picked up from her 'Chief of Police' dad. Frank had taught Sheena a lot of things when it came to observing a situation and the people involved. Sheena was in her 'police chief's daughter' mode. When she was growing up she called this her 'Batgirl' mode. Sheena was always a fan of the old 'Batman' television show that aired on the classic television stations. She loved the character Batgirl. Batgirl was the daughter of Commissioner Gordon, and a part time crime fighter. Even her father did not know his daughter was the infamous Batgirl. Even though Sheena's dad was an officer during those years, she still fancied herself as her childhood hero. To Sheena's benefit, her secret detective skills had helped her so many times in her life already.

Sheena sat on the bed as Mimi paced back and forth complaining about what had just happened. She seemed truly upset; not just at the definitive words Rick had blurted out, but she also felt disrespected. Sheena supposed Mimi was truly mad because Moon was not fighting to keep her in the loop. Maybe Moon would not keep her in the loop when he jumps from college to the NFL. Sheena never did see what Moon saw in Mimi. Sheena thought she was a bit of an opportunist; looking for someone to give her that lifestyle she wanted. Sheena would agree that Mimi was a pretty girl, great features and an awesome body…very curvy. However, she didn't think Mimi would be around for the jump to the NFL. While it's true that Sheena did not know Moon the best, from what she did see, Moon was not interested in anything else but Moon right now. He was a great person but Moon was on a serious money hunt; he knew he was good enough to go to the NFL and would probably be drafted either late first round or the early second round. Moon was almost guaranteed to get a contract. Moon was a great football player with the skill set to do some damage over his career. Mimi just didn't strike Sheena as 'wifey' material.

Right now, Mimi was pacing back and forth in the room talking to herself. She could have been talking to Sheena, but it was not really clear. She seemed to be arguing with her own demons.

Sheena got up from the bed and walked over to the bathroom door. First she listened in by putting her ear against the door. Sheena could hear nothing. After about twenty seconds, Sheena mustered up the courage to knock softly on the door.

"Stormy?"

She waited. Nothing.

"Stormy…are you okay in there?"

Just as Sheena asked the question, the toilet flushed. Sheena giggled to herself. It was an 'Archie Bunker' moment. All in the Family was her dad's favorite show. To tell the truth, Sheena thought her dad was a bit like Archie Bunker; raw, a bit insensitive sometimes and a big blowhard. But in his own way he was sweet and a pushover. While Sheena never witnessed her dad use racially insensitive words, she did know that from time to time he relied on stereotypes. Sheena giggled because the toilet flushing after her question reminded her of a number of episodes of All in the Family that she had watched with her dad.

Sheena stood by the door waiting for some sign of movement from Stormy. She wasn't sure if Stormy was in trouble in there, or was just being moody like she sometimes could be. Sheena remained in place, ear pressed against the door, waiting for the tell-tale sign of movement from within.

"What are you doing Sheena?"

"I was just checking on Stormy."

"Is she okay..."

Just as Mimi begins to ask questions about Stormy, a large 'BOOM' is heard. It sounded like a mini explosion. Mimi ran to the door of the room, opened it and slowly stuck her head out of the door. Sheena watched as Mimi slowly walked outside of the room, but staying in front of the room. Mimi's face at first looked perplexed, and then it softened to 'unbelief'. She walked back into the room, closed the door behind her and sat on the bed.

Sheena feared the worse; the only reason she didn't run out of the room in a panic looking for the source of the noise was because of her 'Batgirl' training. First she would stop and ask Mimi what she saw. That way she could prepare herself for what was to come. Sheena quickly left the bathroom door and took a seat on the second bed, across from Mimi.

"What was that noise?"

"They just broke into the room of that guy from earlier...was it Shimisham?"

Chapter 67

"Hello? Is someone there?"

Frank had just picked up his cell phone to call his daughter again. Frank had butterflies in his stomach every time he thought of her. Frank always referred to this as his 'gut', and his gut was telling him everything was not all right with his daughter.

Frank picked up his phone to call Sheena, when he heard a *'clicking'* sound on his line. Frank had been a detective and knew that this was one of the tell tale signs of phone tapping. Frank was thinking his phone had been tapped; someone was trying to keep tabs on him. Frank thought for a moment and the only thing he could think of was this special agent he met at the Sushi restaurant. Frank did not know his name, but he knew that this was how the government did things; it was their M.O.

Frank put down his phone and looked over to the cell phone he kept on the dresser. It was a simple red flip phone. Frank always told his daughter that if there were an emergency, call him on this special phone. The phone was special because only the two of them knew the number. It was their *"secured Bat Line"*. Frank did everything he could to prepare his daughter for the world as he knew it. He had taught her three fighting styles, how to handle firearms and how to be a detective. Sheena was his little *'Batgirl'* and even though it has been many years since they had used that term, it still rang true for both of them.

Frank walked over and picked up the Bat Phone and contemplated calling his daughter again. Even though Frank knew that if she was in an area with no cell phone service she could not reach him, he wanted to be doing something pro-active.

"Dammit, why not? I am the Chief of Police."

As Frank held the red flip cell phone in his hand, the cell phone rang. Frank's face lit up like a Christmas tree; he was so happy that his baby girl had found a way to call him. He had been so worried. Frank sighed and opened up the phone, ready to talk to his daughter and find out where exactly she was.

"Hey baby. Where are you?"

"Thank you for the sincere affection, but this is not your daughter."

Frank recognized the voice; it had been his job to pick up on these types of things for many years. Frank recognized the voice of the agent right away.

"What can I do for you?"

"I am calling to check up on your progress."

"I am still working on it."

"Okay. I see that you have had several murders in your area. Murders that fit the description I gave you. Have you investigated them?"

"Yes I have."

"Look Frank, don't play games with me here. I am not a playful type of guy. Now you know what information I want. I suggest you spill it if you want to continue to be a valuable asset."

Frank thought a moment before he responded. Frank knew he was in a situation where he had to 'play ball'. Frank just did not like to be talked to like a mere employee, like he was expendable. Frank worked hard to get to the top of his trash heap and he was not about to take a dip back to the bottom just to jump onto another trash heap. Frank wanted upward mobility like everyone else; he just didn't want to be treated like a child when he knew his services were of great value.

"No games. I have been to the crime scene of a couple of victims that fall under the terms that you described. I have my team on them and we will find the perpetrator, providing he is still in Virginia. Either way, we will dispatch the information to the surrounding states to make sure we close in on him fast. I think he may still be here; I don't know that, it's just a hunch. But I am on it. I will call you as soon as I have some definitive news."

"Make sure that you do. Remember, after all of this, there is a place for you here in Washington. My boss told me to remind you of that."

"Thank you. May I ask you one question?"

"Fire."

"How did you get this number?"

The agent laughed…not a demeaning laugh, but an honest to goodness laugh…

"Just your tax dollars at work. Talk to you soon Frank."

Chapter 68

"It ain't no fun...if the homies can't haa-aaa-aaa-ave none..."

Moon was in his own world, settling into the relaxing groove of a blunt of marijuana. Moon wishes he had a bong with him, but alas he didn't. Moon had grown up smoking his weed in a blunt- a tobacco leaf. Once he got to college and hooked up with a few of his fellow teammates, Moon learned the bliss of the water bong; and became its biggest fan quickly. But for this weekend, blunts it is.

While Moon was singing and smoking, Bobby was sitting on the bed across from Moon. They all had been searching the room for any sign of the stranger to no avail. Moon questioned whether they were in the right room because this room was so pristine. Nothing was out of place, nothing was messed up...not even a soda cap in the trash can. Rick was finishing up the bathroom, not a trace of Shemi. Rick walked out of the bathroom and stood in the room with Bobby and Moon.

"What the hell is going on? Did he just disappear?"

"Not a trace of this cat."

Bobby had his head resting in his cupped hands as he looked around the room and then at his friends. He was clearly emotional; Rick and Moon looked at each other to see who would console Bobby. Rick mouthed the words...

"Go talk to him."

Moon looked back at Rick and mouthed back the words...

"I'm high."

...and proceeded to smoke his blunt.

"It's not your fault Bobby. Whatever happened, it's not your fault.

We're all going to help you and Stormy get through this."

Bobby was looking at Rick and looking through him at the same time.

"She told me she didn't want to stay here but I didn't listen to her."

"That wasn't your call Bobby. That's on all of us, Stormy included because she voted too."

"Yeah, but I should have known..."

"Should have known what? You can't predict the future any more than the rest of us. How did we know something like this would happen? You couldn't have known. The current question is; what are we going to do about it?"

"Something did happen and I wasn't there to protect her."

Moon sat on the dresser smoking his blunt and watching the two of them converse. Moon could see value in each side; maybe not, maybe it was just the chronic. Moon watched the two of them like he was watching a reality show on TV.

"Listen Bobby, let's do this. Let's go back to the room and get everyone together. We'll talk with Stormy and see how's she's doing. Then we will let Stormy tell us what she wants to do and we'll back her one hundred percent. I'm telling you Bobby, we can work through this...together."

Chapter 69

"Here she comes."

Sheena was standing by the bathroom door and quickly jumped back a few steps and onto one of the beds. She could tell that Stormy was about to come out of the bathroom because the water stopped running and she heard movement. Once Sheena landed on the bed, she turned to Mimi to pretend she had been talking with her all along.

"So what did they tell you...Stormy, hey girl, you okay?"

Stormy walked out of the bathroom and into the room with the two girls. Of course they were staring at her; Stormy knew that would be the case when she walked out of the bathroom.

Stormy sat in a chair by the room's window, resigning herself to telling the story since the guys were not in here. Stormy recounted to them the entire ordeal. Stormy was a masterful storyteller, recounting the intense attack she experienced. The girls sat with their faces twisted in horror as Stormy told how she was beaten and raped. They consoled Stormy, who until this moment had not had a chance to grieve for herself. Mimi then explained to the two girls how she had woken up this morning completely naked and had to put on her clothes and wake Sheena up to put on her clothes. The girls compared notes and thought it was interesting how Sheena and Mimi both seemed to have a dream about having sex with that guy Shemihazah, but can barely remember the details of the dream. Neither Sheena nor Mimi mentioned how explosive the dream was and how they felt like a well had opened up in them causing them to feel completely drained and completely exhilarated at the same time.

After the women talked and shared, the door to the room burst open and the guys walked back in. Moon took a flying leap and landed on the bed with Mimi, who shot up in the air like she was on a trampoline. Rick took a seat on the bed next to Sheena and Bobby sat in the small fold up chair that was on the wall beside Stormy. Bobby looked at Stormy but she never returned his gaze. Bobby was hurt; *how could he have let this happen?*

Bobby reached out his hand towards Stormy.

"How are you baby? You all right?"

Stormy moved her hand and looked away from his eyes.

Sheena looked at Bobby and tried to help ease into a conversation.

"So, did you find him?"

"No, he wasn't in the room."

"Who the hell was he?"

Bobby shook his head 'no' in response to Sheena's question. Sheena turned to Rick to ask a question, but as she did Rick looked like he had an idea.

"Hey guys, remember that guy we meet earlier today?"

"You mean the guy we almost killed with the car?"

"Don't start that shit again Sheena..."

"Screw you Moon."

"Listen! Moon, where's his bag? Maybe there's a satellite phone in there or something."
"I'm on it."

Moon gets off the bed and exits the room.

"Stormy, you know we need to talk about this."

"I don't want to talk to you Bobby."

"Don't be like that Stormy. I'm here now. I'm sorry I couldn't stop it, but I am here and I want to help you get through this. Just tell me what I need to do."

If Stormy did tell Bobby what he could do, he wouldn't like it. Stormy doesn't even want to look at Bobby. When she thinks of this whole situation, all she can see is Bobby's face…and he is coming up short.

Before Stormy can decide how to respond to Bobby, Moon comes back into the room with the green tote bag. He tosses the bag to Rick, who looks around the room before he unzips the bag.

"Maybe this can help us in some way. This guy Shemi could be connected with the guy we saw earlier today. I know it's a long shot, but maybe we can use something in here. Let's see what we're working with."

Rick unzips the bag and places it on the bed. He is the first to look in and pull out an item. Rick pulls out a book that looks like it could be a hundred years old.

Moon is next to dig into the bag and he pulls out a small black case. Moon opens the case and finds a syringe, filled to the brim with some type of green liquid.

"Anybody want a hit?"

Sheena digs into the bag and pulls out a few vials with red liquid in it. It looks like it could be vials of blood.

Mimi is the last one to dig into the bag and she pulls out the last item; it is a simple cross on a chain. The cross is silver and the chain is silver. The cross has a tag attached to it and the tag reads;

"…not by power or by might, but by my Spirit."

The four students look at the treasures in the bag, wondering what the items are for. The room goes silent. Rick is perusing through the book and eventually comes upon a text with a large circle around the title, '*Enoch and the Watchers*'.

"*I remember this. I remember hearing about the Dead Sea scrolls and some other old books they found. One of them was the book of Enoch.*"

Sheena has never been to church but remembers hearing something about Enoch's book as well.

"*Yeah, I remember hearing that Enoch's book was some wild book talking about giants and fallen angels and a bunch of other stuff.*"

Rick was happy that someone knew what he was talking about and readily filled in more information;

"*Yeah, this Enoch dude was in the Bible. I think he was Methuselah's father or something like that...maybe Noah's grandfather. Anyway, the Bible doesn't say much about this dude except he was so righteous that he didn't even die; God took him up to heaven just like he was.*"

"*You believe in that stuff Rick?*"

"*Hey, I'm just telling you the story.*

"*Yeah right.*"

"*Serious. This dude wrote a book talking about things like; where the stars are placed and what happens to them if they don't do what they are supposed to do. He wrote about some crazy things.*"

"*So read us something.*"

"*Okay.*"

Rick looked back at the book to read. He thought he might as well read the passage that was right here in front of him. Rick took a deep breath and began...

'Now it came to past, when men began to multiply on the face of the earth and daughters were born to them, that the Sons of God saw the daughters of men, that they were beautiful and they took wives for themselves...of all whom they chose. Shemihaja approached the other Watchers with an idea...'

"Look at their movements; sweet, seductive...like flowing waters- full of life. None of creation can rival this wo-man."

"We should be the ones with woman companionship. So that we can live eternally with our own begotten ones...and so shall we create life eternally."

"Come, let us choose for ourselves wives, and beget us children. I will go into this woman and lay seed with her and mingle flesh and spirit. But you, I fear you two will not go through with what we decide and I alone will have to pay the price for such a great sin."

Rick took a pause before continuing. Even this short silence was unbearable to Moon.

"Is that it?"

"No, There's plenty more... *'Then swore they altogether and bound themselves by mutual imprecations upon it'*"

"Come on man, can we fast forward this story a bit. I mean what does this have to do with what we are facing right now?"
"Why don't you let him talk?"

"Just be quiet Moon."

Moon stared at Sheena and Mimi like they had went crazy, talking to him like that. Moon had a mind to tell them both off just for the hell of it, but he didn't want to ruin his high.

"Okay, okay...continue."

"Guys, relax. Let's not turn on each other. Here's what I say. Give me a bit of time to read up on what this book says and I will lay it out to you. As a matter of fact, here."

Rick thumbs through the book and rips out three portions of the book. One portion had the title of *'Secret Serum'*. Rick handed that portion to Moon, who had picked out the syringe. The second portion had the title, *'lifeblood'* which Rick handed to Sheena who had the red vials. The final portion was titled, *'warning signs and the cross.'* Rick handed that portion to Mimi who had already laid claim to the cross. It was perfect. The four of them would read and find out what these things were for. They could each read their chapters and they could all report and come up with a plan of action. Bobby and Stormy were the only ones not actively participating in the research frenzy, but they both had their own issues to overcome. Best to let them work on that.

After an hour and ten minutes passed, Rick began to stretch and look at the rest of the group.

"Well people, it's time. It's time for us to figure out what we are going to do. First I'd like everyone who read up on something to report what they read and what they think it means. Let's try to see all angles and piece it all together. Sheena, we need you to ask the hard questions okay?"

"Why me?"

"Because you're good at asking questions. Okay, so I'll start. There are a couple of chapters in this book. The part I read to you earlier seems to talk about these angels that were supposed to watch over humans but who came down and either raped or seduced the women instead. The women had children, but because the fathers of the children were not flesh and blood, the children

were not exactly human as we know it. They were abnormal; some were beautiful to look at, somewhere hideous, some were giants and others had special gifts like super-strength. Eventually they tried to destroy all of mankind; they wanted to eradicate us from the face of the earth. There were around two hundred angels or so who went through with it. They molested humans, plants, fish in the sea and animals in the fields...everything..."

"I guess that's where the saying, 'he'll screw anything that moves' came from."

"Moon."

"Okay, my bad. Continue..."

'Well, it didn't work out to well for them. They got caught, all their children were killed and they were punished severely. But, then there is this whole new section called, 'Nimrod Reborn'. First it goes over some interesting information from different cultures around the world. It talks about the Annunaki- some type of beings that came down from the sky. It talks about some of the esoteric information from Egypt and it talks about some dude named Nimrod, I guess he turned himself into a giant somewhere along the line. Then there are equations and a bunch of stuff that I don't really recognize, but I get the feeling I know what this is about. If you believe in this stuff, it seems to track a course from 'angels' or 'aliens' interfering in human affair and creating some type of half-breed children. This part about Nimrod with the equations and all would seem like they are trying to do some kind of experiment. Maybe they are trying to do what this guy Nimrod did- figure out how to turn himself into something 'more than human.'"

"Damn Rick, you got all that in an hour? I know you need a beer."

"Okay Moon, so what did you find out?"

"Well, it seems like this is some sort of special poison. The writing says specifically that it will immobilize Shemi-version one."

"Shemi version one?"

"That's what is says."

"Well if Shemi stands for our friend, I know this sounds crazy, then maybe he is connected to this angel named Shemihaja, who was supposed to be the leader of the two hundred angels that came to earth and had children with human women."

"So, would that mean that Shemi is the son of Shemihaja?"

"How could that be? The stuff in the book couldn't have just happened. That had to be like thousands of years ago right?"

Rick stopped and really considered the question. Between the two of them, Sheena and Rick, Sheena was the natural detective. But Rick had spent his former years doing some very devious things and knew how a devious mind works first hand.

"Here's what I think. It's going to sound crazy, so don't shoot the messenger. If we applied all the information in this book to everything has happened to us, this guy Shemi is the one this book talking about. I think Shemi is a creation. I think they created him in a lab somewhere. Somehow they found a way to get super human DNA into his blood. Now he is on a rampage and he's focused on us."

The room went silent. No one dared to speak until Moon offered up his input,

"Yes and this syringe contains the poison that can immobilize him. It won't kill him, but it will stop him. The book says twenty four hours, so I guess that's how much time we have from the time we give him this stuff."

"How are we supposed to get that stuff in him? I don't think he's going to roll up his sleeve for us and donate blood."

261

"No, it says that if he comes in contact with the liquid, it will cause him to go numb and stay in whatever state he is in, whatever the hell that means. If we inject it into him then he will be comatose, not able to move or do anything."

Sheena shakes her head yes.

"Okay, that helps. This section is icky. It is about 'lifeblood'. All it is talking about is how life is in the blood and about co-mingling blood...it's disgusting. To tell you all the truth, I think these red liquid vials are vials of Shemi's blood."

"I have the section on this cross. It seems that this is a blessed cross. I don't know who blessed it, but it is supposed to be used in some sort of 'spiritual battles'. Also, it is supposed to do something weird like turn colors or hum when a half-bred is near. Not sure what this half-breed thing is about but if it turns colors or vibrates, something is wrong ya'll."

"So, now that we read all of this, what are we going to do? We need to come up with a plan Rick."

"Moon is right every one, we do need a plan. What do you guys think?"

Mimi has an idea…

"Let's hitch a ride."

Bobby, who is becoming increasingly agitated, interjects into the conversation.

"Hitch a ride, that's a laugh. There hasn't been one car to pass by here since we hit that chump yesterday."

"Okay, well maybe two of us could go out and walk. Maybe we'll see another establishment, maybe find some people, then we'll come back to get you."

"That's even dumber than the first idea. We have no clue where we are. We are in the middle of nowhere, what did you call it Moon, Boonesfuck? We have no idea if there is anything around here. We could just be walking into the Hills Have Eyes."

"Well I don't see you coming up with any plans!"

Stormy can't stand it. She jumps out of her chair and storms out of the door. Bobby sighs deeply and gets up to follow her. Sheena reaches out, touches Bobby on the shoulder and shakes her head no. Sheena gets up and follows Stormy out of the room.

Chapter 70

Sheena walked out of the room and winced slightly in the sunlight. She turned her head and spotted Stormy standing on the opposite side of the van from her. Sheena slowly walked over; allowing the sounds of the heels of her shoes on the concrete give Stormy the warning she needed for company. Stormy might not want company right now, but she needed it. Sheena was afraid that something horrible happened to her last night as well but Stormy's situation was different; she had a violent encounter with a stranger and was violated. There is no amount of sorrow or words or pity that will get Stormy right. Sheena knew from her father that the road ahead for Stormy would be long, lonely and hard. Although Sheena did not consider Stormy a close friend, she would not wish this on her worse enemy.

As Sheena arrived on the side of the van where Stormy was standing, Stormy turned to look at Sheena and Sheena could see that Stormy was crying. Perhaps this is why Stormy ran out of the room, to have a moment to herself to mourn.

"How you doing girl?"

"Not good."

"I am so sorry you went through this."

Stormy looked Sheena in the eyes. Sheena almost felt like she was in an interrogation with those eyes; watching her for inconsistencies, looking for a weak link.

"Have you thought about what you want to do?"

"I want to leave...I want to get out of here."

"I think they are inside figuring out a plan now. I'm sure Bobby and the rest of them are going to figure out something."

At the mention of Bobby's name, Stormy drops her head into her hands and begins to shake her head. Sheena knows something is up and figures that Stormy is blaming Bobby for what happened. Sheena is not sure if that is fair or not, seeing how she has little memory of the night before and woke up butt ass naked herself. She needed more information.

"Stormy, tell me what's wrong."

"I can't stop thinking that this is all Bobby's fault."

"Why? Was he there; was he awake when it happened?"

"I told him from the start I didn't want to stay here. I told him I didn't even want to come on this trip. I came because of Bobby. He just had to have his way and now I'm the one who has to pay for it."

"Are you ready to leave?"

"Yes! But how?"

"We can start walking, you and me. Let's walk away from this place."

"Walk where? Further into the woods with no cell phone and now with no car? No, let them walk. Maybe that guy won't come back, maybe we are safe now.

"Do you really believe that?"

"No. I want to leave, but I'm scared..."

Sheena looks at Stormy and is about to say something, but then censures herself. Stormy would not let Sheena off the hook.

"What?"

"It's nothing."

"Say it."

"I have a feeling, a gut feeling that this isn't over."

"I have the same feeling. Like something even more terrible is about to happen."

Stormy burst into tears again. Sheena nudged Stormy's head until it rested on her shoulders and she stood there with Stormy and let her cry. The women are both thinking the same thing even though no words are spoken. *'Pregnant; am I pregnant?'*

The two women stood there in the sun. Stormy cried on Sheena's shoulder as Sheena contemplated, *'what would Batgirl do?'* With this sudden thought of Batgirl, Sheena couldn't help but smile just a bit in the middle of her nightmare.

Chapter 71

"...bubble hard in the double R, flashin' the rings...with the window cracked, holler back, money ain't a thang..."

As T.J rolled down the road doing eighty miles per hour, he screamed out the words to this song. It was Jay-Z and Jermaine Dupri singing their collaboration, 'Money ain't a thang'.

T.J was not normally into rap music. He said, *'It's too quick and didn't give you a chance to figure out what they were saying before they started talking about something else.* T.J was anti-establishment about everything. If it was new and exciting, T.J hated it.

"See that's what I'm talking about, these stupid rappers. All they want to talk about is what they got; ooh look at me I have a fancy car, oh I'm so special I have gold and diamonds...come be with me, I have millions of dollars. Shit, damn idiots. Take away all that money and jewels and fancy cars and what do you have? Me, that's who. And how the hell them two idiots get them fine ass women anyway? Have you seen them? I mean really looked them in the face. Jay-Z got Beyonce and he acting a damn fool; shit, he look like a damn fool...like one of them court jesters, but he could use his real face! And that bobble head Jermaine Dupri with Janet Jackson...Janet Jackson! Where they do that at? If there was ever an alien living on earth, Jermaine Dupri is it! Have you seen that big water head his neck is holding up? Look like if he trip, his head will take him down! He is an alien for true, that's why Janet left him. She didn't want to have alien babies with big ass waterheads like Dupri...with the windows cracked, holla back, money ain't a thang..."

T.J was fully loaded. He had been talking for about an hour now, only stopping long enough to take the occasional swigg or two from his bottle of Jack Daniels, a man's best wingman.

"...so anyway, I told her that I would be getting out of prison the day I went in. I only had to do ten years. What, is ten years to long to wait for the love of your life? It went by fast as hell...see, here I am now and it's only been ten years."

T.J takes another drink and looks into the rear view mirror.

"...so like I was saying, we inside the store, right. And I'm over in the back, trying to buy a beer. I turn around and see this dude up in the front sticking up the store. I say 'damn, my man is putting it down right now'. So I walk up to him, you know I ain't no player hater, so I walk up to him to give him props. He got his thing going right; face mask, black pants black jacket...but he got on some new Jordan's...some crazy green color. So I'm trying to help the young man and I'm gonna tell him that his sneakers will get him caught. But does game recognize game? Hell naw, cause he turned his gun towards me talking about 'freeze' and all that...'he telling me to back up because he trying to rob a store'...see what I'm saying, some people are all about themselves. So I'm standing there trying to tell man-man to chill and he screaming at me to get on my knees. Shit, I tell him I don't get on my knees for no one, except that one time in prison, but that was a killer ass dude. So I'm telling young dude to just rob the store and get it over with so I can get my beer and go home. He start waving around his gun like he Clint Eastwood, Dirty Harry so I took out my gun and we start shooting. Him and me, mano-y-mano. We getting it in. Anyway, I pop him in the head and in the chest and he falls to the floor. I walk up to the register to get my beer, and the dude behind the register has this relieved look on his face. He had a deposit bag sitting on the counter filled with cash; I guess he was going to make his drop today. It's all sitting on the counter and I'm staring at the money and he's staring at me and the guy on the floor. He said some shit about, 'Thank you so much for helping me sir. I can never repay you, you saved my life.' I didn't want to hear that shit; there was the money on the counter. So I slapped him upside the head with my gun, took the money and ran out of the store. Cops pull up and catch me a few blocks away. I ended up getting time because dumb ass store keeper fucked around and died, can you *believe that? This wimp ass cat dies and they charging me. Anyway, I did my time and now I'm back baby, ready to be a productive citizen; make my way in life and live good...as soon as I figure out if my damn wife is cheating on me. Ohh she better be at my apartment when I get there. I know my landlord held my apartment for me, It's gonna be just like I left it. And she better be there when I get there!"*

T.J takes another swig of Jack and looks into the rear view mirror...

"So what's on your agenda?"

Chapter 72

"Hey guys, come on over, we got a plan."

The rest of the group walked out of the room conversing among themselves and seem to have come to an agreement on something. The group walked to the van, where Sheena and Stormy were standing.

Bobby looked different. Perhaps he had gotten his bearing back somehow and was taking the lead on coming up with the plan. The students stood in a circle as Bobby talked. Sheena couldn't wait to ask the obvious question,

"So what's this brilliant plan?"

"Well, Moon and Mimi are going to start walking and see if they can reach someone. The rest of us are going to prepare for this guy in case he get back before we get help. We have a bag full of weapons of some sort, so we might as well use them."

Since Sheena was not in the room when the plan was made and since the group dubbed her the 'queen of questions', Sheena took up her mantle and began the ritual.

"Why are you sending Moon and Mimi out by themselves? We don't know how far they'll have to walk before they find help."

"We are sending them because they are the best choice."

"Why doesn't someone else go with them?"

"Because we are going to need all hands on deck to fight this guy off. Besides, going by themselves was Moon's idea."

"That's a stupid idea; we shouldn't split up, especially not now."

"We have to prepare, and we are going to need you and Stormy to help us."

When Bobby stops talking, all goes silent. Sheena is visibly upset and begins walking towards the road. Bobby turns to Stormy and asks,

"Can I talk with you for a minute?"

Stormy rolls her eyes and walks away from the group in the direction Bobby is pointing. After they walk about fifteen feet from the others, Bobby tries to put his arm around Stormy, who shrugs off his advances.

"Come on baby..."

"No."

"Stormy, I'm sorry. Look, I know I should have listened to you. I know I should have listened, but just let me know what I can do to make it better."

Stormy looked at Bobby with tears in her eyes.

"I don't know Bobby, and that's the truth."

Stormy collapsed into Bobby's arms and began to cry her heart out.

Sheena was watching everything; always observing. She watched as the students interacted; she saw Stormy collapse in Bobby's arms. Sheena also noticed the one lone car that was coming down the road in their direction...

"Car."

The rest of the group looked at Sheena with puzzled looks on their faces. It reminded Sheena of a scene out of 'Coneheads'.

"Car..."

Bobby finally opened his mouth to interject the needed words for this moment,

"Huh?"

"A car is coming damnit."

With those words, Sheena bolted out into the middle of the road to flag down the driver.

Chapter 73

"...so anyway, what I was saying is this. You don't need to have funeral per se, if there's no body, right? I had this guy in my car earlier that was just a jerk. He wore those..."

T.J looked up ahead and saw somebody jumping up and down in the middle of the road waving their arms like they were trying to flag down a jumbo jet.

"Damn idiots."

T.J put his foot on the gas and speeds up towards the person in the road,

"Ten points for me."

As T.J got closer, he could make out the person's features. It was a woman...a damn good looking woman at that, even if she didn't have enough sense to get out of the middle of the road. T.J could use a little break from driving; he had been at the wheel for at least eight hours already. He still had another four hours ahead of him though, not enough time to be messing around with some random chick by the side of the road.

"But damn she's fine.' I could at least see what's got her panties in a bunch...maybe I can un-bunch them for her."

T.J took another drink of liquor and laughed out loud as he approached the woman at about eighty five miles an hour. T.J decided to stop, slamming on the breaks and turning into the parking lot of the hotel. If Sheena had been wearing a dress, it would have been a Marilyn Monroe moment. As the car flew past Sheena, who barely moved in time enough not to get hit by the rear of the car when it made its sharp turn, Sheena ran back towards the group and into the waiting arms of Rick, who shoved her behind him as any true protector would.

The car came to an abrupt and screeching halt. Before the dust had a chance to settle, T.J was out of the car and standing in front of the group.

"What the hell is your dumb ass doing in the middle of the road? Don't you know you could get killed playing in the streets sweet thang?"

"Look mister, you got to help us, we need to use your phone."

"I got to help you? Who the hell are you? Lady Elizabeth and her merry band of idiots? I don't have no damn phone."

Bobby was not about to miss this opportunity to make things at least a little better.

"The hell with a phone, we need to use your car and get the police!"

"Oh hell no, I don't even like cops."

Mimi jumped in, confident that Moon would have her back.

"Didn't you hear her? We need to use your car. The hotel manager is already dead and we think a guy's coming back to kill us!"

Mimi was correct; Moon did indeed have her back. Moon did them all one better,

"Man move, we need your car."

Moon pushed past T.J who was a little wobbly on his feet by now. His wingman Jack might have put him in a bad situation. T.J turned around and grabbed for Moon. Moon was a wide receiver and a good one at that. Moon had a knack for getting people to let go of him while he was running. Now, since Moon was trying to commandeer a vehicle and save their lives, there was no way

Moon would be stopped.

Moon whirled around, caught T.J by the arm and brought him in close. Moon then grabbed T.J by the neck and slammed him up against the car so hard that it broke the driver side window. Moon squeezed T.J's neck as he moved in closer to his face...

"Listen man, I will kill you where you stand right now. We need this car. I'm taking this car, and there is nothing you are going to do to stop me. Everybody, get in the car!"

Moon held on to the man's neck with a grip that would not be denied. All T.J could do was grab at Moon's hands and try to pry them free. Mimi jumped in the passenger's seat as Moon picked T.J up by the neck and tossed him away from the car, maybe ten feet.

"Let's go!"

Moon jumped in the driver's seat and sped off in the car, wheels screeching like a drag race. Mimi yelled out of the window...

"We'll be right back for you!"

T.J stood up and ran a few feet towards the car before he was stopped by Bobby.

"Wait, wait, there's somebody else in the car!"

"Who's in the car? What are you talking about?"

"The man in the back. I was giving him a ride. He was on his way to kill somebody just like me. That's why I gave him a ride."

The car traveled fifty feet and screeched to a halt. The car sat there for a moment and the group stared at its tail lights. Suddenly the passenger door flies open and Mimi jumps out, screaming and running full speed back towards the group...

"He killed him, he killed him…"

Mimi ran into Rick's arms screaming to the top of her lungs.

"Mimi, what happened? Who killed who?"

Just as Rick spoke those words, the driver's door of the car opened. The first thing they saw was a pair of boots hit the ground; a pair of cowboy boots. It was Shemihazah. Shemi got out the back seat of the two door car, pulled Moon's lifeless body out of the driver's seat and let it fall limply to the ground. While the group stared at Moon's lifeless body on the ground, no one noticed that Shemi had disappeared.

Actually, he had not so much as disappeared as turned into a black inky liquid substance, which moves as freely as the wind. The students didn't think of Shemi at all; they were focused on Moon. They stared at Moon until they were snapped back into reality when T.J let loose a high pitch scream. Looking at T.J, you wouldn't think he could reach a pitch that high with his voice. T.J could hear his own voice; T.J thought he sounded like somebody was pinching his balls. T.J screamed for maybe three or four seconds before he fell limply to the ground. When T.J fell, all the students could see Shemi standing in their midst; smiling and holding T.J's still beating heart in his hand. Shemi had taken T.J's heart out through his back somehow. Mimi saw this and ran back into the room, leaving the group outside with Shemi.

Rick went into action. He swung at Shemi with all his might, but Shemi was easily able to sidestep his punch and deliver a solid blow to Rick's chest. Rick flew back about ten feet from the blow, clutching his chest as he got back up to continue his fight. Bobby moved out of the way as Shemi came near him, barely escaping a slashing blow from those sharp, long nails that Bobby didn't remember Shemi having last night. Rick ran back towards Shemi, who let his hand grow to five times its normal size. As Rick threw another punch aimed for Shemi's face, Shemi used his enlarged hand to completely envelop Rick's fist…then Shemi began to apply pressure, intending to slowly crush the bones in Rick's hands to dust.

As Shemi was squeezing Rick's hands, Mimi came back out of the room with one of her fists balled into a tight knot. Mimi walked pass Bobby; pass Sheena and Stormy and right to Shemi. Shemi smiled at her as she approached.

"Aww, look-a-here. Looks like she had more balls than all of you combined."

Shemi raised his hand to lift Mimi up in the air and slam her back to the ground, but somehow it didn't work. Shemi marveled at his sudden loss of power as Mimi reached her arm as far back as her body would allow and swung with all of her strength at Shemi's face. Shemi was not scared; Shemi knew that her punch would not hurt him. It would be a love tap.

Mimi's fist connected with Shemi's eye and immediately there was the sound of a solid hit…and then a *squish*. Mimi's fist had destroyed Shemi's eye! Shemi screamed in pain. Shemi has never known pain from personal experience; he was always the one causing the pain. Somehow Mimi was able to hit him, *to hurt him*, as he had never been hurt before. Mimi swung again and again, cracking ribs and tearing flesh away from bone with every blow. Shemi had to put Rick down; he actually threw Rick down to pay more attention to dodging these blows that was inflicting damage on him. Shemi tried to sidestep Mimi but she was locked in, unable to miss. Mimi sidestepped with Shemi and continued to throw haymakers with every ounce of her strength. Mimi had tears running down her face, but she wasn't crying…she was focused. She swung and swung with all of her heart.

As Shemi reeled back from every blow that Mimi threw, he finally figured out what was happening.

"The bag, you have the bag!"

With this realization came fear; Shemi knew that the items and information in that bag could bring about his demise. Armed with these items and information, Shemihazah was in danger of being wiped off the face of the earth; he would fail his mission!

Shemi couldn't have that. Shemi stopped trying to defend himself from the blows and he stopped trying to sidestep Mimi. Shemi had a new idea; *run*! Shemi had to get away from them and now. They have all of the items. While Shemi didn't think they could figure out what the items were and read all the information about him, he knew that he had misjudged them. *'If they didn't read the book, then how did she know to grab this item and attach him with it?'* Shemi needed to regroup and get his *mojo* back. Now that Shemi knew where the bag was, he could retrieve it and still have his children. It would take an hour or so for his body to heal up from this assault, but Shemi knew that he couldn't wait longer than that no matter what. They could drive off again and it would take him more time to find them and that bag. Shemi had to retreat now and come back later to finish them off. He would try not to kill Mimi and Sheena, since they are carrying his seed, but they are expendable. His main focus was on Stormy; she would provide the perfect womb for his seed and she would yield him many. Shemi allowed himself to change to his ink form and Shemihazah blew away in the breeze.

When Shemi disappeared, the students finally could let down their guard to tend to other things. Mimi ran over to Moon's body to check for vital signs. She knew there would be no life signs; she saw Shemi twist Moon's head from the backseat and she heard it the moment Moon's neck snapped.

Mimi knelt by Moon's body, that was lying on the ground. Mimi laid her head on his chest to listen for a heartbeat but no heartbeat was detected. Mimi lay on Moon's chest for a few moments, content for now to live in this space. Mimi picked up Moon's upper body and laid him on her lap, rocking back and forth; overcome with tears.

Bobby slowly moved to where Mimi was holding Moon's body. He stared down at his fallen friend and the woman who was holding him. The sight was breaking Bobby's heart...

"Come on Mimi...come on Mimi, we got to go inside..."

"No! No! Leave me alone!"

Bobby could understand her pain. Mimi pushed Bobby off of her like he was a rag doll and leaned back over Moon's body.

"Come on Mimi, we have to go back inside and regroup."

"No! We can't just leave him out here like road kill!"

"Come on Mimi, me and Rick will get him right now and bring him in the room. We're not going to leave him out here. Come on Mimi, we have to go inside."

It took a minute for Bobby to wrestle Moon's body out of Mimi's lap and to get her up off the ground. Bobby let Mimi lean on him for support and walked her back to Sheena and Stormy. Bobby asked them to take Mimi inside while they get Moon's body. The girls held Mimi, but they did not move towards the room. Instead, they watched as Bobby went back over to Moon's body and stood over it; looking rather broken up himself. Rick slowly walked over to Bobby, trying to give him a few extra moments to make sense of this tragedy. Bobby bent down and placed his hand on Moon's neck, checking for vitals. After a few seconds Bobby stood up and looked towards the sky,

"Can we get a little help? Tell us what to do. Help us make it out of here..."

Rick walked over to his friend Bobby and placed his arm on Bobby's shoulders. The two friends looked at each other; their eyes expressing the grief that their mouths could not speak. The two friends stood over Moon's motionless body and bent down to pick him up. The girls watched as Rick and Bobby picked up Moon's body and carried him back to the room. The girls watched and grieved as Rick and Bobby laid Moon's body on the bed closest to the wall. Moon looked like he was sleeping; just a quick nap to ward off the tiredness and stress of this trip. As Rick laid Moon's body across the bed, Bobby took the blanket off of the second bed and laid it over Moon's body. All of the students were now in the room; the women were holding each other as Bobby stood over Moon's body shaking his head in disbelief. The group looked around the room at each other; knowing that this had just gotten more serious and that anyone of them could be next because Shemi would be back soon. Bobby and Rick went back outside, collected the body of T.J and placed him on the bed next to Moon. Although T.J was not a friend of theirs and he didn't help them when they asked, it just wasn't right to leave his body outside. They had to do the right thing and move T.J's body into the room as well.

Once they got T.J into the room and placed him on the bed next to Moon, Rick moved over to the second bed which was still holding the green tote bag and its contents. Rick looked inside the bag and removed the book. Rick looked around the room at his friends; wondering if they still had the *moxie* it would take to confront their stalker and take him out of this world. Rick wasn't sure where exactly they stood on the issue, but he knew that now is the time for them to muster their strength and fight. Now is the time to summon whatever courage they can find and prepare for the battle of their lives. Shemi was coming back and he was going to be hell to deal with. They may all die or they may make it out of this ordeal alive. But one thing was for sure; they must fight.

Chapter 74

"I will not let fear control my thinking..."

Frank was sitting at his desk doing routine paperwork. Although he was moving through the paperwork very quickly, he was distracted. Frank had not heard from his daughter and he had not found this killer. Frank felt like things were getting out of control and Frank did not like when things were out of control. Frank was a control freak; not being in control made Frank a very anxious man.

Frank opened his bottom drawer to retrieve his weapon so he could go out. Frank was not sure what his destination was, but he had to move; he had to do something active to find his daughter. All Frank could think was that Sheena was somewhere in danger or maybe hurt and calling out his name. Dave told him that Sheena was most likely on a weekend excursion with her boyfriend Rick. The verdict was still out on Rick. Frank was the Chief of Police and of course he had done his homework. Rick had his share of run-ins with the police; his record was substantial, but it was mostly dumb kid stuff. Fighting, stealing, and threatening adults...Rick was a violent young man.

However, Rick did have changed in the last few years. No more arrests or run-ins with the cops. He went to school and had a few community service projects he worked on without being sentenced to do them by the court. Frank didn't like that Rick was dating his baby girl, but there didn't seem to be any problems. Frank had him over for dinner a few times and Rick seemed like a young man with his head on tight...but Frank still didn't trust him. That is not saying much though, because Frank didn't trust anyone.

While looking through his desk drawer, Frank's cell phone rang again. Frank looked at the caller screen and saw that it was Carol.

"Hey Carol, I thought you forgot about me."

"Hi Chief, never that. The computers were down overnight for regularly scheduled maintenance. They are good to go now and I have good news for you; I located that phone."

"That's the best news I've had all day. Where is it?"

"It's on a secluded road going towards the Blue Ridge Mountains. I'm sending the GPS coordinates to your cell phone right now."

Just as Carol said those words, Frank's phone beeped with an incoming message. Frank looked at the phone for a second and saw that it was from Carol.

"Thank you Carol. I appreciate this. Let me get on it."

"Chief, before you go..."

"Yes Carol, what is it?"

"My brother stopped by with some tickets to the Washington Wizards game against The Kicks. You know the Knicks are going to win the championship this year right?"

"So you say."

"Yeah, well...I have two tickets...floor seats. You interested?"

Frank took a moment and thought about it. He had been so involved with work for the last few years; he had not even allowed himself to date much. Frank did like Carol, she was a great woman. Frank knew that Carol was married, but he had little respect for her husband.

"I'd love to Carol. Dinner's on me."

"Alright then. Bring a good credit card, because I'm not the 'salad and water type of girl'."

"Sound good. I'll give you a call later tonight. Thanks again Carol."

"Don't mention it Frank. Talk with you later."

By the time Carol hung up the phone, Frank was already at the elevator. Frank thought the elevator was taking too long, so he dashed for the staircase and ran down the stairs. Frank burst through the front door of the precinct and dashed over to his car. In a flash Frank was gone; car screeching on the pavement all the way down the street. Frank left so fast that he forgot to ask for backup, so he called it in on his radio. When asked how many cars he wanted to back him up, Frank screamed back into the radio

"All of them Damnit!"

Chapter 75

"It's time to man up."

The students are in the room finalizing their plans for Shemihazah's return. They all know he is coming back and that it will be soon. Fortunately they know they have the perfect warning signal. Since Mimi used the cross to punch Shemi's face in, Shemi knew they had it as well. Rick was sure that Shemi knew all of the items in the bag and was at least afraid that they could use these items against him- that had to be why he ran off. Rick admitted that the '*black ink*' thing was amazing. Shemi's body liquefied or changed to some type of substance in the blink of an eye. '*How the hell did he do that?*' Shemi was definitely not human and Rick had a hard time believing Shemi was created in a lab by men. Rick knew there was a lot the government and scientists were doing behind closed doors, *but what the hell*?

Rick, Sheena and Mimi look up as Bobby walks out of the bathroom.

"It's ready. You got those condoms Rick?"

Sheena turns and looks at Rick as he pulls a twelve pack of Magnum condoms out of his pocket. Sheena shakes her head and laughs,

"You must have thought you were doing some damage this weekend, huh?"

Rick gives a weak laugh, a little embarrassed by the revelation. It is true- he did plan on doing some damage this weekend, but Rick wished he had thought to take the condoms out before Bobby asked. Rick handed Bobby a handful of the Magnums and they all walked in the bathroom behind Bobby.

"So what I did is dilute about one fourth of the contents of the

syringe into this water in the sink. I mixed it well and even said a prayer over it to bless it. Hey, every little bit counts. What we will do is put this liquid into the condoms and use them as projectiles. From what we read, it should be enough to at least immobilize him a little. Then we can get close enough to inject the syringe into his body and incapacitate him. Maybe we can kill him somehow from there."

"And tell me again why we don't just jump into the car now and leave? We could have been miles away from here by now and gotten some help."

Sheena brought up a good point. It would be nice to run, to get away from here. But Rick knew better. Rick knew that they had to take their stand.

"Mimi said the tank was almost on empty; the gas light was on. If we get in that car and don't make it far, Shemi will have us out in the middle of the woods and I don't see us faring very well. We know he's coming back. So we should stand out ground right here. At least we know these surroundings. If another car comes through that would be great, but we can't keep running. We have to end this or we'll never be free...he'll hunt us for the rest of our lives and kill us the second he gets a chance."

Everyone knew Rick was right. They all watched as Bobby was able to put the diluted liquid into three of the condoms. They now had three projectiles; they needed at least one of the first two to hit him, then they could accurately hit him with the last condom and get him immobile enough to get the syringe in him. It was a hell of a plan, but it was the best they could come up with. The cross that Mimi used and now had around her neck would let them know when Shemi arrived. Sheena took two of the condoms and Stormy took one. Rick thought Sheena would be least likely to freeze up at the *moment of truth*.

Rick wanted to go over the plan again. Rick wanted this to be as precise an operation as they could muster. This was their chance of making it out of here alive. Rick had always heard that term in movies, but it was never as powerful a concept to him as it was now. *Alive; they wanted to stay alive.*

In the movies there is always a little more time. There was time to go over the plan, time for the corny chit chat about the determination to survive...the five extra minutes for the characters to get that last quickie in. Not so today, there was no more time. The cross around Mimi's neck was turning red...blood red. They all knew what that meant from the books. They all knew Shemihazah was back. Rick stretched out his hand in the middle of the floor...

"Bring it in everyone...."

The rest of the students came in close and put their hands on top of Rick's. Rick looked around at all of them ...really took time to look each one of them in the eyes.

"There are no more goodbyes today. Alive; let's stay alive."

The students all agreed and lifted their hands like a basketball team getting ready for the opening tip. As the students moved towards the room door, Sheena pulled Rick to the side.

"Listen, I love you Rick...but you're going to have to work on your game time pep speech."

Chapter 76

The students file out of the hotel room one by one and stand to face Shemihazah, who is standing about forty feet from the end of the hotel building. Rick is the last one to exit the room. He closes the door and walks up until he is about twenty feet away from Shemi. The rest of the group slowly walks with him, staying just a few feet behind Rick as they walk.

Shemi is standing in front of them with a cigarette in his mouth. He retrieves a lighter from his jacket pocket and lights his cigarette. The students watch Shemi as he inhales a breath full of smoke and exhales it in their direction. The smoke somehow reaches Rick's face before it dissipates. Shemi laughs out loud and takes another drag.

"So that's what ya'll want to do, stand there in defiance of me?"

Shemi takes another long drag of his cigarette and exhales. Rick looks straight at him without blinking.

"Whatever it is you want you're not getting it from us."

"Really? How do you know that I have already gotten it?"

Every person there knew exactly what Shemi meant, but none took it more personal than Stormy. Rick looked back at Stormy and could see the storm brewing in her eyes. Rick held up his hand and caught Stormy's attention and helped her remember to stay calm and focus on the plan.

"What do you want?"

"Hmmm, what do I want? Just the whole world and everything in it. That's all. Then I'm going to pass it down to my heirs and they will rule this place forever."

"You're not getting us to help you."

"You don't have any choice."

Shemi points at Stormy,

"...and you're the one who's going to bring it to pass."

Bobby had enough. He rushed at Shemi, closing the distance in mere seconds. Shemi was ready for him though and sidestepped Bobby's lunge. As Bobby dove past, Shemi turned around and grabbed Bobby by the neck and displayed him to the group. Bobby elbowed Shemi in the solar-plex. Shemi let go of Bobby for a second and Bobby fell to the ground- just as Rick rushed towards them and jumped up with a flying kick. The kick hit Shemi square in the chest and sent him reeling back, just as Bobby grabbed Shemi's feet. Shemi fell straight to the ground and his head hit the pavement with a solid thud.

Rick tried to stomp Shemi while he was lying on the ground, but Shemi rolled away in time. Shemi kicked Bobby in the top of the head, the pain forcing Bobby to let go of Shemi's feet. Shemihazah got up just as Rick was lunging towards him again. Shemi snatched Rick out of the air and slammed him to the ground. Bobby jumped on Shemi's back, but Shemi easily shook Bobby off who fell to the ground next to Rick. Shemi slammed his foot down on Rick's chest, preventing him from getting off the ground. Shemi reached down, grabbed Bobby by the head and put him in a headlock. Bobby let loose a muffled scream, the full sound blocked by Shemi's arm as it cut off the air to Bobby's windpipe. Bobby took a small hunting knife out of his pocket, the knife he never left home without, and he plunged it into Shemi's calf muscle. Shemi screamed out in pain and put more pressure on Rick with his foot. Shemi took his other hand and reached around to Bobby's head and snapped his neck. As the women screamed in horror, Shemi picked up Bobby's lifeless body and raised it over his head to throw. Before Shemi had the chance to throw Bobby's body, Rick used all the strength he could muster and screamed out,

"Now!"

As Shemi threw Bobby's body into the air towards the van, Sheena and Mimi threw their condom balloons at Shemi. Rick took hold of the knife in Shemi's calf and began to twist on it until Shemi screamed in pain and lifted his foot off of Rick. Rick rolled to the side and watched as Shemihazah began to grow right before his very eyes! It was like watching the incredible hulk or one of those movie character burst out of their clothes as they grow enormous muscles and turn into a psycho monster.

However, just as Shemi's body started to grow, the condoms began to hit him. Sheena's condom hit Shemi on the right leg and Mimi's condom hit Shemi in the abdomen. Shemi continued to grow…seven feet, eight feet, nine feet, teen feet…the group stood there in amazement watching this automatic growth spurt. Rick scrambled as far away from Shemi as he could. Since Rick was crawling away on his hands and knees, he was waiting for Shemi to slam his foot down on top of him again and squash him to paste.

But something started happening to Shemi. Shemi was screaming and holding his abdomen where the condom hit him. Shemi also started to lean as the weight on his leg seemed to be too much for the leg. Shemi screams again as his right leg starts to shrink…his body was still growing but his leg and now his abdomen was starting to shrink. Shemi screamed in agony again before he lost his balance and fell over on the side of the hotel. By this time Shemi was fourteen feet tall; when his body hit the hotel, it crashed right through! Shemi's fall took him through the ceiling and into the last two rooms of the hotel, the two rooms directly next to the student's room. As Shemi crashed through the hotel, the pain caused him to roll and flail, which completely destroyed the room. Shemi tried to get up again, but to no avail. Shemi had to reverse his growth spurt and return to his regular human size. Shemi began to shriek again, until he was the size he was when the students first met him- about five foot five inches tall.

Once Shemi was on the ground and had returned to his regular size, Stormy snapped. She looked around and saw Bobby lying on the ground dead, then looked back at Shemihazah with hate in her eyes. Stormy spoke the first words she had spoken in the last few hours. He words were simple and full of passion,

"Let's kick his ass."

With that, all three of the women rushed in on Shemi. Sheena started kicking Shemihazah in the ribs and Stormy took the tire iron that she was hiding and started pounding on Shemi's abdomen with it. Mimi took the cross off of her neck, put it inside her balled fist and started wailing on Shemi's head.

Each one of Mimi's blows to Shemi's head was causing major damage; breaking bones and gristle. Mimi hit Shemi three times quickly; breaking his nose, knocking out three of his teeth and swelling the other eye. Shemi screamed and opened his mouth. His mouth grew four times its size in mere moments and was filled with razor sharp teeth. Shemihazah lifted up his head towards Mimi and took a big bite out of her neck. Mimi grabbed her neck as Shemi leaned back his head with her flesh and windpipe in his mouth. Mimi fell to the side clutching her neck.

"Use the last condom!"

Rick's voice reminded Sheena that she did have another condom with the liquid in it. Sheen took out the condom just as Rick grabbed Shemi's right arm.

"Help me!"

Stormy grabbed hold of Shemi's right arm with Rick as Sheena threw the condom on Shemi's left arm. Stormy and Rick held onto Shemi's right are for dear life. Sheena took the syringe case out of her pocket, took out the syringe and plunged it into Shemihazah's veins. Immediately after she pushed the poison into his system, Shemi went comatose; he could not move. The students collapsed on the ground where they were. Rick, Sheena and Stormy; that's all that made it. Soon sunlight turned to blackness- the blackness of eyes hidden behind eyelids. They all passed out.

Stormy was the last to awaken after about thirty minutes or so. She looked around and saw that Shemihazah was still lying on the ground, immobile with that stupid blank stare. Bobby's body was gone and Mimi's body was gone. Stormy sat up and looked at the damage to the hotel. It like one of those drone attacks you see on television in the Middle East that hits a civilian's house. As Stormy stood up, Sheena walked out of the room and to her. Sheena had been helping Rick move the bodies into the room; the bodies had piled up. Sheena led Stormy to the room because she knew Stormy would want to make her piece with Bobby.

When Rick saw Sheena and Stormy enter the room, he nodded to Sheena and put his hand on Stormy's shoulder. Rick left the room so the women could have a moment to themselves.

Rick went to the van and stood with his back against the hood. As Rick stood there, the women came out of the room and stood next to him, one on either side. Rick put his arms around them both and they leaned on him, allowing themselves to feel safe for the first time since they arrived at this place. In the background, sirens could be heard. Sirens! That means they were going to be rescued. Rick let the ladies go and ran towards the road looking both ways to see from which end the help was coming. Rick finally saw the source of the sirens, it was the police. Sheena's father had found them. Sheena was glad that she was alive to see him…he was late! When the police arrived, they arrived in force. There were ten cop cars, not counting the Chief's. The police got out and got busy doing what they do. Frank got out of his car and saw Sheena. Sheena ran to him and he ran to her and took his baby girl into his arms and held her tight. Sheena sobbed in his strong arms, grateful for this moment. Frank looked around to survey the place and saw Stormy standing near looking at Frank embrace his daughter. Frank smiled at Stormy and gave her a nod. Stormy smiled and ran over to Frank, allowing him to envelope her in his embrace. Stormy was hurting too and needed the strong arms of someone she could trust to hold her. The three of them stood there for a few minutes, just hugging and letting themselves be hugged. Frank saw Rick standing by the hotel room door. Frank looked at Rick in the eyes,

"Come here young man."

When Rick arrived to where Frank was standing and holding the two women, he stood still to see what the Chief wanted.

"Yes sir?"

"A lot of death here today."

"Yes sir."

"Is any of this caused by you?"

"No sir."

"Did you stand up like a man and protect my daughter."

Rick looked at Sheena. A stream of tears ran down the side of Rick's face; silent tears- no sniffling, no blinking or wiping them away. These were proud tears; the proud tears a man shed for knowing that he stood his ground and protected his woman.

"Yes sir, I protected her with my life."

"Well then, seeing as to how she is here and you are still here, I'd say you did one hell of a job son. I appreciate it. Bring it in..."

Never let it be said that men are not emotional. Rick walked over and fell into Frank's embrace right along with the women; Rick shed his own tears right along with the women. The four of them stood there and hugged...and it felt good.

Shortly after they stopped hugging, Frank took out his phone and made a call he was hoping he would be able to make.

"Hello, this is Frank."

"Do you have good news for me Frank?"

"Yes. I am sending you the coordinates when we get off of the phone. I have your property."

"Is it intact?"

"I would say yes."

"Good job, I'll be there in an hour."

Chapter 77

"Good job Frank, very good job."

The agent that Frank had spoken with at the Sushi restaurant was back. He brought his team with him to retrieve the body of Shemihazah, all of the victims in the hotel room and the remaining items from the tote bag. The agents pulled up in four black Escalades and the lead agent himself came in on a helicopter. Once they got all of the items, they left the scene.

Before they left, the agent that Frank had talk with came over to him to congratulate him on a job well done.

"You know, this is going to be a good thing for both of our careers."

"Is that right?"

"Sure Frank. Our government was depending on us and we came through. You should be proud of yourself Frank."

"I'm just happy I got my daughter back and that this whole mess is over."

"As you should be. If I were you, I'd be expecting a call. I'm not sure when it will come in, but it will come. A lot of people have been keeping their eye on this situation and you have made a lot of friends in high places today. Just watch what you say. Be smart when you write this up and it will all be swept under the rug. But if anyone talks about it; you, your daughter, this Rick guy...if any of you say anything, the full weight of your friendly government will come down on you like bricks falling from the sky. You get my meaning?"

Frank shook his head in agreement.

"Good. So I'm off. By the way, my name is Mike. We'll be getting to know each other better in the near future."

With that, Mike walked towards the helicopter that was waiting for him.

"Mike..."

Mike stopped and turned towards Frank.

"When you see me, will I see you?"

Mike smiled,

"Definitely...as long as you don't talk."

EPILOGUE

"...twenty-two, twenty-three, twenty-four...plus a triple word score...seventy-two points- read it and weep."

Frank and Sheena played Scrabble together for years. They had not had the chance to play in the last couple years; both of them often too busy to fit it in their schedules. It's interesting how a quick brush with death can serve as a reminder of how precious our time is here on Earth. You never know what going to happen; and the things that we don't know that *are* happening all around us can be kind of mind-boggling.

Frank writes down the points from his daughter's word. She is winning the game but that is nothing new. Frank hasn't been able to beat his daughter with any consistency since she was in junior high school. Sheena had an amazing mind and it would take her far in life. She was resilient, intelligent and beautiful; and Frank was a proud, if not biased father.

"So dad, where are you going on your vacation?"

Frank was thinking of taking a vacation. What he wanted most was to take some time off and go to Italy with his daughter. She had always wanted to go to Italy. Frank supposed it was because of some book she read somewhere. Life is short. Frank wanted to tell her tonight about the vacation…if he could just make a word in Scrabble that would give him a good lead into the subject.

"Well to tell you the truth honey, I had an idea about my vacation…"

Frank's work cell starts ringing and he puts his daughter on hold for a moment to take the call.

"Hello, this is Frank."

"Hi Frank, this is your President."

"Mr. President, hello."

Frank jumped up and started waving frantically at his daughter. Sheena jumped up in amazement when she heard that her dad was speaking on the phone with the President of the United States…and the President called him!

"I understand you did a great job in the field for us recently. I told you that if you were able to take care of this situation for us, your government would be very appreciative."

"Yes Sir."

"Well Frank. I am having a small get together at the White House next week. Just my wife, my daughters and a few close friends. I would like to personally invite you and your daughter to the diner. What do you say Frank?"

"Absolutely sir!"

"Great. I will send you the details. I also have a few things I want to talk with you about. I am forming a new committee and I want you to be involved with it. We'll talk over the details when I see you next week. Does that work for you Frank?"

"Absolutely Sir."

"Oh yes, and make sure you bring that brave daughter of yours, we would love to meet her. I think my daughters would love to meet her as well."

"I will bring her with me Sir."

"Great. I'll see you next week. And tell your daughter congratulations for me."

"Congratulations, Sir?"

"Yes. I hear she's expecting. Just know that she and her child will have the best care your government can provide. Please let your daughter know that Stormy will be here too. It is great talking with you again Frank, Goodbye."

Sheena watched as the blood rushed out of her Father's face. She thought the conversation was going so well until that very last minute. *What in the world happened?*

Frank was dumbstruck. *Congratulations? Was Sheena pregnant? Why hadn't she told him?* That seemed unlikely since they had the type of relationship that she would come and tell him this sort of news. Frank didn't know what to do…should he confront his daughter about it? *Perhaps.* The first sparks of anger started to seep into Frank's chest. But wait, *if Sheena was pregnant, how the hell would the president know about it?*

Frank looked at Sheena long and hard. Sheena stared back at her dad, wondering if he was having a heart attack or something.

"Dad, what's wrong? Are you okay?"

"That was the President. He invited us to the White House for dinner next week. He also wants to talk to me about joining some type of committee he's creating…"

"That's great dad, I'm so proud of your!"

Sheena rushed across the room and jumped into her dad's arms. Frank held his daughter and accepted her love. After a moment of hugging, Frank continued,

"The President also told me to tell you congratulations."

"Okay, congratulation for what?"

"He seems to think you are pregnant. Is there anything you want to tell me sweetheart?"

Sheena looked back at her father, stunned... and then memories of her recent ordeal a couple of weeks ago began to surface. She thought of the conversation she had with Stormy about her rape and Sheena's dream. Sheena thought of the things Shemihazah kept saying about bringing his own children into this world and she remembered the other morning when she was thinking her period was a bit late. Sheen thought about waking up in the parking lot naked and she involuntarily began to rub her stomach as dread closed in around her. Sheena looked at her father and shook her head as her eyes began tearing up. Frank looked at his daughter and hugged her...

"Shhh, we'll go to the doctor's office first thing in the morning. I love you baby."

****

About the Author

Elliott Eddie is a world renowned speaker and Toastmaster's 2013 International Speech Competition Semi-Finalist. He is a worldwide distributed filmmaker, an award winning writer and actor with three self-help and one Science Fiction books in print. As an Entrepreneur, Elliott has established several businesses including; Superior Tax Prep stores, P&E Realty Development Company, a professional speaking company and he is currently serving as Chairman/C.E.O of DM Media Inc.

Elliott is currently on tour as a motivational speaker; giving insight and information to help the masses understand how to use information to increase their lot in life. As an entrepreneur, Elliott shares how to start companies and corporations. He educates groups on how set up businesses, strategize ground level marketing techniques and grow businesses into self-reliant organizations. The end result is to free your life and fill your pockets. As a speaker, Elliott gives information and instruction on how to find and hone your individual talents and turn those talents into a vehicle for emotional and financial success.

1/19

Made in the USA
Charleston, SC
04 March 2017